THE BURNING ALCHEMIST

TEMPORAL ARMISTICE BOOK 5

MATTHEW S. COX

DIVISION ZERO PRESS

ISBN (ebook): 978-1-950738-40-3

ISBN (paperback): 978-1-950738-41-0

CONTENTS

1

GRANDMA

Coping with major life changes rarely earned much more than an 'okay whatever' out of me.

Being lazy has a few advantages, after all. Freaking out and getting worked up takes effort and honestly doesn't do much but make people think you're crazy. End result is, whatever blew up is still blown up, plus now you're tired and people are avoiding you. Not me. Even when the trailer home I grew up in burned to the ground when I was twelve, my reaction more or less amounted to 'well, that sucked.'

One might think surviving a fire that should've killed me as a child would forever be the most shocking event of my lifetime. Nope. I'm special. Not long ago, the truth of *how* I survived the fire came out: I'm not fully human. My dad's a Shaar'nath. Most humans mistake us for demons, but we're not. Discovering I'm more or less a being from another plane is a bit of a big deal. More recently, I've become mom to a six-year-old daughter.

Sometimes people have kids they didn't know about come out of nowhere and surprise them… but it doesn't usually happen to the *mother*. It's a whole lot harder for a woman to have a kid she doesn't know about than a guy. Nine months plus labor tends to leave a pretty strong mark on the memory. Usually, it's a guy who goes on a one-night stand, forgets the woman's name the next morning, and years later, a surly teenager shows up asking for money. Okay, bit cynical. Sometimes the kid's hoping for a real connection.

Anyway, point being, I went from only having to worry about myself to being a mom—in a literal instant. Well, it might've been more like a minute or two, but I blacked out from the pain. To split another technical hair, she's not really my daughter as much as an exact copy of me. Biologically speaking, she's my twin sister. Main problem with my being mom is I'm only twenty-three. Pandora is six. Yeah, sure, it's possible to have a kid at seventeen, but as soon as someone thinks I got knocked up as a teen, they tend to make certain assumptions about me. Assumptions that both piss me off and aren't true. No, a different 'not true.' I had plenty of sex by that age, but I'm not an idiot. I'd been careful.

Pandora doesn't really care either way whether I'm big sis or mommy. She calls me 'mom' which is both easier and much less annoying than 'hey you.' It wouldn't bother me if she called me 'Brook' or 'Brooklyn,' but some people get weird about little kids calling adults by their name. I've never been one to let a small argument fail to escalate. Someone tries to give me 'parenting advice' about the kid's manners and I'm going to be in their face. Anyway, seventeen years from now, we'll look like identical twins. Weird thing about half humans, at least when mixed with Shaar'nath—we stop looking older not long after twenty.

Speaking of moms, it's time for Pandora to meet our mother.

She lives in Allentown, which is a little over an hour north of Philly by road. Sprinting, I can fly it in about ten minutes. In the past, we'd have taken a PEPTA—Philadelphia Enchanted Public Transportation Authority—portal, but they only open them once an hour. Sure, the travel is instantaneous, but the wait for the portal mages to do their thing is tedious. Both Pandora and I are getting a ton of practice using our psychic abilities to remain unnoticed whenever we do obviously inhuman things. My dad managed to force an entire city block to remain unaware of me roasting a creep to ashes. Then again, he's had thousands of years of experience. Still, it's not too difficult for me to force humans close enough to recognize me to ignore my presence.

This lets me fly around as much as I want. Pandora's even gotten the hang of it. You know what they say about kids... brain plasticity or something. They learn stuff much faster than adults.

Wow, am I in for a heck of a ride watching over her.

Her powers aren't as fully developed as an adult's though. For example, she can't 'sprint' at 350 MPH like me. Maybe it's some kind of evolutionary thing. Like, baby Shaar'nath would get into a lot more trouble if their parents couldn't catch them. Whatever. So, our flight takes a little longer. Pandora adores being able to fly. I still haven't told her about my disastrous first attempt. It ended with me kissing the side of a high-rise building. I used to be afraid of heights. Not so much now.

For the flight, we shift all the way into our Shaar'nath forms—which means armor plating—mostly so our eyes turn into pools of dark blue energy, impervious to high-speed wind. Sprouting wings and a bladed tail is also kinda destructive to clothing. Thankfully, Natalie made us multifunction enchanted amulets. Not only can they create illusions of clothing, they teleport anything we happen to be wearing into safe storage in an instant. It's *way* less hassle to use wings when I don't have to manually take my shirt off.

Flying north to Mom's place in Allentown is as fun as going for a walk with my kid in a park or on a nature hike. We don't exactly take a straight as-the-crow-flies path, deciding to meander around and investigate anything interesting. Her laughter is simultaneously awesome and a little heartbreaking. It's only sad because I didn't laugh much as a kid. Speaking of maudlin, Humberto made a weird remark at the station yesterday. Something got him all philosophical and stuff. He wondered if it would be better to know when you reached your last day of life. Like, what would people do if they woke up one day and got a notice they'd started on the last day of their life and would be dead in exactly twenty-four hours? Some of the guys talked about touching base with everyone they ever knew to say their farewells. McCafferty thought it'd be a bad idea because some people would go completely crazy. For some people, the only thing holding them back from chaos is fear of punishment. If they're going to die anyway, they'd lose all fear.

He's got a point.

Whatever. No time for bad thoughts today. I wave for Pandora to follow and turn back on course for the final few minutes of the flight.

Time to play the ultimate prank on my mother.

WE DIVE OUT OF THE AIR AND LAND ON MY MOM'S FRONT PORCH.

I'm still radiating psychic energy so no one notices us, apparently effective since a handful of kids and parents in the area don't react whatsoever to a pair of winged beings in what appears to be form-fitting white body armor. Pandora and I shift back to appear fully human. Less than a second after all our extra body parts have gone into hiding, our enchanted amulets replace the illusionary clothing with our physical outfits. Shaar'nath don't have a concept of clothing at all, at least on their home plane of Imbreleth. Kinda happens when the place you live is full of fire. Much the way I put up with clothing, whenever they visit the mortal world, they deal with it to avoid attracting unwanted attention. I'm still not sure how they do it, but they can simply conjure the appearance of clothing... maybe they're using psychic projection to cause people to see them dressed? It's hilarious sometimes when full-blooded ones pop into this world and attempt to mimic fashion. They have zero concept of style. One dude who tried to kill me a few months back looked like a reject from an Eighties hair metal band. Another guy clearly hadn't visited this realm since the Sixties.

"This is where you grew up?" Pandora gazes around, making a face of confusion. "I don't remember it."

"You remember the trailer?"

She scrunches her nose. "Not really. Don't remember anything before having all the buttheads standing in a circle around me."

"Mom only bought this place three years ago, after she got the book deal." I ring the bell and stand off to the side, leaving my mini-me directly in front of the door.

Pandora barely contains her giggles. Yes, she's totally in on the prank. It's not every day you get the chance to make your mother think some crazy time stuff happened. I managed to find a plain coral-colored dress similar to the style Mom bought me years ago. Didn't have too many dresses, but she'll remember this one. Hey, this counts as a special occasion, right?

A minute or so after I ring, my mother opens the door. "Oh, hi, Swee—" Mom blinks, dumbstruck at the little me staring up at her. Time has been fairly kind to her. She's forty-four but could probably pass for mid-to-late thirties, amazing considering how hard she worked for most of my life.

"I lost my keys again," says Pandora in a spot-on impression of me wanting to cry but acting angry to hide it. "That butthead Miguel threw my backpack up in a tree."

The little bastard teased me incessantly from third to fifth grade. Judging by the look on Mom's face, she doesn't remember six was too little for Miguel to pick on me. And yes, I told Pandora to complain about Miguel. It's not some weird embedded memory.

Mom mumbles something incoherent and faints.

"Crap!" I telekinetically catch her before her face smacks into the floor.

"Oops." Pandora glances over at me. "I think we broke her. Can I laugh or would that be mean?"

I levitate Mom to the sofa, walking in behind her as she floats. "Close the door. Don't laugh yet. After she knows what happened, you can laugh."

"Okay." Pandora follows me, closes the door, and scampers over to sit on the sofa beside Mom.

It takes my mother a moment to come to. She looks up at me as I'm patting her on the cheek. "Oh, Brook... I thought I saw—"

"Hi!" chirps Pandora.

Mom looks to her right at the grinning child. "*Ay! Dios Mio!*"

"Easy." I squeeze her hand. "Sorry. Just playing a little trick on you."

"Trick?" Mom looks back and forth between us. "What kind of trick is this? That's *you*."

Pandora makes a 'so-so' hand tilt.

I sit on my mother's left. "Yes and no. Relax, Mom. I'm not here to drop her off. Not going to put you through raising me a second time but I might ask you to babysit occasionally."

Pandora cracks up laughing at the 'oh shit' look on my mother's face.

I'm not insulted by it. Honestly, I know the kind of terror I was. My mother's expression would fit a combat veteran who spent ten years as a POW then went through hell to escape and go back home only to be asked to do it all over again. I sit with her and explain how Melisandre and a group of Elestari and Shaar'nath lured me into a trap and basically cloned me using magic. No point going into detail about the level of pain involved. It would upset her too much.

"So, basically, she's me around like five or six, but already showing a few small differences," I say.

"Differences?" asks Mom.

Pandora lets her wings out with a *fwoof* like a pushbutton umbrella snapping open. In the same instant, her dress changes to a frilly, black, 'sparkle goth' thing—Natalie's illusion courtesy of her amulet.

"Gah!" yells Mom, grabbing me.

Pandora laughs. She loves jump-scaring people. Then again, so do I.

"Considering she spent her first moments of existence surrounded by Elestari and Shaar'nath... she already knows what we are."

"Yep." Pandora flashes a cheesy smile while extending her horns.

They're adorable, really. At her age, they're only like two inches long, slightly curved, but still sharp.

Mom appears torn. Mostly, she has a look of 'aww' in her eyes, but she's still kinda hung up on the whole 'demons are evil' nonsense.

"How old is she really, you think?" I ask.

"Umm." Mom gets up, coaxes Pandora to stand beside her, and looks her over. "She reminds me of your size on your sixth birthday. You always were a little small for your age."

"Yeah." I smirk. "Exactly why Miguel used to give me a hard time."

"Until you got a little older." Mom winks.

I stare at the ceiling.

"Why would he stop picking on her when she got older?" asks Pandora. "Did she beat him up?"

Mom and I exchange a conspiratorial glance.

"Almost did." I examine my fingernails. After years of teasing me constantly, the moron thought I'd date him without at least a serious apology.

"So, Brook." Mom stares at me. "What are you going to do here? Children don't just come out of thin air."

"It's handled." I wave dismissively. "Took some liberal swinging of the charm hammer, but legally, Pandora is my daughter. You dealt with raising me once, and that's a lot to ask of anyone. I can't do it to you a second time."

Pandora giggles.

Mom gives me this long sigh. She'd totally be willing to 'raise me' again, but can't hide a little bit of relief she doesn't have to. Then again, she's relatively stable now financially—and works from home—so a lot of the headaches I gave her wouldn't apply now. It's a real pain in the ass to raise a grade-school-aged child when you have to work ten-hours a day all week long.

"What do you mean by charm hammer?" Mom gives me the same look she always used to hit me with whenever the police showed up: sadness, anger, and the doubt of 'should I yell at you or expect not to see you for a few years?'

I've already tried to explain how demons aren't really a thing and Dad isn't evil, but talking about that stuff only upsets her. If she ever accepts the truth of what the Shaar'nath really are, it won't be a quick process. "Having Pandora made legally my daughter required I *encourage* a few city workers to just trust me on some unverifiable information."

Mom gasps. "What do you mean?"

"I can generally coerce people to go along with my desires. Go figure, the city workers have like this serious problem faking documentation." As a half-Shaar'nath, I am psychic and have an array of mental powers like charm, knowing the intention of anyone by looking at them, and the 'don't pay attention to me' radiance. Straight-up mind control is a bit beyond my skill set, though. Fortunately, I didn't need it there. Getting people to believe a plausible lie isn't difficult. Oh, their computer must have had an error. Of course Pandora Amari must be in the system. I must have lost her birth certificate when I moved. Look at us and tell me this isn't my kid. That sorta stuff.

Mom covers her mouth.

Pandora giggles.

"You falsified legal documents?" Mom raises both eyebrows.

"No." I make a super innocent face. "Technically, a city clerk did."

She gasps.

"Umm. Do you have a better idea?" I tilt my head. "Not like I can tell anyone what really happened without getting into the whole existential mess. Date of birth? Oh, she wasn't born. A bunch of crazy Elestari made her out of thin air."

"Shaar'nath, too," mumbles Pandora. "A whole *team* of buttheads."

Mom mulls for a moment, then sighs. "I suppose you do have a point."

"Anyway, Pan's already registered in first grade. Just going to proceed like she was always here. Though, if anyone questions me having a kid at seventeen, I'm going to admit she's my sister in confidence."

"Well, she's welcome here as often as needed. Suppose I am a grandmother." Mom gives me side-eye. "Is she exactly like you?"

"Quite similar, but not completely exact. Different experiences will give her a unique personality."

"Rawr," deadpans Pandora, showing off her fangs.

"And..." I gesture at her. "She's fully aware of what she is, so there's that."

"Oh dear," whispers Mom.

I grin. "Honestly, I think it will help. Growing up, I always felt like something wasn't right. Like I didn't fit in. You know how when you think you forgot something but can't remember what you forgot? My whole life. *Now* it makes total sense. She's not going to grow up with the constant question marks in her head."

Mom nods.

"Anyway, Mom, I figured you'd enjoy spending some time with your granddaughter since you had to work so hard you didn't really have the time to enjoy with me."

My mother stares at me, seeming hurt.

"Not blaming you." I smile. "Not at all. You did what you had to do, and I'm beyond grateful for everything."

Mom chokes up.

"Oh, great." Pandora fake rolls her eyes. "Now, we're gonna get mushy and hug."

I snicker.

"She's got your sarcasm." Mom glances at the child.

"Yeah. She's totally joking."

Pandora jumps into a hug, wings and all. Surprisingly, Mom doesn't seem to mind. Oh, sure. When *I* sprout wings, it's scary.

I swear. Grandkids can get away with anything.

2

MISCHIEF

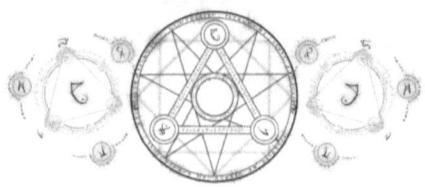

Sunday mornings are usually relaxing, and today's no different. No pressure to get up and go anywhere early, nowhere specific to be. Just a day of rest. My mother still wakes up at the butt crack of dawn on Sundays and goes to church. Not me. Sleeping late is too appealing. Even before I knew how the world really came to exist, I didn't really get too into her religious stuff. Something always seemed off about it, and more than half the people there radiated bad vibes.

By vibes, I mean their intention. As a kid, I had no idea about the Shaar'nath stuff, but I did believe in being psychic for two big reasons. One, I figured out telekinesis pretty young. Two, every time I looked at someone, whatever their intentions were became known to me. Took me awhile to call it 'psychic' stuff. Back then, I thought I just had some really sharp 'kid intuition' or something. They say children can smell bad people like dogs can. Sure worked for me. And no, I'm not saying the people at my mom's church are bad, more like sanctimonious and insincere. They simply weren't as into it as my mother. She *truly* believed. Everyone else, not so much. Most of them only went there to be *seen* there. They preened over it. It's one of those things that made me think the whole thing sounded 'off.' Pride supposedly being a sin and all yet here's a whole building full of people so damn proud to be in that building every week.

Anyway…

I'm cleaning up after breakfast—Pandora and I woke up late, like almost ten in the morning—when it occurs to me the apartment is too quiet. I'm not referring to my next-door neighbor Tracy, either. She hasn't engaged in MMA fights with a boyfriend in a while now. The only sound is coming from the television in the living room, some news program. No, the quiet in my apartment at the moment is of a more worrisome breed. A six-year-old lives here. Silence is dangerous. Silence is evil. Silence means something is about to burn or bleed.

"Pan?" I call.

No response.

I wander into the living room. "Pandora?"

"… increased sightings of magical creatures within city limits," says the news anchor on the screen. "People are becoming concerned."

A smaller frame floating on the screen to the man's left shows security video from an office where a bunch of what look like gnomes run around the cubicles, leaving behind trails of papers and random office supplies they appear to be trying to steal.

"Some people are blaming mages," says the co-anchor. "Accusing them of deliberately smuggling illegal beings past the Aether Wall to 'take over.'"

I head down the hall and check both bedrooms and the bathroom. No sign of her. Admittedly, her room isn't terribly big. It's more of a huge closet than another room. Still, it's enough space for a kid's bedroom, about the same as I had growing up. Mom let me have the bedroom in the trailer we used to live in, while she slept on the couch.

"Pandora?" I yell, not quite at the point of freaking out yet.

Upon returning to the living room, I notice the patio door is open. Hmm. Seems she went for a late-morning fly. Odd, she up and jumped off the balcony without at least telling me.

The television's now showing a panel of experts: Ladonna Steele, a lawyer for the Academy; Sidney Stafford, jackass representing FRUM (Foundation for the Responsible Use of Magic), and Rachel Feuerstein, a rep from the SPCMA (Society for the Prevention of Cruelty to Magical Animals).

They're in the midst of discussing an increasing number of sightings of magical creatures inside Philadelphia city limits. This is no secret to anyone who lives here. A few weeks ago, a cockatrice ended up on the bus I used to take to work. Sidney is arguing with Ladonna over the idea that 'mages' are letting creatures in on purpose to 'take over.'

"Take over what?" blurts Rachel. "Magical creatures have been on Earth longer than we have."

"The Aether Wall is over 150 years old." Ladonna holds up a placating hand. "Nothing, not even magic, lasts forever without needing repairs. You can abandon your crazy conspiracy theories. A few creatures slipping past the ward is not in any way a plan to 'take over.' Philadelphia is the only city in the world to have an outright barrier to block magical beings. Other major metropolitan areas rely on repelling magic."

"Hah." Sidney shakes his head. "Crazy monsters all over the city the police can't handle? Of course it's a play for power. Mages want to make ordinary citizens dependent on them. Citizens and cops can't cope with fire-breathing giant crows. We're going to need *mages* to protect us soon. Mark my words."

"Numerous conspiracy theories argue there are people, likely mages, actively sabotaging the barrier," says the anchor. "But there has been no evidence of it put forward."

Rachel rolls her eyes. "Some of those creatures are quite helpful. Others are wonderful companions. And, like Ladonna said, occasional creature sightings are the norm everywhere else. Repelling spells aren't perfect."

"And they're far less trouble to maintain." Ladonna smiles.

"You're ignoring the danger," yells Sidney. "Sure, magical creatures have been all over the Earth for thousands of years, but back then, we didn't live in giant cities. There are too many people living too close together for them here. One dangerous creature can do a lot of damage."

"Same could be said for an empty talking head convincing gullible people to believe nonsense," snaps Rachel. "Or politicians."

Pandora swoops in and lands on the patio like some giant goth faerie, a big paper cup in each hand and a two-pack of chocolate cupcakes hanging from her mouth. Seriously, the illusionary dress Natalie gave her is extra as hell. The kid steps inside, telekinetically closes the patio door, then walks over to me, offering one of the cups. After I take it, she climbs up to sit on the couch. I can tell from the style of the cups she went to Kwan's Market.

"You flew to Kwan's?"

She lets the cupcakes fall from her mouth to the sofa beside her. "Yep. One of these is yours."

"We just ate breakfast."

"I know. But coffee needs chocolate."

Relieved she's okay—as is anyone who might have crossed her path—I sit. "Did you shoplift this stuff?"

"No. I gave him money. You don't like stealing from Mr. Kwan."

I sniff my coffee. Wow. Kid got the perfect balance of cream and sugar. "Where did you get money?"

"From some rich guy. He won't miss it." She sips from her cup. "I gave him the wallet back."

I chuckle.

She glances over at me. "You're not mad?"

"Nah. I shoplifted a PlayStation when I was eleven. Be kinda hypocritical of me to yell at you for swiping a ten-spot."

"Was a twenty," mutters the child.

I fake gasp. "Oh no. That's grand theft."

She snickers, then extends a claw to slice open the packet of cupcakes, taking one and handing me the other. The scent of hot cocoa wafts from her cup.

"Hot chocolate?"

She nods. "Yeah. I'm six. My tastes haven't changed to coffee yet."

Heh. I flip the TV off the news to a kid's cartoon. We sit there sipping our hot drinks, nibbling on chocolate cupcakes, and watching little cartoon animal astronauts run around for a while.

"Wanna do some mischief?" asks Pandora once a commercial starts.

I grin. Ooh, little temptress. Makes me feel like a kid again. "What are you thinking?"

Pandora twirls her hair around one finger. "I dunno... maybe pranking people by making stuff move?" She still struggles with the word 'telekinesis,' so she avoids trying to say it. Hey, she's only six.

"Works for me." I sip coffee. Yeah, so not the most responsible parenting, but if I knew I could do this stuff at her age... wow. Took me a few more years before chairs started to slide mysteriously out from under nasty teachers. Also, she doesn't do anything mean. Just messes with people. It's cute.

And a shitload of fun.

3

EXPECTATIONS

W eekends have a super annoying habit... of not lasting long enough.

Even though my schedule gives me a three-day weekend all the time, it goes by too fast. Sunday shot past in a blur of laughter. The kid and I spent hours roaming the city randomly messing around using telekinesis to prank people. Probably not the smartest thing since everyone is on edge over magical creatures sneaking in. We had a few people scream when they saw something move by itself, though we kept everything in good fun. Nothing dangerous or intentionally scary.

Monday, I suffered through the curse of adulthood after Pandora went to school, meaning I did a lot of cleaning around the house, laundry, and so on. Even went grocery shopping. Blergh. Spent the second half of Monday keeping an eye on Pandora and Ashley. My Mondays have been 'kid days' for a while now, ever since I ended up making friends with Tracy next door. Ashley is adorable, and the girls are as close as sisters.

Also, on Monday, I received a letter from Pandora's school. It appears to be a form letter sent to all parents, informing us that the 'parties unknown' responsible for carving 'Miss Randall is a butthead' in the cinder block wall of the gym will eventually be found. They also ask for the responsible student to turn themselves in, promising less punishment. Hah. If they had any clue who did it, they wouldn't send this letter. Also, what kid could possibly *carve* writing into cinder blocks?

Hmm. Let me think... one with a magically sharp tail blade and claws?

I laugh for a good half hour over the letter.

Anyway, the inevitable aftereffect of Monday occurred, that is to say: Tuesday. Tracy returns the favor of childcare, watching Pandora while I'm at work. If she's busy—which is often—Natalie takes over. The girls *adore* hanging out at her enchanted item shop.

Being a firefighter often feels like a career of extremes. Either we sit around bored, or all hell breaks loose. In reality, it's not quite as polarized... but the mind focuses on the strongest signals, so to speak. We have a few minor calls: kitchen fire, smoking car on the side of the road, teenage girl stuck in a washing machine trying to take a 'funny selfie', and even a cat up a tree—yes, seriously. Only, this cat turned out to have wings and flew away as soon as I got close to it.

Can't really say things are significantly weirder than usual. Sure, there likely is an increase in magical creature sightings, but going from one every few months to one a week isn't the end of the world. Freaks people out, but it's not a big deal. Unlike Shaar'nath or Elestari, society at large knows about the existence of magical creatures—people in Philly just don't expect to see them downtown. Everyone who's lived here their whole life has the distorted perception this stuff only exists on television documentaries.

Right when I think the day is about to be routine, we get a call to assist with a fire at an ACME market across the street from Philadelphia's Magic Gardens. Apparently, the magic went haywire and chucked a fireball across the street. Due to the bad timing of the alarm —less than twenty minutes before my shift would have ended—I call Natalie on the ride to the fire site and let her know what's going on. She's cool with continuing to watch the kids.

The fire is not too destructive. It jumped through a hole in the wall of a parking deck in the same building as the ACME. I'd been expecting rows of burning groceries. Instead, we got a bunch of melted cars. Something weird about the fire keeps it burning despite us throwing water on it. For the most part, we hose down nearby vehicles and the concrete, trying to keep it from disintegrating. Eventually, someone manages to locate a pyromancer who's able to dispel the persistent flame. As calls go, it ended up being fairly tame. Only some property damage, no one hurt. Still, by the time we're able to leave the site, get back to the station, and finish cleaning up the trucks and gear... it's dark.

Doesn't help we are a bit light staffed. My boyfriend Jason and Bill Lancaster are away for a couple weeks, along with ten other people from various stations around the city, attending a firefighter event in Germany. Groups from all over the world are having this competition type thing plus sharing techniques and stuff. Sounds kinda fun, but way too much effort. Not for me. The last thing I need is to call attention to myself in a competition where a woman my size breezes through events guys as big as Brian Herlihy struggle to pull off. Inside a burning building when someone's real life is on the line, no one's gonna see me kick a door off its hinges or walk unharmed through the flames. I'll risk being discovered in an emergency, but not for bragging rights.

Once everything's calmed down, I head home... walking off in the general direction of the bus stop before ducking into an alley. As soon as I stretch my wings, the amulet swaps my polo shirt, pants, and work shoes for illusions. Damn handy. No one pays me any attention as I cruise into the sky, pull up to about 500 feet, and swing around toward home. My apartment might be in one of the less nice areas, but it's at least fairly close to the station. Taking the bus had been a little annoying, but flight reduces my commute to about five minutes at a lazy glide.

I could cut it down to under a minute, but 'sprinting' is effort.

Generally, on the way home from work, one thing I don't expect to see is a half-dressed blonde Shaar'nath hanging out on the roof of a high-rise apartment building. At least, I assume she is one. Girl's got wings and a tail quite like mine. Main difference is her skin tone is more natural... like an Elestari. From what I've seen thus far, my kind have generally inhuman skin colors: paper white like me, crimson, black, blue, and so on. Fortunately, Ireland exists, so people don't freak out when they see me. Some humans are almost as pale as I am.

Curious, I circle closer.

This woman is more or less like the Norwegian blonde Valkyrie super-model type, except for the wings, tail, and horns. I've never seen a Shaar'-nath with 'ordinary' coloration before. Okay, gotta ask. I land next to her.

She gives me a casual 'oh, there's someone else here' glance, then resumes staring into space. I'd peg her for mid-twenties, but she could be centuries old. The woman's almost wearing one of those killer shimmery red evening gowns. I say almost because she's pushed it down to her waist, no doubt to allow her wings out. If not for her having wings and being obviously not human, her glum expression and perch on the side of a building might worry me she's considering a jump.

"Sorry to intrude on your melancholy," I say. "Mind if I ask you a stupid question?"

"Go right ahead. Doesn't mean I'll answer it."

I chuckle. "How'd you dye yourself Caucasian?"

She laughs. "Okay, wasn't expecting that. You must be young."

"Yeah. Relatively. Look, if you're having a moment, I'll screw off and leave you alone."

"It's fine. Just…"

"Breakup?"

"Sort of. It's not like you're thinking. I couldn't do it."

I raise an eyebrow. "Go all the way?"

"No. Eat him." She sighs. "The reason I look like I do is because I'm what the humans call an eater-of-men."

"Succubus?"

"No. Those aren't our kind. I literally eat them. Strip the flesh off their bones and everything." She makes a nauseated face. "I'm kind of bored with it."

"Bored?"

She nods. "Yeah. You try eating the same thing every meal for a thousand years. I can't even bear the thought of touching man again without getting sick. Started off tonight like any other feeding night.

Found a guy, hit him up in a club... went back to his place... and blech. Couldn't do it."

In my youth, I often ate the same sorts of foods all the time since it's what Mom could afford... but getting sick of it wasn't an option. Still, what she says makes sense. "So, what did you do?"

"Screwed his brains out and left. Now I'm starving and ready to throw up."

"Great, you're a Hollywood actress."

She chuckles.

"Ever eat a hamburger?" I raise an eyebrow. "Do you *have* to eat humans?"

"I..." She blinks. "Don't know. I've never tried."

I sit next to her. Damn, the concrete's cold. Illusionary clothing has its shortcomings. "So, the only reason you keep devouring men is because it's what everyone expects a man-eater to do?"

"Seems so."

"That's not a good reason. Embrace your inner chaos. Society's expectations of us don't mean anything. Hell, I'm a firefighter. There are still tons of people who think it's weird for a woman."

She rolls her eyes. "Humans. What they do for their jobs is not the same thing as our inner nature."

"Did you not just tell me you aren't a succubus?" I grin. "Your inner nature is Shaar'nath, not man-eater."

"It's complicated." She holds up her arm. "It's why I look just like them. Not a snowdrift like you."

I stick out my tongue. Mature, right?

"You've spent all your time among humans. The easiest way for me to explain it to you is being part of a sect."

"Sect or subspecies?"

"Sect."

I smile. "So that means it's just a social club. Try a cheeseburger. You don't have to buy them drinks first."

She laughs. "You aren't what I was expecting at all."

"You expected me?"

"Didn't expect to meet you, but I've heard of you. You're the one who's supposed to destroy the Armistice, right?" She sighs. "I can't believe they're *still* trying it."

"Ugh!" I gaze at the sky. "Yeah. Seriously. Morons. And no, I have no intention of doing it."

"Must be nice," mutters the woman.

"What?"

"Being able to decide."

"Yeah. You don't *have* to be a man-eater. That's old folkloric bull-shit. Shaar'nath existed for thousands and thousands of years before humans happened. It's ridiculous to think you can only eat them. Like I said, just because people expect you to be something, it's no reason you *must* be that something. If cheeseburgers don't work for you, try tacos. They're a lot easier to get, taste better, and no one will scream if they see you eating one."

"Trying to decide between Italian or Chinese for dinner used to mean something way different for me." She laughs, then sighs. "I've been trying to cut down. One a month. Maybe I will experiment with something else."

"Another stupid question."

"Hmm?" She glances at me.

"What do Shaar'nath usually eat? I mean, when they live in Imbreleth."

"There are all sorts of edible creatures. Lava worms, desolate strid-ers, pulsating quons."

I cringe. "Sounds… fascinating."

"Hah. Yeah. Another reason I've spent the past eleven centuries here." She sulks. "I can't even look at a man without getting sick to my stomach."

"You'd be surprised how many women feel that way, and they don't even eat them."

She laughs. "Ioeth."

"Pardon?"

"My name."

"Oh. I'm Brooklyn. Nice meeting you."

"Same."

"Which, erm, side are you on?"

Ioeth raises an eyebrow. "Side?"

"About the whole destroying the world bit."

"Oh. Against. Would you support a group of lunatics trying to blow up the only restaurant you liked?"

I laugh, despite feeling a little unnerved. Wow. It takes a lot to creep me out. At least she's not an enemy. So, so weird this woman doesn't feel like a murderer to me. Even if she only ate one guy a month… after a thousand years, her kill count has to rival that of the insurance industry. However, trying to apply human law here is like chickens accusing people of murder for consuming them. Such a weird moral slope.

"Fair point. Anyway, speaking of food… I have a little one who's waiting for some."

"All right. Any suggestions on where I should try these 'tacos'?"

I stand and give her the address of a little place about two blocks from my apartment. Little 'hole in the wall' next to a laundromat called Juan's. Almost as good as my mom's cooking.

"Thanks. I'll give it a shot. I'm absolutely starving." Ioeth waves, then lets herself fall off the building onto her wings, cruising away to the northwest.

Hmm. Did I just bring an end to a serial killer's spree or help a woman with a crisis?

Whatever. Time to go home.

4

UNDER THE BED

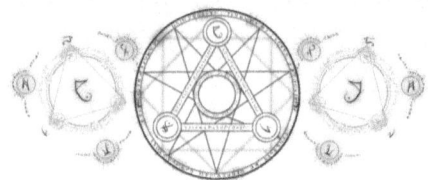

A shrill scream wakes me in the middle of the night.

It takes me a moment to process the meaning of a child shrieking in terror. Oh, right. I have one of the little buggers living with me now. She screamed. Probably means something bad is going on. Considering I don't see or smell fire, no earthquake, nothing's roaring, and our apartment is presently quiet, the most likely culprit seems to be a nightmare.

This, at least, I have some experience with. Having nightmares, I mean. Being on the other end and doing the comforting is new. Surprisingly—well, not so surprisingly in hindsight—being trapped in a burning trailer didn't give me nightmares. Even before I knew what I was, fire didn't scare me. I had more mundane nightmares… usually me running away from packs of bullies, including teachers. Being poor sucked. Being so poor I had to wear the same clothes all week long sucked even more. You'd think the school administration would do something about teachers making fun of students.

Anyway, the child screamed. Time to investigate.

I get out of bed and make my way to her room. It's catty-corner at the end of the hall to my room, so close I can stand with one foot in each bedroom and not fully do a split.

Pandora is awake, sitting cross-legged on her bed, her back against the corner of the wall. She appears reasonably calm. Wings, tail, horns, and claws are out… which is normal for her at night.

"You okay?"

"Fine," says the child.

"What's with the screaming?"

"There's a monster under my bed."

I take a step into the room, suppressing a yawn. "Are you being serious or did you have a nightmare?"

"Serious."

"Must be a scary one for you to scream like that."

The kid gives me a 'bitch please' face. "I didn't scream."

I crouch and peek under the bed. Two baseball-sized yellow eyes stare at me from the deepest corner against the wall, attached to a creature resembling a partially deflated giant frog. Thing's about three feet across, mostly mouth, and covered in spots of varying green shades. Bunch of little horns stick out here and there as well. And… it's quivering.

"Don't let her get me," whispers the monster.

I lean up to look at Pandora.

The child examines her claws. Greenish blood drips over the back of her right hand. "He shouldn't have pulled my tail."

I peer under the bed again.

"It draped over the side, fair game," whispers the monster.

Pandora snarls.

"Eek!" The monster attempts to cram itself deeper against the wall, its body deforming like a Jell-O mold.

Hmm. This has to be one of the 'under-bed' monsters that feed on a child's fear and don't actually hurt anyone. "Okay, go on. Get lost." I wave it out.

"Leave Ashley alone or I'll rip your face off," says Pandora.

The monster emits a whimper before blurring into a green smear and disappearing into the closet. Well, he certainly won't be back in *this* apartment.

"Great." Pandora sighs at the ceiling. "Now I have a closet monster. He's gonna sit in there and stare at me."

"Hah. Doubtful." I sit on the edge of the bed. "Closet monsters are a demotion. But the bed monsters still use closets to move around. He's gone. Go back to sleep."

"Okay."

"You're not scared, are you?"

"Pff." She rolls her eyes.

Grinning, I ruffle her hair. "Didn't think so."

She scoots under her covers and curls up like an adorable little creature from the outer planes of the Abyss. I tuck her in, kiss her atop the head, and return to my room. Oh, screw it. Maybe the kid's on to something. I pull my long T-shirt off and spread my wings, careful not to swat anything off my shelves or dresser. After extending my tail, I, too, crawl into bed and curl up like some odd mini-dragon.

Hmm. Yeah, this *is* kinda comfortable.

5

DADDY ISSUES

Something I've been putting off for too long needs to happen.
It's time for me to introduce my father to Pandora. The only reason it hasn't gone down yet is irrational paranoia. Nothing about my father. I'm merely afraid calling him into the world is going to jinx me into having to deal with Melisandre or the warmongers sooner than they'd have otherwise made assholes of themselves. No basis in fact. Pure superstition. Some of the people who believe in literal demons and angels think if one side makes a move in the mortal world, it gives the other side permission to do something, too. It's not true, but, again, superstition.

On Wednesday, I go straight to Tracy's apartment from the fire station after my shift is done. Wednesday is her 'light' day, meaning she has only school to worry about, no job hours. Consequently, she watches the kids. More to the point, she tries to do homework or study while keeping one ear and half an eye on them. As soon as I get home, the kids come over to my place so she can focus on her nursing degree.

When I walk into Tracy's, she gives me the same sort of stare a person trapped in a burning car does when they see me rip the door off. Oof. Guess the kids are in the midst of a sugar rush or she's got a ton of work.

"Guys," calls Tracy. "Brook's here."

"Okay," chorus the girls from down the hall. A moment later, they run into view. No odd smells, no burns, blood, or visible injuries. Good.

I point to the right at the wall separating our apartments. "If you hear some strange noises in a little while, don't freak out. It's just my father."

Tracy and the girls all stare at me.

"You have a father?" asks Tracy.

"Uhh, yeah." I chuckle. "Everyone does. He just lives kinda far away."

Pandora gives me a 'wow really' look while Ashley smiles. She's already met him. I should probably be mildly concerned that an eight-year-old's reaction to a powerful 'demon' showing up is an 'ooh!' Then again, he's not a bad guy. I think he's vicariously recapturing the 'dad-ness' he missed being part of my childhood with her… which means he's going to flip out over Pandora.

"Oh." Tracy gives me a knowing nod. "Gotcha."

"Have fun studying. You wanna pop over for food when it's ready or did you feed them?"

"Got absorbed. Food would be amazing…" Tracy apologize-grins at me.

"Not a problem. I'll knock on the wall when it's ready." I head for the door. "C'mon, guys."

The kids follow me out of Tracy's apartment and into mine. I make a quick stop in the bedroom to trade my uniform for a tank top and comfortable skirt. Jason needs to hurry up and get back from Germany. The most pleasurable sensation in my entire week shouldn't be taking my shoes off. When I cross the apartment back to the kitchen, the girls trail after me, intent on helping. They're both a bit too little to really do much in terms of cooking, though Pandora loves cutting vegetables. No, I am not letting a six-year-old handle a knife—she's using her claws to shred peppers, onions, and mushrooms. Yes, I made her wash her hands first. Honestly, her tail's significantly sharper and more dangerous than any kitchen knife… kinda silly not to let her use knives. While she does that, I show Ashley how to measure out the seasonings for the rice.

Fajitas aren't too much of a pain in the ass. I have the stuff on hand, and it's a good choice for an unexpected large dinner. Add some rice and beans on the side and no one will be hungry. While working on food, I explain to Pandora about my (our) dad, who's the reason we have all our neat powers. Mostly, I tell her the 'buttheads,' as she refers to the warmongers, threatened to hurt me if he showed himself, so he never got to be 'dad' to me when I was little. The girls listen intently. Ashley's a little jealous, but not too much so. She doesn't even remember her father. Dude ran off on Tracy when the kid was only around two. We have that sort of in common. I didn't meet my Dad until a few months ago. Little did I know, he'd always been watching me from a distance. Stupid Elestari.

Anyway, I want to make this a little bit special for him, so I put Pandora up to hiding in her room for a minute and surprising him. Giggling, she hurries off down the hall. Ashley stays put in the kitchen.

Okay, here goes. I close my eyes and concentrate on wanting to communicate with him. The exact way it works is a bit of a mystery to me, but knowing the real name of a Shaar'nath lets us sorta talk to them. He may or may not hear my words as I think them, but he'll be aware of me attempting to make contact. My father's real name is Baal'nethiel. Talk about a pain in the ass finding gifts with his name printed on them. Dad? If you're not super busy, can you pop in for a bit? I continue thinking about wanting to talk to him for another minute or so. Another thing I'm fuzzy on: the exact rules for how Elestari and Shaar'nath can jump back and forth between the human world and their home planes. As far as I know, either side can freely enter this world, but if they're killed here, they can't come back for a few decades.

I'm in the middle of explaining to Ashley how to time rice cooking when Dad appears out of thin air in my living room. He turns in place, looking around until he spots me, then walks into the kitchen.

His human form is so over the top, but it's irresistible. He's basically 'the most interesting demon in the world'. The human form he's chosen makes him look like he's in his early fifties, salt-and-pepper hair. He simply radiates coolness. I'm starting to recognize this image as 'dad,' so he no longer strikes me as smoldering and sexy. Yeah, I know, eww. Bear in mind the first time I saw him, he *was* basically a complete stranger. He's going for this old-school kind of 'coolness.' Part of me thinks it's a little lame, but I suppose it's normal for most people to feel their parents are lame when they try to act cool.

"Brooklyn..." He strides over into a hug. "Hope all is well? Staying alive, I see."

"Yep."

"Not destroying the world. Good girl." He again glances around. "I half expected to appear in the middle of a battle."

"Hah. No. Not this time." I pantomime wiping sweat from my forehead.

"Hi, Brook's dad," says Ashley.

He spins to smile at her, then scoops her up and swings her around once before setting her back down. For a minute or two, he talks to her about random stuff, basically acting somewhere between a mall Santa and surrogate grandpa. Ashley adores the attention. Even if she has to get it from a ten-thousand-year-old being from another reality, a positive male presence in her life is sorely needed. Much better than the parade of assholes Tracy used to date.

Normally, I wouldn't interrupt them, but I don't want to make Pandora hide all night. "Dad, there's something I needed to ask you about."

"Of course." He winks at Ashley in a 'be right back' manner, then straightens up to his full height, facing me. "What's on your mind? Are the idiots up to something again?"

"Yes and no. This is more of a personal situation. You know how you couldn't really be around for me when I was little?"

He deflates, nodding once.

"No blame. Just stating what happened." I pat his arm. "My emotional baggage is unpacked. Hate's on them, not you. So anyway, got a little surprise the other day and figured I ought to share with you."

Pandora peeks her head out of her room. I grin at her, which she takes as a 'go'. She steps into the hall, creeping toward the kitchen while trying to be quiet. Not difficult. She's barefoot on carpet and doesn't weigh much. I doubt she did it on purpose, but the jeans and *Moana* T-shirt outfit she has on makes her look exactly like me from seventeen years ago. The few dresses I owned only came out for special occasions. Except for *Moana* not being a thing back then, she's totally going to give Dad a flashback to watching me from afar when I was little.

"Surprise?" Dad exhales, then shakes a fist in a random direction. "I still desire to disembowel the ones responsible for threatening Reya and your lives were I to reveal myself to you."

"The last thing we need is more reason for war. So, the jackasses tried something, and it didn't quite work out the way they expected."

He chuckles. "Fools. Melisandre is getting desperate. I'm not surprised a reckless plan failed. What did they do?"

Pandora stops about two steps behind him, clasps her hands behind her back, and stands there trying not to laugh. Ashley bites her arm to keep herself from giggling. Dad glances at her, raising one eyebrow in confusion.

I examine my fingernails, pretending to be annoyed. "Melisandre appears to have finally accepted he's not going to be able to convince me to blow shit up, so he decided to make another agent of doom."

"Another one?" Dad pinches the bridge of his nose. "Fool."

"Yeah."

He lowers his arm. "We'll need to do something about them, preferably soon. How much do you know about this new demihuman?"

"A lot. You might even say I know everything about her."

Dad regards me with a suspicious look for a moment. "Where is she?"

Just to be weird, I lift my tail up and point the barb over my shoulder at Pandora. "Right behind you."

Dad blinks at me once, then turns around in a gradual, somewhat defensive stance.

Pandora makes her eyes super wide and puts on the most innocent face imaginable for a tiny destroyer of the universe.

"Wha...?" Dad whispers.

"Melisandre tried to copy me. He did too good a job. She kicked him square in the balls."

Pandora giggles. "Hi."

Dad seems to choke up, since he doesn't say anything.

Pandora sprouts horns, tail, and her wings with an audible *fwoomp*, the amulet saving her shirt from being ripped apart by swapping her outfit for the illusory dress. The kid grins wider, showing off her fangs.

You know the movie with the rabbit cop and her fox buddy? *Zootopia*, I think. Yeah. Remember the face the pudgy cheetah cop made when he saw something cute? As soon as Dad mentally processes the sight in front of him, he does a nearly spot-on impression of him, straight down to bringing his hands together at his chin.

Ashley sniffles and grabs onto me, having an attack of the 'awws.' Honestly, seeing my father's reaction is making it kinda hard for me to talk, too. Once the initial shock wears off, he picks Pandora up and holds her like a big doll. The expression on his face is totally 'this is mine, now.' I'd make a joke about it being damn difficult to make a demon cry, but we're not demons and honestly, Shaar'nath are *highly* emotional... at least compared to Elestari. You know, ruled by our baser instincts while the 'angels' consider themselves all intellectual and aloof. Dad's not crying *too* much, but his eyes are misty.

He sits at the kitchen table with Pandora in his lap, trying to make up for all the times he wanted to talk to or hug me, and he couldn't. She tells him about 'the buttheads' and kicking Melisandre in the groin, running away, and me finding her in the park later on. It doesn't take long for Ashley to also hop up in his lap. He knows she's desperate for any sort of father figure and is all too happy to oblige. Weird thinking of this guy as the same Baal'nethiel who used to lead massive armies into brutal, savage combat.

While cooking, I give him the story about what Melisandre and a group of warmongers did to me that resulted in Pandora's existence and bring him up to speed on my plan to have the human world consider her my daughter.

"I got a bit of static from the clerk's office. They didn't seem too inclined to accept my explanation for having a six-year-old come out of nowhere with no birth certificate or other documentation. Hopefully, my charm won't wear off."

He waves dismissively. "I'll pay them a visit tomorrow to make sure."

"Awesome. Thanks." I exhale, relieved. His psychic abilities are a lot more advanced than mine. He could probably make the county clerk declare Lawrence my son, and the man looks old enough to be my grandpa. "How come they didn't just try to conjure a 'destroyer' before?"

"Humans are an unexpected occurrence. The ancient magics responsible for the existence of this world did not specifically create them." Dad shrugs one shoulder. "I'm sure if the fools knew *how* to conjure a demihuman properly, they'd have done that instead of involving your mother. As far as your twin sister is concerned, I doubt they'll be willing to attempt anything like this again."

"So sure?" I shift the fajita stuff into a big serving bowl, then knock on the wall to let Tracy know food's done.

"The ones who participated in the ritual, casting the spell to create her, will likely have drained themselves severely. It will take them at least half a century to recover from it. And"—he bounces Pandora on his leg—"since the effort failed spectacularly to do what they wanted it to do, they'd be foolish to repeat it."

Doorbell.

Pandora puts away her extra parts. Her fancy black goth dress shifts in an instant back to the *Moana* T-shirt and jeans.

"I got it!" Ashley jumps off Dad's lap and runs to let her mother in.

Just because things have been crazy lately, I keep an eye on her, prepared to telekinetically drag her back from harm. Fortunately, it *is* Tracy at the door. Dad stays for dinner. In fact, he's probably going to stay all night. Can't really blame him. I probably should have introduced them a little sooner, but admittedly, I'd been slightly worried how he'd react. Glad to be wrong. And hey, on the positive side, I will never be in a situation where I can't find a babysitter.

6

AN INCONVENIENT INOG

Afew minutes after four in the afternoon on Thursday, we get a call for someone being stuck.

Usually, 'stuck' means large person sat on the toilet with the seat up or someone climbed into a washing machine, or a crawl-space, or something along those lines. I hop on a small truck with Humberto, Lamar, and the new probie, Alex Edison. He's about my age, friendly, and a total gym rat. Only bad thing about him is his habit of constantly wanting to talk about how many reps he can curl.

Yes, it's a bit annoying how a new guy swoops in and no one's giving each other weird looks, wondering *if* he can do the job... like they did with me. Whatever. Only an idiot of a woman joins the fire department and doesn't expect to put up with at least *some* bullshit. Maybe if I stood six feet tall with broad shoulders and a buzz cut, they'd have taken me more seriously. To a point, I get it. No one looking at me would think a girl my size could hang here. No, I'm not abnormally tiny... I'm just not big. In a job where not having the ability to carry the dead weight of an adult man around could be the difference between life and death, it makes sense for people to have questions. And yeah, when I *do* pick a dude up and haul him around, they have more questions, but that's not my problem.

We stop in front of a row house on Bosnall Street. Since this isn't a fire call, it's not surprising we find no smoke. Humberto checks the address we got from the emergency dispatcher, then heads over to the front door.

"Hello?" He bangs on the door a couple times. "Fire department. Someone stuck?"

No response.

Can't see much from the front. Just a solid brick wall running the length of the block. These rowhouses are basically one enormous building separated into individual living spaces by thick interior walls.

"Fire department," shouts Humberto, pounding on the door again. "Mr. Campos?"

A chorus of voices yell. Sounds like two adults and at least one child trying to say 'in the backyard.'

"Dammit," mutters Alex. "Do we have to break the door down?"

Humberto rattles the knob. "It's locked."

"Give me a sec." I walk up to the building, extend my claws when they can't see my hands, and climb. There ought to be a backyard space between this set of rowhouses and the next one over. All these places usually have at least a tiny attempt at a yard. Most aren't much bigger than an average living room, though. If the family is somehow stuck in their yard, the back door ought to be open. I can go up and over the building and enter via the rear.

It's nice being so strong my bodyweight is a triviality.

The guys stand there watching me scale the wall like a spider. Claws turn the bricks into decent handholds, but I do take advantage of windowsills. The second story window directly above the door is open a few inches. I push it up the rest of the way and slip inside. Easier than going over the roof.

It's a kid's room, likely a boy's. I don't pay much attention to anything and hurry out into the hall, down the stairs, and to the front door. After opening it to let the guys in, we head through the house to the kitchen and back door.

The yard is maybe twenty square feet, if that. It's got a tree in the corner, and a whole lot of opaque white spooge smeared everywhere. I really don't want to say what this stuff looks like. Yeah. That. It looks like Godzilla had sex with this backyard. The goo is all over the place, draped from the tree, on the ground, even adhered to the back wall of the house. A man, woman, and two kids appear to be trapped in it. The poor guy fell over backward and landed on a thick trail of gunk that's about two feet wide and three inches deep. It appears to have the consistency of thick glue. The son, who I'd guess to be around nine, is stuck by the hands to his father's arm... and has one foot trapped in the unknown substance. A girl around ten or eleven stands in the middle of the yard, her bare feet sunk to the ankles in the slime. Pink shoes sit atop the stuff one step behind her. Looks like she tried to run across it fast but the gunk stole her sneakers. Wow, poor kid's lucky she didn't face plant. Mom, who's constantly praying in Spanish at a near whisper, is stuck sideways to the back wall of the house like a mounted trophy, three feet off the ground, her head closer to the door.

"What the hell?" I ask.

"Help!" shouts the girl. "It's gonna rip my feet off. It's too sticky!"

Humberto slips past me, grabs a broom from the porch and hesitantly goes down the two steps to the yard, stepping into one of the few areas of ground *not* covered in gunk. He prods the end of the broom handle into the slime, then pulls. It appears to take damn near most of his strength to get it unstuck, and there are splinters left in the slime.

"Damn," whispers Alex. "Yeah, that's gonna peel skin off."

Both kids whimper.

"Where did this stuff come from?" I ask.

"A monster!" yells the boy.

The daughter reaches for us. Tears stream down her face. She looks as terrified as a mouse caught in a glue trap, knowing it's going to be stuck there until it starves to death.

"What kind of monster?" asks Alex.

"A big worm," yells the boy.

"Looked like a slug." The father grunts, probably trying to move. He's so thoroughly glued in place, his attempt to move isn't obvious as anything more than a facial expression.

I step off the porch, careful to put my boots down on clear dirt, and make my way over to the daughter. Except for Mom hanging on the wall, she's the closest to the house. "Hang on, sweetie. We'll get you unstuck... eventually."

She grabs my arm, clinging and shivering. "I thought I could jump over it, but I couldn't."

"Ariana," says the man, who I assume to be the 'Daniel Campos' indicated on our call notes as the property owner. "Don't touch her, or you'll get her stuck, too."

"My hands are clean, Papa!"

I look back at Lamar and Alex on the porch. "One of you guys call back to dispatch and tell them we need a mage out here. None of our equipment is going to touch this gunk."

The ground swells up near the back corner of the yard in front of the tree, forming a large anthill type mound. It rises to a little over two feet in height before the top ruptures, exposing a bright lime green slug as big as an adult hog. Giant pores all over its body exude a continuous supply of the same sticky residue. A pair of eyestalks wave around briefly before focusing on the boy.

"¡Mierda!" yells the kid. He pulls at his father's arm in a frenzy. No idea if he's trying to unstick his dad from the ground or merely attempting to flee. Either way, I don't blame him. The slug could eat him in three bites. Regardless of what he's trying to do, his hands are *not* coming unstuck.

His mother gasps.

Humberto, Lamar, and Alex all scream, as do Ariana and her mother.

The slug undulates out of the hole, slithering toward the panicking boy. Fortunately, it's not terribly fast. We probably have about a minute and a half until it reaches him.

"Be right back. Getting an axe!" shouts Alex before darting into the house.

"Axe is just gonna stick to it, man," calls Lamar.

Every now and then in a girl's life, circumstances line up to create what I call a 'fuck it' moment. One such moment was the day I stole the PlayStation. Figured I'd probably get away with it, but even if I didn't, the result of success would be worth the risk. I'm having another one of those moments. No way am I going to sit here and watch some giant slug thing eat a little boy in front of me. Explanations and excuses can come later.

I raise both arms, pointing my palms at the oblivious monster slug. Within a half second of me attempting to summon Imbreleth fire, a fat stream of dark crimson flames projects outward from my palms, incinerating the disgusting slug. Haven't measured how hot this stuff is exactly, but it's *way* hotter than ordinary fire. I've used it to completely cremate human remains to ash particles in a few minutes. The slug lasts about ten seconds before no trace of it is left.

"Whoa," whisper Humberto and Lamar simultaneously.

"Wow," says the boy. "Is that why they call you firemen?"

"She's not a fire *man*," snaps Ariana.

I chuckle. "No. I'm special. Not all of us can do that."

"Oh, thank you," says Daniel Campos. "Can you burn this glue off?"

"No. What's worse than glue so sticky it'll rip skin off?" I ask.

He stares at me.

"*Boiling* glue so sticky it'll rip skin off." I frown and gesture at the area where the slug had been. A puddle of opaque white spooge bubbles and smolders. It didn't catch fire, merely became slightly less viscous. "Sorry, but this is going to take a mage to get rid of. Just try not to move."

"I can't move," says the guy."

"My skin is peeling off," whimpers Mrs. Campos.

"Sit still and stop struggling." I tap my foot. "You're only hurting yourself."

Lamar hurries around and braces her, resulting in himself becoming stuck... but her weight is no longer hanging on glue. She breaks down sobbing and thanks him.

I grimace, realizing how much pain she must have been in.

Alex appears on the porch brandishing a big fire axe. For a second, he seems confused, then... disappointed. "Where'd it go?"

"Brook invited it to a barbecue." Humberto chuckles.

"Aww, guys." I smile at them, throwing off a heavy dose of charm. "No need to mention that to anyone. We need to get a mage here to clear out the slime."

The guys give me dazed looks. With any luck, they won't feel inclined to mention me going full flamethrower to anyone.

"I'll go call it in." Alex rushes into the house.

Humberto looks up from his Scry enchanted phone. "That's an inog."

"What the heck is an inog?" asks the father.

I gesture at the spot of boiling slime. "That *was* an inog."

"Ground burrowing giant slugs, known to leave a sticky residue, which they use as a trap to catch and eat small prey," says Humberto, reading from the Scry.

"Wow." I whistle. "Small prey? Someone needs to update the article."

"No kidding, right?" Humberto whistles and puts the Scry back in his coat.

We stay with the family, trying to keep them calm. About twelve minutes later, two cops and an aethermancer in a blue police robe show up. Ordinary people refer to them as 'wizards,' but mages find the term slightly demeaning. No idea why. Guess it's like calling a doctor a 'bonesaw.' Anyway, an aethermancer is a mage who doesn't have a strong affinity for a particular element, such as pyromancer or hydromancer. They use more generalized magic. Some even call them 'arcane' mages. They do all the fun stuff like opening portals or making stuff levitate.

The cops are more or less here only as an escort to guard the mage. That Sidney Stafford guy and his FRUM organization have stirred up something of an anti-mage faction. Even though this guy's a cop, some nutjob might throw a brick at him for being a mage. People are stupid.

He mutters something under his breath, then bobs a few inches off the ground before floating over to me in the middle of the yard.

"Inog," says Humberto.

"Ahh, yes. Troublesome nuisances." The mage nods once at me. He rests his hand on Ariana's head and mutters, "*nilax desporum.*"

The girl emits a faint gasp and looks down.

"You can lift her out of the residue now," says the mage.

I grasp Ariana under the armpits and lift her. The girl's feet slip out of the slug trail as easily as if from cake icing. While I carry her to the safety of the porch, the mage heads toward the boy. By the time I've deposited Ariana on the steps and returned, the boy's clinging to the mage's back and the man's helping the father up to his feet. Okay, I'm impressed. A mage letting the boy cling to him. Most mages I've run into except for Natalie are kinda stuck up. Got the impression this guy was the same when he told me to pluck Ariana out of the ooze.

Soon, we get the mother off the wall and bring the family out front to a waiting EMT crew who checks them over. None are seriously hurt. Soon, the mage has all the slime gathered into a giant wad, which he appears to destroy using a few splashes of an acid-based spell.

"Another day, another weird," mutters Humberto.

"Wow," says Alex.

"Welcome to Philly." I pat the new guy on the back.

"Crazy." Alex shakes his head.

"Nah." I laugh. "This? This is tame."

7

INITIATION

E ven though I didn't get any inog slime on me, it's still tempting to shower once we get back to the station. At least the stuff didn't have a noticeable odor. The four of us stash our gear and return to the 'ready room,' which is a fancy term for a hangout spot. If we're not cleaning something, repairing something, asleep in the barracks, or out on a call, we more or less hang out here waiting for the alarm to go off.

"How'd it go?" asks O'Keefe as we walk in.

"Giant freakin' slug," says Humberto. "Thing was as big as my dick."

"So, you picked it up with tweezers?" asks McCafferty.

Humberto gives him the finger.

"Sticky mess all over the place. Poor woman was stuck to the wall." Lamar shakes his head.

"You talkin' about the call or what happened in Humberto's bedroom last night?" Rich Baker cackles.

"Yeah, yeah…" Humberto flops on one of the sofas.

O'Keefe groans. "Sticky slug? Yeah, we had one of those yesterday. Damn thing crawled across the Schuylkill Expressway over by Ritner

Street. Left a slime trail like a speed bump. Poor bastard in a F250 hits the glue, and it's so damn sticky, the tires stopped dead on contact, rest of the truck kept going, flipped up and over."

Everyone whistles.

The guys start discussing how likely it is a whole nest of inog are in the area and could become a serious problem. Within seconds of me flopping on the sofa facing the big TV, Brian Herlihy leans on the couch behind me, giving me the 'hey I got an idea' look.

I peer up at him.

"Hey, wanna mess with the probie?" he whispers.

Heh. "What are you thinking?"

He waves dismissively. "Nothin' too bad. Ya do the mental thing and lift me up the pole when the moment's right."

I have poor impulse control, so I hold up a fist.

He bumps it. "Excellent."

A few minutes later, when Alex returns from the bathroom, Brian walks over to him. He's our resident giant red-bearded Viking... and he's almost as bad as Pandora for mischief. My current boyfriend, Jason, also happens to sport a ginger beard, but he's more 'lumberjack hipster' in terms of looks. Brian's beard obeys no comb, nor the laws of physics. He's also freakin' large, so when he yells 'oy, probie,' the whole room gets quiet.

"Time ta let ya in on one of the little secrets." Brian throws a conspiratorial arm around Alex's shoulders. "Assumin' ya don't know how ta go *up* the pole."

"Up the pole?" Alex raises an eyebrow. "You guys climb the pole?"

"Nah." Brian waves dismissively. "It's a li'l bit o' magic in the post. Lot faster'n goin' all the way ta the stairs."

Of course, by now, the other guys know he's up to something because he's exaggerating his accent. Under normal circumstances, Brian has no accent. As soon as he starts to sound half Irish, half Scottish, people who know him expect bedlam. Everyone more or less drops what they're doing to follow Brian as he leads Alex out from the ready room to the pole. Yes, fire stations usually have one. It's not just a Hollywood myth. Anyone on staff during the overnight shift sleeping upstairs uses it as a shortcut down to the garage. Also, yes, I had to deal with quite a few 'pole dancing' jokes when I first started. You know, because a woman in a fire station must be a stripper-gram, right?

Ugh.

My former lieutenant even tried to 'soften' the remark by saying the guys only teased me because I didn't 'look like' a female firefighter. Meaning, not a she-hulk. Double ugh. I had many reasons to dislike Lieutenant Pirelli. Amazing how often the man's chair slipped out from under him or his coffee bumped into his lap. Back then, none of the guys knew I had telekinesis.

Brian approaches the pole. "Now, watch carefully."

Alex folds his arms in a suspicious way, seemingly not buying the buildup.

Brian flicks the pole twice making soft pinging sounds, mutters, "Nerble nervit," then grabs on with one hand and strikes a pose.

Guess that's my cue. I telekinetically lift the big guy straight up. He's gotta be at least 250 pounds, which is a noticeable exertion... but not so much I grunt or strain visibly. Brian appears to levitate up the pole until he disappears into the hole in the ceiling. Faking curiosity, I step closer to keep him in view until he can step off the pole into the barracks upstairs.

Alex appears gobsmacked.

O'Keefe and Baker barely manage to keep straight faces. They know about my telekinesis. Humberto should know, but he looks equally baffled as Alex. McCafferty, I don't think knows about it. He also appears awestruck. Lamar just shakes his head.

"You try it," says Brian from upstairs.

Alex flicks his finger at the pole twice, says, "Nerble nervit," and grabs on.

Brian gives me a head shake, so I don't do anything.

"Takes a few tries. Gotta pronounce it just perfectly to activate the spell," says Brian.

We watch Alex repeat variations of 'Nerble nervit' for about five minutes. At one point he says, "Burble mervit,' and O'Keefe loses it, almost falling over he's laughing so hard.

"No, no, no." Brian, still watching down from the hole in the ceiling, waves both hands then overenunciates, "Ner-bull ner-vit."

Again, Alex tries about six or seven times before looking like he's going to give up.

"Dude, you just gotta lean a little bit on the 'er' part." O'Keefe walks up to the pole, does the tap, says, "Nerble nervit."

I float him upstairs.

Humberto finally catches me staring at O'Keefe and clamps a hand over his mouth to stop himself from laughing.

"Grr!" Alex grumbles and resumes flicking the pole while chanting that nonsense.

We're all more or less cracking up at this point watching a grown man continually baby talk at a pole while waiting for him to notice we've basically sent him to get a 'bucket of steam.' Poor guy seriously thinks there's something magic about the pole and keeps trying.

Lawrence Ellis walks in. It's as good to see him as it is an 'ugh' moment. The only reason he'd be here is if he wanted to ask me for help investigating another suspected arson case. I don't really mind helping. The ugh comes from knowing the guys are going to tease me about it plus guilt over Lawrence getting put in the hospital last time I helped him. Predictably, he walks right over to me, smiling bemusedly at Alex muttering nonsense at the pole.

"Hey. Good to see you," I say.

"Good to be on my feet again." Lawrence chuckles. "Hope I'm not interrupting anything."

"Not really."

Brian gives me a thumb-up.

Next time Alex says, "Nerble nervit," I lift him about halfway up and hold him there.

Everyone, except Lawrence (and obviously Alex) claps.

"Shit, I'm stuck," yells Alex.

"Uh oh. That's not good," says Brian in an ominous voice. "Only thing you can do now is say Nerble nervit backward. Careful, though... if you mispronounce it, ya might end up in New Jersey."

"Like teleportation?" Alex shivers.

"No, like launched out the roof." Brian makes an explosion noise.

Guffaws come from the guys.

"Uhh." Alex gulps. "Tivren, uhh…"

I flip him over upside down.

Alex yells and grabs onto the pole with both hands. He's not seriously frightened, so I keep holding him there. The feel he's giving off is more like a guy trying to tightrope walk between two houses and almost slipping.

"I'd like to ask you to help out on an investigation… if you have the time." Lawrence smiles.

"Figured. Are you sure it's a good idea? The brass can't be thrilled you're pulling someone my rank over to arson."

He shrugs. "They don't mind. You have special skills."

"Tivren elbren!" shouts Alex.

I float him to the floor.

He leaps to his feet and jumps away from the pole. "Screw that thing."

The guys burst into laughter. Alex looks around, making this face like he knows something isn't right but not exactly who to blame for what. Doesn't take him long to start laughing as well. Least he's a good sport.

Lawrence nods to the side, then walks a safe distance away from the laughing.

Sigh. I follow.

"The fire gutted a six-story apartment," says Lawrence. "Eighteen people died."

"Ugh. I dunno."

He tilts his head. "I thought you said your people aren't evil."

"We're not. I'm just extremely lazy."

Lawrence opens his mouth, likely to point out again how eighteen people are dead, but I cut him off.

"Okay." I half smile. "You know I'll help."

"You remind me of asking my son to take out the garbage when he was fourteen." Lawrence purses his lips. "He'd grumble the whole time, but he'd do it."

"I'm not really grumbling, am I?"

"A little. Not as much as Byron used to."

I raise both eyebrows. "He stopped grumbling?"

"Heh. No. He grew up and moved out." Lawrence hooks his thumbs in his pants pockets. "You'll need to run it by your lieutenant, of course?"

"Yep… but I don't think Sims will object."

8

THE STEDMAN BUILDING

I am becoming far too comfortable with flying.

Riding in Lawrence's department SUV to go somewhere is tediously slow. The property in question is in Fishtown, like two blocks away from Northern Liberties. It's kinda far away from my station's response zone, but the arson investigation team is city-wide. I've trusted Lieutenant Sims with a few of my secrets, one of which being my ability to fly kinda fast, so he doesn't mind me going off with Lawrence. If there's an emergency, all I need is an address and a smartphone, and I'll probably beat the fire crew to the scene.

"Site's mostly out now. Might be some smoldering spots," says Lawrence.

"How bad?"

He winces. "Six-story apartment building. My estimation is the fire broke out in a ground floor apartment, but it too-rapidly jumped to the space directly above. There's an almost simultaneous spread on the second floor. I've already interviewed the people who made it out. A resident of a ground floor apartment adjacent to the origin point described hearing a sound like a loud flamethrower."

"You're thinking another spell bomb type thing?"

"Yes. And it likely shot straight up, burned through the ceiling, and ignited the second-floor apartment at the same time as the ground level."

I exhale out my nose. We're not even at the place yet, and already, an uncomfortable squirm is seeping into my consciousness. Something about this fire is bad… or maybe it's my imagination. My discomfort could be imagination. Subtle psychic hits are basically indistinguishable from random thoughts. Talking about eighteen people dying in a fire *is* plenty morbid enough to give people the creeps. Me, not so much… which is why I'm thinking this sense of ominousness is outside information.

"Guessing you have nothing to go on, so you're hoping for a long shot?" I grin at him.

"More or less." He chuckles. "Been all over the building as much as is safe to do. Haven't discovered any evidence of accelerants or any clear ignition source. Got the landlord pestering the city about demolishing what remains of the place before it collapses and does damage to adjacent properties or hurts someone and opens him up for a lawsuit."

I shake my head. "Always comes down to money. Sounds kind of suspicious to me he's pushing so hard for the building to be torn down. Almost like he's trying to conceal evidence."

"Could be. I let the detectives know my thoughts. They said they haven't seen anything suggesting the man had a motive to burn the place."

"Low income units. Maybe he wants to replace it with more expensive ones?"

He whistles. "Could be. No way to prove what the man's thinking."

"Maybe not prove it, but I might be able to tell." I wag my eyebrows.

"Heh, now that's damn tempting." Lawrence gives me a conspiratorial wink. "Can't do nothin' with it in court, but least it'll let us know if it's a waste of time to go digging around. We can pay him a quick visit once we're done at the site."

"Okay. Still not exactly a master of mind reading, but I'll do my best."

LAWRENCE PARKS NEAR THE CORNER OF EAST WIDLEY AND DAY STREETS.

We're in front of the burned ruins of a six-story brick building. Even before the fire, it looks like it definitely saw better days. In front of us, a long swath of strange, green wooden garage doors takes up most of the block. They all look pretty beat up, like one good storm would tear them all down. So bizarre. The curb isn't ramped, so they can't be for cars. Wonder what's inside. Meh, not my concern.

A few cops hang out in the area around the Stedman Building, the one that burned. Could throw a rock from where we parked and land it on I-95. Yeah, this is definitely not an expensive part of town to live in. Lawrence hands me a pair of blue nitrile gloves, which I put on.

"Still worried about fingerprints?" I ask, smiling.

"Nah. It's to keep the nasty stuff off your hands. If you gotta touch something to get a read, go right on ahead. But any stink you can't wash off is your fault." Lawrence gestures in an 'after you' manner.

"No stench waiver?" I chuckle.

"Not this time."

The cops nod in greeting as we cross the property and go in the front door.

"Careful," says Lawrence. "The structure is liable to collapse. If you feel something pulling you upstairs, it might be a problem. Anything above the second floor is really too unstable for us to go tromping around."

"No problem. I—" My voice catches in my throat as an incoming wave of psychic 'mood' hits me.

The strange green doors spanning the next block leap into my mind's eye. It's the middle of the night. Flames fill the dark sky. Someone stood by those doors watching the fire and listening to people scream. A loud metal *clank* precedes a long, loud wail. The fire escape broke. Someone fell to their death. Disappointment. The watcher wanted the man to burn, not go splat.

"Sick bastard," I whisper.

"I'll assume you're not talking about present company." Lawrence smiles.

"You showed me a little model of a grandfather clock a while back... I think it's the same guy."

"Oh, damn." Lawrence hangs his head. "We been after this guy for damn near a decade. Are you sure?"

I hold a hand to my forehead until the dizziness fades. "As sure as random mental images can be. Guy had the same twisted pleasure listening to people scream. And he watched it."

Lawrence sets his hands on his hips. "Yeah, sure does sound like him all right."

"Yeah, the sicko who got off on hearing people burn to death." I shudder. "Definitely feels like the same guy. The energy in the walls feels just like that little clock."

"Didn't find any devices here."

I glance over at him. "How thoroughly did you look? The building's going to come down at any minute, right?"

Lawrence tilts his hand in a so-so gesture. "We conducted a reasonably thorough examination of the fire, accounting for the safety of all personnel."

That's him saying they rushed. Well, kinda rushed. It's not like Lawrence to half-ass anything. I'm sure he's genuinely worried about having five stories of brick, wood, and concrete fall on his head. Good chance something like that would be the end for me, too. I'm tough, but not *that* tough. Hell, they burned Joan of Arc to death.

My thoughts wander as I make my way deeper into the building. The Elestari tried to make a 'world destroyer' like me before, only last time, she was a half-Elestari. Did Joan have strength like me? Obviously, she didn't have armor, at least not without putting metal on. Elestari fly much faster than us. The girl probably had wings. Maybe magic. Of course, the poor thing had a seriously bad case of 'the myths.' Worse than my mother. Even if she had magic, I doubt she'd have used it, considering it evil. She most likely thought being burned at the stake was 'God's will' for her and didn't even put up a fight.

It's funny, really. I laugh only because it didn't *truly* kill her. She ended up in Aesinor as a full Elestari—and, according to my father, did *not* handle learning the truth well at all, that the whole religion thing she'd dedicated her life to amounted to stories made up by humans. And yeah, the 'angels' are assholes. For the most part. Laniah is the exception. *She* doesn't consider humans to be mold growing on the side of a fish tank.

Wonder if Joan could've fought her way out of being burned at the stake if she wanted to? How potent is a half-Elestari?

My thoughts shift gears when a sudden urge to take a left turn grabs me. I follow the odd feeling down a corridor, climbing over tons of debris that fell down from upper floors. A few meters past a huge chunk of fallen ceiling, I walk through the steel frame of a former doorway. There's no more wall around it, nor apartment in front of it. Just a steel rectangle I went through to be weird. The ground is still wet, mushy ash mixed with particles of drywall, paint chips, and wood bits. Everything reeks like someone threw a pair of old boots in the oven and left them there until they caught fire.

Grunting, Lawrence makes his way down the debris-strewn corridor, grabbing onto cinder blocks for balance. He steps off the long ceiling slab behind me, then avoids the door frame. "I'm impressed."

"I haven't done much."

"You found the origin point." He points up.

The ceiling is entirely destroyed, basically turning this space into a two-story tall vaulted cathedral. Even the ceiling of the second-floor apartment directly above me is mostly gone. "How do you know anything shot straight up? There's nothing left."

"Burn intensity of the surroundings on the floor above us. The fire spread outward from this apartment as well as the one above it at roughly the same rate. If no sort of magical fire penetrated from here upward, it means we had two simultaneous ignition sources in two separate apartments triggered within thirty to forty seconds of each other. Considering you suspect it's the same man we know who uses little time bombs…"

"Right." I look around. Come on, Brook. Do a psychic. I poke myself in the leg. "Is anything still here?"

"Hoping you can find something. Even if it's a vision."

I smile back at him. He's certainly a lot more open to the idea of psychic phenomenon than he used to be. Granted, he's seen me go all out… armor, wings, the whole deal. My knuckles kinda ache when I think about punching a stone golem in the face.

Eyes closed, I try to focus on the icky thoughts of the man watching the fire, opening myself to whatever psychic energy might be imprinted on the area. This is potentially a bad idea since eighteen people died here. According to some research I've done recently, violent deaths tend to leave powerful psychic imprints on the surroundings. They call the technique of reading psychic imprints out of objects 'psychometry.' Lucky me, it seems to be something I'm capable of. Gotta brace myself for a mental sledgehammer of anguish. Sure, I often find death hilarious, but I'm not a complete bitch. Someone dying is only funny if they deserve it. I can't laugh at a bunch of innocent people getting roasted in their sleep. Some dude stuffs a gun up my nose in Kwan's Market? Yeah. Him French kissing a speeding bus is totally hilarious.

I'm drawn to a spot on the floor where the gloopy ash-gunk residue has formed into a series of mounds. Looks like a model landscape for a science fiction movie about a desolate alien planet. I crouch and reach out, allowing my subconscious to guide my telekinesis. My brain latches onto the sense of an object I can't see, guided by my psychic fixation on it. It's under at least a foot of muck. Not too heavy. Small. I pull it up toward my hand.

Goldish metal breaks the black surface. Glittering ruby eyes stare at me from the face of a six-inch-tall owl statuette. I pluck it out of the ashy sludge, stand, and back away until I'm next to Lawrence.

A *thud* comes from overhead. Probably a piece of ceiling or wall collapsing.

"Got something."

"I'll say." He whistles. "Is that gold?"

"No clue. I'm not a jeweler."

"Think we can get out of here before it comes down on top of us?"

I nod. "Yeah. After you."

We climb back down the jammed corridor. Every creak or clatter in the distance overhead kicks me a little more in the butt to move faster. It's tempting to pick Lawrence up and haul ass, but it only sounds like small stuff dropping. Damn sure the instant I start to hear anything like cracking or feel the floor vibrating, I'm going to grab him and make a new hole in the wall to get out.

Fortunately, the Stedman Building decides not to crush us. Once we're outside and over by his SUV, I peel off my right glove and gently touch one bare knuckle to the owl's beak. The instant I make contact, my surroundings change.

It's as if I've teleported two blocks down the same street. I'm facing the Stedman Building, and it isn't burned. No, I'm walking toward it. Rather, watching someone walk. This is a vision. I'm not in control here, merely observing. Soon after crossing Day Street, a guy in a UPS uniform walks up to 'me.' He appears to be in his later thirties with jaw-length light brown hair. Kinda has a half-stoned look to him. He hands 'me' a small cardboard box. Something about the dude feels wrong. He's extremely creepy, like the kind of creepy to randomly stab sharp things into nearby animals on a whim. Fortunately, he doesn't do anything more than smile and walk away after handing 'me' the box. The vision tilts down to look at the package. It's addressed to Joyce Underhill, Apartment 104.

"...ooklyn?" Lawrence gently shakes my shoulder. "You with me?"

It takes me a moment to collect myself back into my head. "Yeah. Whoa."

"Vision?"

"Yep."

"You're getting better at this. Didn't pass out."

I chuckle.

Lawrence keeps his hand on my shoulder as if I'm about to fall over. I'm not, but it doesn't bother me. I don't have too many friends, so it's nice to be reminded he cares. He waits for me to shake off the disorientation of feeling like someone else, then gives me an expectant look.

"I... think I saw the dude. He dressed up like a UPS guy and handed a package to someone named Joyce Underhill."

He stares at me like I just gave him winning lottery numbers.

"What?"

"Ms. Underhill is the woman who lived in the apartment where the fire broke out."

I slump. "Damn."

"What did this man look like?" Lawrence takes the owl statuette by grasping it in a plastic baggie.

"Late thirties, maybe. White guy. Light brown hair down to his jawline. Seemed kinda high or maybe just so sociopathic you can see it in his eyes. Definitely a 'do not leave unsupervised with small animals or children' type of guy."

Lawrence winces. "One of those?"

"No, not a pedo. More like anyone he doesn't feel threatened by, he'd torture them to death for fun."

He shudders.

"My feelings exactly. But… I saw his face."

"Well, that'll come in handy if we happen to run into him." Lawrence examines the owl in the bag. "Nice find, though. Doubt we're going to get prints off it. None of the others had any."

"Worth a try?"

He shrugs. "So's asking you to fly around Philadelphia in circles looking for him."

"Hah."

"Welp, we may as well get back." He climbs into the SUV.

Looks like my work here is done. Helping him out is kinda like watching someone else's child. I get to have all the fun parts of hanging out with a kid, but the responsibilities—in this case, paperwork and testifying—are someone else's problem.

I can deal with that.

9

DEADLY ALCHEMY

We get back in the SUV and sit there, I dunno, maybe waiting to see if the Stedman Building collapses. It's surprisingly fascinating to watch the place, wondering if it's going to implode at any moment. The structure is definitely unstable, giving a bit more credibility to the landlord being so insistent on receiving the go-ahead to proceed with demolition. I could probably help it along with a telekinetic slam in the right spot, but other buildings are too closely packed here. If this thing comes down uncontrolled, it's definitely going to ruin someone's day.

"You mentioned the guy wanting to demolish what's left of it before?" I ask.

"Yes. Now that you've gotten a chance to feel around the place, I can't think of much reason to preserve the site for investigation. I imagine Mr. Maxwell will be quite eager to speak with us when I tell him I only have a few quick questions before closing the investigation and releasing the property back to him."

I nod. "Okay. Let's do it."

He makes a phone call. "Hello. This is Lawrence Ellis with the Philadelphia Fire Department. Is Mr. Maxwell available?" He pauses. "I see. Well, can you let him know I'm the chief investigator on the fire at the Stedman Building. The investigation is almost complete. I just have a few questions I'd like to ask him in person, then we can close things up so he can do whatever he needs to do with the property." He pauses. "All right." Lawrence holds the phone to his chest and whispers, "I'm on hold."

Heh.

In under a minute, he nods in response to a voice on the phone. "All right. I'll be there as soon as traffic allows. Thank you."

He hangs up.

"We're going to see him now?" I ask.

Lawrence shifts the SUV into drive. "We are."

WE ENTER THE OFFICE OF MAXWELL PROPERTY MANAGEMENT ABOUT twenty minutes later.

It's on the forty-fourth floor of an office building in center city, sharing space with multiple other smallish businesses. At a quick glance around, my guess is Charles Maxwell has two, maybe three employees: a receptionist and an accountant... and possibly someone in a tiny side office. Anyone's guess what they do. Maybe a dispatcher for maintenance requests.

The receptionist hurries us into the largest office in the space, which isn't too large.

Charles Maxwell looks to me like any other fiftyish white dude in a suit. He could be a lawyer, a stock trader, a VP, or the strange guy at car dealerships who watches everything from a back office but never talks to anyone. He stands as soon as we walk in and shakes hands with Lawrence. I get a somewhat offbeat smile and nod. My first impression is the guy probably inherited a pile of money and or real estate and is in the pool a bit over his head. Not picking up any sort of malice or deceit off the guy. Genuine hope.

"Good afternoon, Mr. Maxwell," says Lawrence. "I apologize this investigation has taken longer than usual. Just trying to be thorough. This is Brooklyn Amari. She's helping me on the investigation."

"Hello." I force myself to wave like an adult rather than give a two-finger off the head surly teen salute.

"I understand." Charles leans back in his chair. "Hope you've got some good news for me."

The good thing about not having to do any of the talking is it makes concentration easier. I focus on the guy's mind, trying to barge in on his outermost thoughts.

Lawrence opens his notepad to the handful of questions I suggested. "We do. Just a few procedural points to get out of the way first."

"All right," says Charles.

"Please understand this is all routine stuff." Lawrence smiles. "You've been pretty insistent on wanting us to hurry things along so you can proceed with demolition. What is the rush?"

His thoughts jump to worry about lawsuits.

"I went there as soon as they got the fire out and saw how unstable it is. The building's old. They put it up in like 1922, if I remember right. It's close to other properties. My concern is liability. If it goes down in an uncontrolled collapse, it could hurt people."

Lawrence jots down some notes. "True. Can you think of anyone who might want the building to burn down?"

The name Donald Huxley appears in Charles's thoughts, shrouded in maybes. He's not convinced but has this 'if anyone might have *wanted* it to burn' feeling.

"Well..." Charles leans forward, resting his elbows on the desk. "There's some ongoing disputes with a tenant's organization, but I don't think any of them would escalate things to the point of burning the building to the ground. There's something else. It's probably nothing, but no harm mentioning it, I suppose."

"What's that?" asks Lawrence.

"About six months ago, a developer contacted me about buying the Stedman Building. His offer was low, and he also admitted to me he intended to demolish the building to make way for some manner of new development. I have no idea if he was planning on more expensive apartments or something commercial. It didn't seem right to displace thirty families so some guy in a high-rise office could make a buck."

Says 'some guy in a high-rise.' Ironic right? But this guy is thinking of Huxley. Charles is also considering selling the guy the property now if the man keeps his initial offer. He'd rather get the money than go through the hassle of replacing the building himself. It sounds reasonable to consider this Huxley dude might have something to do with the fire... except for knowing a psychotic serial arsonist did it. 'Grandfather clock guy' has a string of fires going back a decade. He's the sort of case that gets passed on from one detective to another, spanning multiple careers and might never get solved. Psychos like him sometimes end a detective's career. Or maybe I've just seen too many melodramatic cop movies. Sooner or later, they say every criminal makes a fatal error and gets caught. Hope this guy screws up soon.

"Very noble of you, Mr. Maxwell." Lawrence tucks his pen away. "I think that about covers it. Soon as I get back to my office, I'll be finalizing the paperwork. You should be receiving an official notice returning custody of the property to you either by close of business today or early tomorrow."

"Great. Thank you." Charles stands and offers a hand.

Lawrence shakes.

"Did you figure out how the fire started?" asks Charles.

"It appears to be intentional." Lawrence stuffs his notepad in his pocket. "Jury's still out on motive, though. It may be a random event. Won't know more until the police have a suspect in custody. For now, though, there's nothing more to gain from the property itself. I agree with you it's a hazard and ought to be dealt with soon."

"I appreciate your help. Thanks." Charles nods at us.

We return to the SUV. Lawrence gets into a friendly conversation with a parking enforcement agent. Apparently, the meter here was in a bad mood and didn't realize our vehicle is an official one. A three-way argument ensues between Lawrence, the enforcement officer, and the meter troll. It's honestly closer to a tiny stone golem on a post, but the thing's got a bad attitude. It knows it messed up calling for an officer and it's trying to come up with all the lame excuses it can. Argument's not the best word. Lawrence and the agent are on the same side, bitching at the meter. It's stupid of me, but being around someone in a 'police like uniform' in the middle of a spirited debate makes me nervous, like they might notice me and find a reason to give me trouble. Can't call it a guilty conscience because I haven't done anything... recently. I stay quiet and remember the guy's not a real cop, just a meter attendant.

Eventually, the stupid mini-golem decides to pout and shapeshifts back into an ordinary-looking meter. The cop laughs and goes on his way. Lawrence and I get in the SUV, shaking our heads.

"Well, there's twenty minutes we won't get back." I rub my eyes. "So, are we done here?"

"More or less."

"Pity we can't talk to the owl woman."

Lawrence glances at me. "Why not?"

"Uhh, because she lived in the apartment where the fire started. She's dead."

He chuckles. "No, Mrs. Underhill survived. She wasn't home at the time the fire broke out. Not sure where she is now, but she's definitely alive."

I blink. "Lucky."

Lawrence pats the baggie containing the statuette. "Hopefully, in a few months, we'll have more of an idea of what happened."

"A few months?"

"Detective mages are backed up. It's going to take them a while to get around to looking at this."

I point at the window. "C'mon Lawrence, you know me better than that. Go to Natalie's. She'll look at it for us."

He taps at the GPS. "Remind me?"

"Enchanted Evenings in Kensington."

"Odd name for a magic item shop. Sounds like an escort service." He chuckles.

I laugh. "I've told her that a dozen times."

AFTER AN OBLIGATORY STOP AT REANIMATOR COFFEE, LAWRENCE AND I walk into my friend's store.

A pair of tween boys in the toy area amuse themselves with the 'remote control' faeries, flying them around the shelves at high speed. I can't tell if they're racing or pretend fighting. One little girl about Pandora's age is riding the toy unicorn up and down the aisles. Another, somewhat older, girl plays soldier with the 'laser gun' Natalie made. It fires bright, harmless bolts of light. Super unrealistic as lasers go, but it looks pretty.

Four adults browse shelves of more domestic enchanted items... appliances and so forth.

Wow. This is the most crowded I've ever seen the shop. Fortunately, no one is talking to Natalie at the moment. She's observing the goings on from the counter, smiling wide. Having more than one customer in the shop at the same time is cause for celebration.

"Can't believe the department seriously doesn't have people for this."

"You know mages. They love the glory. 'Arson investigation' doesn't command the same kind of ego being a detective for the police department does. Cops have a team of arcane investigators, but it takes them forever to get around to anything and tons of paperwork."

"Ugh."

Natalie spots me and waves.

I walk over and hand over the strawberry latte I got her. "Here ya go."

"Ooh. Thanks. Mmm. Strawberry. My favorite. It's almost like you know me." She hugs me. "Hey, Lawrence."

"Hah." I chuckle.

"Hello, dear." He smiles. "Sorry to keep visiting you only when we need something."

"Aww, it's okay. What's up?" She sips her coffee.

Two faerie toys shoot past me at bullet-like speed. The boys wearing the control rings lean over the waist-high wall surrounding the play area, guiding their minions around the entire store.

"Guys!" calls Natalie. "Be careful. If you crash them into something it could blow up."

Both kids yell 'sorry' and steer the faeries back to the play area as well as slow them down.

The girl playing with the 'rifle' tries to shoot the other girl zooming around on the tiny unicorn. The mini-horse is astonishingly lifelike, but small. Compared to a six-year-old, it's about the size of a normal horse to an adult.

"We were wondering what you can tell us about this." Lawrence holds up the baggie. "First question being, is this thing still dangerous?"

Natalie takes the owl. She sets it on the counter, waves her hands over it, and whispers a few magical phrases. Faint light appears in swirls around her fingers, connecting them to the statuette. "It's no longer dangerous. This is an alchemical device."

"It turns lead to gold?" I ask.

She sticks her tongue out at me. "No. What I mean is, it's not an enchanted item. Alchemists are closer to mages than enchanters, but they don't really cast spells. They create things like this owl. The same way a pyromancer would throw a fire spell, an alchemist creates a little item that contains a fire spell… then later, the item is used to release the magic. It doesn't necessarily have to be the alchemist to use it, either."

"You're saying alchemists make items like an enchanter?" asks Lawrence.

"These aren't 'items' as much as basically grenades." Natalie ducks a high-speed faerie toy. "The things I create are permanent. An alchemist's talismans only work once. It's exactly like a mage casting a spell but pausing it to use later. Usually, they carry a whole bunch of trinkets around, all basically pre-cast spells."

"Oh." Lawrence rubs his chin.

"Excuse me," asks a later-thirties woman approaching the counter. "Is the sign for the unicorn correct? The price is $8,000? Not $800?"

Natalie makes the same face she always does when her guilt gets in the way of her survival. "Yes. The price is based on materials, the amount of time it took me to make it, and rarity. I'm willing to negotiate a bit on the price if you're interested in buying it outright."

I expect the woman to cringe and run off, but she merely says, "Give us a few minutes to talk about it."

"Of course." Natalie smiles. "Bear in mind, it will last for a few hundred years if it's treated well and doesn't need food, won't make messes, and so on."

"Treated well?" asks the woman. "How delicate is it?"

"It's not brittle. I mean, if no one runs it over with a car or abuses it." Natalie smiles.

The woman nods and walks away.

"So, hand grenades," I mutter.

"Yep." Natalie wags the owl at us. "Alchemists blow stuff up or make bath bombs. I make useful things that last for decades or centuries. Anyway, this owl appears to have been an amplification spell. It's a complicated talisman that's a mixture of clockworks and alchemy."

"Not a fire spell?" Lawrence scratches at his eyebrow.

"Nope. I'm assuming because it's in a baggie, you don't want anyone touching it for fingerprint reasons. Without being able to take it apart, I have to guess, but it looks like the mouth is an opening to a mechanism inside. Most likely, the guts of this thing contained a phial with a hypergolic potion, and the alchemy spell infused in the owl magnified the potency of the burn by about five times."

I stare at her. "Once more in English? Hyper-what?"

"Hypergolic usually refers to chemicals that spontaneously combust when exposed to the air," says Lawrence.

"Ahh. See? This is why I don't feel qualified officially becoming an arson investigator." I wink. "Need at least a few more years of school."

"You should consider it." He smiles, then shifts his attention back to Natalie. "This is not an enchanted item?"

"No." She shakes her head. "There's no magic left in it. It's presently a brass owl. Probably has some wind-up bits inside to smash the phial and release the potion."

"Can you tell what determined when it went off?" I ask.

She makes a series of faces at the owl. "The alchemist who makes a talisman can set them off whenever they want, as long as they are close enough. I'm not really sure how it works since I'm not an alchemist, but they somehow *feel* every active talisman they've created. It's why you don't usually see them selling their stuff. They can only make so many talismans at once before they exhaust themselves. You know how mages get tired the more spells they cast?"

"Yeah," says Lawrence.

"These guys, they make themselves tired when they create a talisman, and don't get un-tired until the talisman is spent."

"Ouch. Gotta suck." I whistle.

She nods. "Yeah. Supposedly, they can have way more active talismans than any mage can throw magic before they pass out from exhaustion, but it takes them a while to make each one."

I lean on the counter. "Something tells me this guy doesn't keep a large stock of talismans around. He probably makes them and uses them fairly soon."

"Could be." She shrugs. "If an alchemist isn't going to toss their talisman like a literal grenade, they can set them off almost like remote control."

"From how far away?" I ask.

"Not really sure. Probably not so far they couldn't see it. Definitely not from miles away."

I frown. "This guy definitely likes to be close so he can watch the show."

Lawrence's cell phone rings. "Excuse me a moment."

I nod at him, then take a few gulps of coffee, making Natalie wince since it's still—to her—too hot to chug.

The woman who asked about the unicorn returns with a well-dressed man and the little girl who'd been riding it. To my astonishment, they agree to purchase the unicorn and begin haggling over a cash price. The girl, who's around six or seven, gives off a sense of disbelief. She's super excited. Okay, I understand the world has some people to whom dropping eight thousand bucks on a kid's toy is not a big deal. I wouldn't really notice spending $80 on something for Pandora. Some people in some parts of the world would look at me doing that the same way I'm looking at this couple. I keep my mouth shut but still think they're crazy. When Natalie first made the unicorn, I called it the 'Tantrum Generator.' Every kid who saw it would want it and no parent would ever pay so much for a fake horse with a horn. I mean, the stupid thing doesn't get any bigger. The girl's going to outgrow it in a few years... at least as far as riding on its back goes. Maybe it'll follow her around and act like a pet dog. Who knows?

They agree on $6,500. Knowing Natalie, it probably cost her about one grand in materials. *Lots* of her profit margin is based on time and artistry. For example, I could smear paint on a canvas and no one would pay for it. Some big-name artist smears paint on a canvas, it's worth a fortune even if both 'paintings' look like something a four-year-old made.

Lawrence walks over to me as Natalie's finishing up the transaction. "Found Mrs. Underhill. She's staying at a homeless shelter for the time being until the insurance kicks in and she can find a new apartment. Feel like paying her a visit?"

I give the rich couple serious side eye. Meh. Not their fault they can afford an expensive toy when some people have nowhere to sleep, or kids like I used to be never knew *if* they would have dinner.

"Sure." I lean into the conversation going on at the counter. "Gotta go, Nat. Talk later."

She smiles. "Okay. Stay safe."

10

OWLS

Turns out, we're not too far away from where Joyce Underhill is staying.

The homeless shelter is in East Kensington. Think it used to be a video rental place before streaming and Trance crystals killed tape and DVD. Any store not offering Trance crystals to rent went under. Those don't work via the internet or streaming. Unfortunately, they're kind of like the enchanted unicorn toy of the movie world. Players are still around $2,000 and each movie crystal—or trans-speri-ence crystal as the makers call them—is around $350. It's like watching a movie from inside the main character's head. You don't get any control over what happens, but the devices *do* share everything—taste, touch, smell. Some of the newer ones have branching story paths where you can decide how the character acts at key points.

It's not everyone's thing, especially for action movies. Being shot at sucks, even virtually.

Anyway, this particular former video place has been sectioned off into little cubby areas using the same drab grey cubicle walls they do in corporate offices. They're soul-draining in an office, but in a place like this, they make it even drearier. An administrator in a small office near the front directs us to the left side, center aisle. We find Mrs.

Underhill in a small 'room' made of cubicle walls, just large enough to hold a cot, a 'shelf' of three stacked milk crates, and a steel folding chair. She's probably getting close to sixty. Grey at the roots of her puffy afro gives her a cute grandmotherly vibe. A work smock from the Fishtown Wawa lays draped over the milk crates. We appear to have interrupted her reading.

"Excuse me, Mrs. Underhill?" asks Lawrence.

"Yes. Oh, I do love a man in uniform." She smiles, probably teasing him, if her tone is any indication. They're not so far apart in age, really. Lawrence is fifty-two.

He chuckles, looks away for a second. "Sorry to intrude on you at a time like this. I'm Lawrence Ellis. This is Brooklyn Amari. We're with the fire department, arson investigation."

Joyce sits up straighter. Her expression doesn't change, but the shift to defensiveness is obvious to me. No guilt, though. The woman either expects we're fishing for someone to blame or she has suspicions about the owl.

"We don't think you're involved," I say in as soothing a voice my sarcastic self is capable of producing. "Actually, I believe you might be more of a victim here than most. Someone tried to make it look like you started the fire, but we know you didn't."

Mrs. Underhill glances at me, eyes a little narrowed.

"You recently received an owl figurine." Lawrence holds out his cell phone, showing a picture of the statuette.

As soon as she sees the photo, her eyes get huge and she covers her mouth.

"It looks like an innocent figurine, but it's the device that started the fire," I say. "Whoever gave you the statue tried to either kill you or make it look like you were responsible for the building burning."

"Just a UPS man. No one I know admitted to sending it." Mrs. Underhill describes the same guy I saw in the vision when I touched the owl. "Never saw him before. Seemed a bit strange."

"Strange how?" I ask.

"Like you don't wanna be alone in a room wit' him. Maybe I'm paranoid or whatever, but that boy didn't seem quite right."

"He isn't," I mutter. "You have no idea who he is?"

"Nope. Sorry. I'd help ya if I could. Never saw the man before."

"And no idea who might have sent you the owl?" asks Lawrence.

I'm sure no one did. The fake UPS driver is almost certainly the arsonist, possibly alchemist.

"Can't rightly say." Mrs. Underhill shakes her head. "Spoke ta everyone I know. Not one of 'em admitted to it. Thought maybe they didn't want to hear me grumble at them for spending money on me, but now ya sayin' the thing started the fire? Guessin, none of them did send it. Damn thing burned down my home." Tears gather in her eyes.

Sensing guilt, I crouch and take her hand. "Don't blame yourself. You had no way to know."

"It's gotta be that damn lawyer," snaps Mrs. Underhill.

"Lawyer?" Lawrence pulls his notepad out.

"Lennox Bradley. He works for Maxwell. Man's been harassin' me for weeks." Mrs. Underhill scowls at the cubicle wall. "Somehow, I ended up the unofficial mouthpiece of a tenant's organization. Took forever to get anything fixed, and ya make too many maintenance requests in a year, they raise your rent. We've been demanding repairs and an end to retaliation in rent hikes, but all it does is get 'em threatening to take us to court or evict us."

Lawrence and I exchange a glance. Seems a bit extreme to burn down the entire building to make an example of a noisy—rightfully so —tenant. My read on Charles Maxwell didn't give me anything to suspect he had any intention to conceal involvement in the fire. It's possible the lawyer did it without approval, but it's kind of thin. A landlord isn't a landlord without a building full of apartments to rent. Destroying the source of his employer's business wouldn't be a great move on the lawyer's part. See, I'm like smart or something.

"Don't make no sense how the man knew ta send me an owl," says Mrs. Underhill. "I got a thing for 'em. Always been fond o' owls, ever since I's a little thing. Maybe the super went in my apartment when I's not there and noticed all my owl stuff. Guess he figured I'd keep an owl, even if I had no idea where it came from."

"If the building management company was involved," I say, "The superintendent could've planted the owl figurine in your apartment while you weren't home. No need to fake a UPS delivery."

Mrs. Underhill stares into space for a moment, then nods in a 'makes sense' sort of way. "Well, now. I ain't got no idea who'd wanna burn me out. Gotta do somethin' nice for Patty once I'm back on my feet."

"Patty?" asks Lawrence.

"She works the overnight at the Wawa. Night o' the fire, she had a thing wit' her family. Asked me to swap shifts so she could go to her son's thinga-ma-whatever. The young man lives with his wife up in Maine, so she'd be gone a couple days. Patty saved my damn life."

I squeeze her hand.

"Mama?" asks a woman behind us. "The hell you doin' in a place like this?"

Lawrence and I pivot to look at a late-twenties woman in a nice coat. Something about her says lawyer or maybe middle-management.

"Not botherin' no one," mutters Mrs. Underhill.

"Nonsense, Mama." The woman slips past us. "You're going to stay with me and Will until you get sorted."

Mrs. Underhill winks at Lawrence. "My daughter, Mae."

Mae finally decides to acknowledge we exist, giving us each a once-over look. "Why'd you folks dump my mother at a homeless shelter?"

Lawrence holds his hands up in a 'slow down' gesture. "We had nothing to do with that, ma'am. Arson investigation. Fire department."

"Oh." Mae seems to relax. "What's your interest with my mother?"

We explain the basics. Well, Lawrence does most of the talking while I 'listen.' Highly doubtful Mae is involved. The woman's merely protective of her mother. As there's nothing more for us to do here, we gracefully slip away to leave the pair arguing over why Mrs. Underhill hadn't called Mae. Apparently, her cell phone got shut off for nonpayment, thanks to a rent increase she calls punitive.

Good time for Lawrence and I to make a run for it before we get dragged into the 'you should have called me sooner' argument.

11

GOOD MISCHIEF

Does the ability to watch a TV show over and over again without getting sick of it mean I have mental damage? My former college roommate thought so. The past few days have been routine and thankfully unexciting. Couple of kitchen fires, a few false alarms in apartment buildings, and a pair of car accidents. Spent an hour talking to Jason last night. He's having a lot of fun at the firefighter's expo in Berlin. Hearing him talk, he sounds like a big kid at adventure summer camp.

I'm stretched out on my sofa watching *Dead Like Me* again. Love this show… except for the follow on made-for-TV movie they tried to chase it with. Could've done without that. I mean, it's good they tried to give us more, but it doesn't have the same magic as the show. Humanity has spent centuries thinking of demons as evil when the true evil lives among them unnoticed: television executives. Why do they always cancel the good shows?

Huh. Now I got myself wondering.

Are there grim reapers? Given what I now know about reality, it seems unlikely. Human beings are like bubbles. They rise up out of the bathtub, exist in myriad, beautiful splendor for a little while, then pop, falling back into the water only to rise again as another bubble. Every human being to ever live or who will ever live is a reflection of Elestari and Shaar'nath. Both sides poured their energy into the creation of the world. It's not surprising the bubbles act like the soap responsible for their existence. There's no Universe Engine or creator figure churning out an endless stream of new souls, which get run through mortal life like meat through a meat grinder, only to end up sorted into different trash bins at the end. Energy is constant and it keeps going around in circles.

I suspect Elestari and Shaar'nath souls also keep going around in circles. Even humans figured out energy can't be created or destroyed, only changed. I am not, however, bored enough to try and understand stuff. I don't need to know *why* cheese pours out of the machine onto my nachos when I push the button, only that it does.

Haven't thought much about the grandfather clock arsonist over the past couple of days. Lawrence officially declared the fire at the Stedman Building to be arson via magical or paranormal means. He's handed it off to the police detectives to conduct the investigation. Works for me. The remainder of my involvement consisted of sitting with a police sketch artist to help them create a drawing of the creepy guy. Chasing down suspects is the job of the police, not the fire department. Lawrence is what they refer to as an 'expert witness.' His role here is done, at least until any trial happens and he's called on to testify about his findings. Might snare me, too, if the prosecution tries for a long shot attempt to involve psychic discovery. I'm not exactly a legal buff, but even I know psychic phenomena doesn't do well in courtrooms. It's too difficult to prove anything, and no one trusts a 'tribunal of telepaths' to verify anything. People are too afraid establishing something like that would lead to some kind of crazy dystopian world where the mystics control everyone. Maybe they're right. Much easier to just regard psychic testimony as unprovable.

"Mom?" yells Pandora from her room.

The child's voice sounds curious and ever so slightly worried. That's an 'I might have screwed up but need a second opinion' tone. It's a little after six on Friday. Ashley's here tonight and may wind up sleeping over as Tracy's class schedule is overloaded today. And by 'overloaded,' I mean she has two classes after work. Doesn't get home until almost eleven.

I pause *Dead Like Me*, get up, and head down the hall to the little hellspawn's room. The girls look adorable and more or less normal except for my kid having claws. They're sitting on the floor, evidently in the middle of a nail polishing party. Considering they're six and eight, I'm astonished at the relative lack of mess. Most of the polish has ended up on nails—and claws. Pandora's got her knives out, so to speak. Is it twisted of me to find them cute? At her size, the claws are like three-inches long. Pen knives, basically. Significantly sharper, but still. Adorbs.

Ashley's nails are all painted a matching sapphire blue. She waves her hands back and forth, trying to dry them faster.

"What's up?" I ask, leaning on the doorjamb.

Pandora shows off her blue-painted claws. "Will the paint get inside me and make me sick if I shrink the claws?"

"Huh. Good question. I have no idea. Never tried to paint my claws… but I used to wear black polish all the time on my normal nails. Try retracting one claw as a test."

"Okay." The girl nods, then stares at her right hand. Her index finger claw shrinks out from under a layer of nail polish, which flutters to the floor like a scrap of a popped balloon. "Ooh!"

One by one, Pandora puts the rest of her claws away, making nine more strips of dried nail polish.

"Aww, poop." Ashley picks up a scrap, letting it dangle between two fingers. "We wasted it."

I'd tell her not to waste polish painting her claws again, but bleh. She seems to have had fun discovering and learning, it's not wasting anything. Ugh. Since when do I sound like my mother?

Pandora studies one of the dried polish bits. "So weird. Feel it. Like plastic."

"Your nails are plain," says Ashley.

"Yeah." Pandora looks at her hand, then up at me. "Will it stay on these nails if I claw?"

"Another good question." I furrow my brows.

"You never painted your nails?" Ashley also stares up at me.

"I used to. Didn't know I had claws before I stopped painting them."

"Why'd you stop?" Pandora tilts her head.

"Fire department. Some idiot behind a desk somewhere thinks it's unprofessional."

Both girls stick out their tongues.

"You know, I bet the guys would all paint their nails in solidarity if I tried to protest."

They giggle together.

Honestly, I don't really care about nail polish. It's certainly not worth rocking the boat over. However, the idea of watching Brian paint his nails pink or something is almost tempting. He'd totally do it, too. It would be too tempting to resist if not for my laziness holding me back from all the effort it would take to organize. That, and the brass would turn it into a clown act. Oh, look at the woman complaining about nonsense. If we're going to make a big deal about something, it shouldn't be nail polish rules. We should insist the older stations have separate bathrooms and showers installed.

Ashley carefully paints Pandora's index fingernail blue. She waves her hand around to dry it somewhat, then extends her claw. The tiny onyx dagger appears in the usual manner, devoid of paint. When she retracts it, the human fingernail is still painted.

"Yay!" Pandora cheers, then holds her hands out for Ashley to do the remaining nine nails.

They kinda remind me of being little and hanging out with my friend Gina Gonzalez. She's a year older than me. Haven't really spoken to her much since the end of high school. Last I heard, she joined the Navy.

"Oh, Mom? When the polish dries, can we take Ash flying?" asks Pandora.

I shrug. "Sure, why not."

"Yay!" cheer the girls simultaneously.

I head back to the sofa to leave them to their nail painting. Like fifteen minutes later, the girls pass behind the couch on their way to the kitchen. I don't think anything of it until the creak of the oven door sets off my sixth sense.

After pausing *Dead Like Me,* I lean over the back of the sofa to look. The child is kneeling on the oven door, half climbed into the oven. Ashley's standing on a chair next to her, reaching for the dial. "Pandora? What are you doing?"

"Gonna sit in the oven so the polish dries faster."

"Use a hair dryer. Oven gets too hot. It'll ruin the polish." I shake my head. "Also, your dress might catch fire. If you're going to sit in the oven, don't wear anything combustible."

Pandora backs out of the stove, twisting to look at me. "Poop."

Ashley covers her mouth, giggling.

The girls close the oven, put the chair back, and scurry to the bathroom. Soon, the whirr of a hair dryer comes from down the hall. I resume watching TV. Eventually, the dryer stops and the kids walk out to stand expectantly in front of me.

"Ash?" I ask.

"Yeah?"

"You know playing with ovens is dangerous, right?"

She nods. "Uh huh. I wasn't gonna get in."

"Good. Just making sure." I pat her on the head. "I don't want you two messing around with the stove until you're at least like twelve."

They both nod.

"Not gonna hurt myself," says Pandora.

"You won't... but Ashley isn't immune to fire. And neither is the building." I tap a finger to her nose.

She starts to smile, then makes this 'oh, oops!' face, then smiles again.

I'm not worried. As a kid, my mischief occurred outside the house. Weird considering my ancestry, but playing with fire never occurred to me. "Guess you guys are ready to go."

"Yeah." Ashley nods so rapidly her hair ends up covering her face.

I pause the DVD again, get up, and head over to the counter to grab the apartment keys from my bag.

"Oh, Mom?" asks Pandora.

"Hmm?" I stuff the keys in my pocket. No need to bring my whole bag for a quick fly around.

"I saw somethin' weird at school today. Was goin' to the bathroom an' saw glowing people whispering."

"Ghosts?" I ask.

She shakes her head. "No, teachers. But they glowed like ghosts. I pretended not to see them. Ms. Groves was scared something might hurt people, but Mr. Sandoval told her not to worry because they had to let it in."

"Let what in?" I blink.

Pandora shrugs. "Dunno. They're gonna do somethin' next Friday night at Rolling Hill Park."

"Glowing?" Ashley scrunches up her nose. "But not ghosts."

"Nope. They're both alive, and they didn't see me 'cause I didn't let them."

"You eavesdropped on your teachers?"

Pandora grinds her toe into the rug. "Not really. They're not *my* teachers."

"You eavesdropped on teachers." I fold my arms.

"Uh huh." She smiles.

I give her a high-five. "Nice. C'mon. Let's fly."

The girls cheer and run down the hall to the stairs, heading for the roof. This is probably going to turn into more than a simple flight. Only question is, are we going to end up at a mall or playing a few innocent pranks on unsuspecting people. Meh. Either way, it'll be fun.

12

NOT QUITE RIGHT

My daughter has issues.

So, we flew around a bit last night and we ended up at the mall. Well, a store full of electronics had a particular movie playing on fifty or so televisions showing a scary little girl with pure white skin and long black hair... so guess what Pandora wanted to do? I bought her a plain white dress, and she proceeded to fling her hair over her face and sneak up on people in the store around all those televisions playing *that* movie. It would have been freaky enough considering we're both literally as white as snow, but she also used her psychic abilities to make people not see her until she got close. So, to them, she appeared out of thin air.

I'm a mature adult.

I also bought a long white dress.

Yeah, we had fun messing with people last night.

There are at least two mall security guards who came to investigate the 'haunting' who are probably *still* drunk. I've never heard a fat guy scream at such a high pitch before. Really, it makes no sense to me. Who the heck finds a little girl scary? Maybe there's something wrong with me, but if I saw some kid climb up out of a well looking all

soaked and stuff, I'd be like 'here, have a towel and some hot chocolate. You look frozen.'

Unfortunately, it's morning. It wouldn't be a big deal other than
being Monday. I'm off from work, but the kids have school. I drag
myself out of bed, put my wings and tail away—you know, the kid's
got a point. I *do* feel better in the morning if I sleep that way. Read
online a few years ago it's healthier to sleep in the nude, so that's
become my normal. Works for me. Course, we have a guest, so it's not
proper to let it all hang out. We're not living in Europe after all. This is
America where society is horrified by the human body. I throw on a
shirt plus sweat shorts, then head to the kitchen.

Ashley slept on a bed of sofa cushions and blankets on the floor
next to Pandora's bed. The girls are still asleep, no surprise considering
they stayed up late talking. My parenting style is 'learn by experience.'
As in, today, the girls are going to experience what it's like not to get
enough sleep. Hopefully, they'll think twice before staying up so late
again. I put a skirt on Pandora, then carry her out to the kitchen and
leave her slumped over the table.

"Hey, Ash," I say, upon returning to the room. "Morning. Time to
get ready for school."

She moans.

I gently prod her shoulder until she opens her eyes.

"What time is it?"

"Time to get up." I pat her on the arm. "Get dressed and go to the
kitchen."

"Okay."

A blood-chilling scream comes from the hallway, specifically the
bathroom. I spare a quick glance at the window to make sure it didn't
crack. Pandora shrieking like that can mean only one thing—except
there hasn't been a man or boy in the place for a week.

"Who left the seat up?" I yell.

"It's not up! I'm small!" shouts Pandora past chattering teeth.

Well, she's awake.

"You fell asleep sitting down, didn't you?"

Her grumbling is adorable.

Eventually, the girls are dressed, barely awake, and sitting at the table waiting for the rune oven to finish their waffles. I'm standing by the freezer debating on which flavor of tragedy I want to embrace this morning. Frozen breakfast burritos are convenient, but they seriously lack flavor. Yeah, I'm comparing them to my mother's cooking. And no, she never makes 'egg burritos.' It's insulting to even call these things burritos. Really, they're American omelets wrapped in a tortilla —nothing Mexican about them.

Boom.

I practically jump into the freezer at an explosion behind me. A wet *splat* follows, then Ashley screaming. My heart's still basically in my throat from the sudden loud noise as I turn to look. A huge tentacle of doughy muck stretches out from the rune oven. It's got Pandora in its grip, waving her back and forth. She's more or less upside down, her arms trapped at her sides, kicking and snarling. Of the three of us in the room, she's probably the *least* scared. Before my brain is even done processing the situation, Pandora extends her tail and begins rapidly stabbing the ten-inch onyx blade at the end into the dough tentacle.

The kitchen smells like a waffle bakery.

I run over, trying to grab her out of midair. The damn waffle-tentacle swings Pandora at me, aiming for my face. Great. My rune oven is trying to kill me, using my kid as a ball-and-chain flail. I duck. It swings her back; this time, I catch her by the shoulders and hold on. Kid's snarling like an angry… something. Sounds a bit more menacing than a housecat or dog, but not quite deep or loud enough to be a mountain lion.

Pandora wraps her legs around the waffle tentacle to hold it still and begins sawing at it using her tail blade. She's not strong enough to free her arms from the gluey mess, which is concerning. Dough shouldn't be this powerful. A thin tendril of waffle extends past her head, going for my neck. My hands are occupied holding her in place so it doesn't smash her into anything… so I do the only thing I can and bite it.

Mmm. Still tastes like blueberry waffles.

Ashley stops screaming and proceeds to stare in awestruck silence.

After a moment, Pandora succeeds cutting the tendril just past her feet. I set her on the floor for the time being and go after the remaining mess with my claws. The severed part reconfigures itself into a blob, evidently smart enough to try suffocating Pandora by covering her face. Bad move letting go of her arms. She goes full woodchipper on it using fangs, claws, and tail. Meanwhile, the upper part, which is still seriously stuck to the inside of the rune oven, is trying to pick me up off my feet using a grip around my neck.

"Ash," I gurgle. "In my room, there's an orange wand on the bureau. Please go get it."

"Are you sure?" asks Ashley.

I slice the dough from my neck to let air in. "Yes, I'm sure. Why wouldn't I be?"

"Mommy doesn't want me touching the wand she has in her room. I'm not supposed to know about it."

"Your Mom has a wand, too?" snarls Pandora.

"Yeah. It doesn't really do anything but make a noise like bzzzz."

I laugh so hard I'm crying.

Ashley gives me this look like I'm nuts, then walks out.

I stand there shredding the dough beast for a moment. Damn, this stuff is sticky… and strong. It's hard to tell if Pandora is winning or not, though she sounds more angry than worried, so I stay calm.

"This is way skinnier than Mom's wand." Ashley re-enters the kitchen holding the dispel magic wand Natalie made for me. "Where's the switch?"

As wands go, it's fairly plain in appearance. Standard twelve-inch wooden rod, about as big around as a finger.

"No switch. Point it at this crazy waffle monster and yell 'knock it off.'"

Ashley aims the wand. "Knock it off!"

A faint white light flickers at the tip of the wand. The doughy mass emits a dull *whump*, then stops moving. Over the next few seconds, it shrinks back into the approximate size of four freezer waffles.

Pandora lays flat on her back, arms and legs splayed to either side like she just fell off the roof of a high-rise building.

"Neat." Ashley smiles at the wand. "It kills monsters?"

"No, it turns magic off. You guys okay?"

"Yeah," says Ashley.

Pandora retracts her claws and tail. Her sparkle-goth dress flickers back to the T-shirt and jean shorts she intended to wear to school today, thankfully neither stained with waffle dough nor ripped. "Yep. Umm, didn't Natalie fix the stupid rune oven already?"

"She tried. Said something like 'holy crap' and started shaking her head. Told me I needed a new one. This one's hopeless."

"Seriously." Pandora dusts herself off and stands. "So, get another one."

"Can't. Building management won't let us replace appliances on our own."

The kid points at the counter. "Get another one, put it there, and leave the cursed one alone. I'm supposed to eat breakfast, not have breakfast try to eat me."

"I got attacked by lo mein," says Ashley. "The oven is bad."

Duh. Now I feel kinda stupid. The lease says I can't *replace* existing appliances, but it doesn't say anything about getting a second rune oven. As long as it's not 'built into' the cabinets, I'm good. "Yeah. Think I'll do that."

I collect the remains of the smoking waffles, toss them in the trash, then grab four new ones from the freezer. The instant I take a step toward the rune oven, the girls both gasp.

"Are you nuts?" asks Pandora.

"Relax. The oven's sketchy, but it's never freaked out twice in a row before."

"Nope." She shakes her head. "Not worth the risk. I know how bad your luck is, and now there are two of us here, concentrating it."

I laugh. "Guess you're okay."

"Yep. Still hungry."

"Me, too," says Ashley.

I reach to put the waffles in the rune oven.

"No!" screams both girls.

I laugh again. "Wow. I just realized I don't own a toaster. Okay…" I toss the frozen waffles back in the freezer for another day. "Do you guys want cereal or do we stop at Kwan's on the way to school? All we have time for before you're late."

The girls exchange a glance, then shrug.

"Cereal's fine." Pandora plops herself down in her chair.

Resignation in her voice sounds so much like me. Does she somehow have ingrained memories of being tight on cash and won't argue about eating food she's not really interested in? Then again, I've always loved cereal. So, Choco-Wizard it is.

I pour out two reasonable portions, add milk, and set the bowls in front of the girls, who promptly attack their food.

"Why do people get rune ovens if they're so crazy and cost so much?" asks Pandora around a mouthful.

"Probably because they don't use any electricity and are supposed to last fifty years or so."

Ashley points her spoon at the rune oven. "How old is that one?"

"Not sure." I grab a breakfast burrito from the freezer and toss it in the rune oven.

Both girls crawl under the table.

"Drama queens," I mutter before spotting an engraving on the edge of the door. "1918."

"What?" asks Ashley.

I shut the door and push the purple gem. The rune oven comes to life. "There's a 1918 engraved on the door. Guessing it means it was made in 1918."

"That's a'most a hundred years old!" yells Pandora.

"It's more than a hundred years. Like 102 years." I rub my chin. "Probably why this thing is so random."

The rune oven beeps. Both girls scream.

"Relax you guys. Nothing exploded."

Pandora and Ashley hide under the table, watching like they expect a demonic beast to leap out of the rune oven and tear my face off. I open the door. The only thing to jump out at me is the smell of pizza. Considering I put a sausage-and-egg burrito in there, the fragrance of pizza is quite unusual. But it's better than having to kill my breakfast.

"Safe." I grab the burrito and take a bite. Sure enough, tastes like pizza… but has the consistency of eggs and sausage. So… so… weird. But, I'll deal.

13

ANIMAL CONTROL

Monday gave me a chance to relax.

I failed at adulting. Spent the whole day playing video games and not wearing pants… at least until the girls got back from school. Poor Tracy. As soon as she showed up at 6:40 p.m. to pick her kid up, I burst out laughing, suddenly remembering the 'wand' thing. She found it considerably less funny, but didn't yell at Ashley.

So, anyway, it's Tuesday again. Back to the usual routine. I land at the fire house in time to see the garage doors open and the lights go on. Oh, joy. Perfect timing. At least I'm not hourly, so I don't need to worry about hitting a time clock. Guess the Starbucks run waits. I dart inside and hop on the truck, fall into one of the seats, and start poking the guys for details. Sounds like a small fire in a residence across the street from Marconi Plaza.

Another ordinary day in South Philly.

We roll to a stop at the intersection of Johnston Street and South Thirteenth. Smoke peels from several windows on a three-story brick rowhouse at the corner. Weird place. Second floor has a balcony enclosed by a waist-high wall and like an ordinary house door. The third floor looks small, probably cramped inside since it has a sharply angled roof. The thickest smoke comes from the single window at the top on the front of the building.

Something inside is making a screeching noise like an angry hundred-pound cockatiel having its first Brazilian wax.

We're in luck, too. Got a hydrant right on the corner. It's four feet in front of the concrete stairs leading up to the front door of the house that's on fire. An older couple on the sidewalk nearby hurry over to us.

"It's in the house!" yells the man.

"Please don't let it destroy our home." The woman gives Humberto the eye as he hooks a hose up to the hydrant. "Do you really need to throw water all over everything?"

Her husband looks at me like 'do what you have to do' while patting her. "Let them work, hon."

While the guys wrangle hose, I grab an extinguisher and make my way inside, zapping a few small spot fires burning on the walls and carpet. The left side of the living room is caught a bit too intensely for a fire extinguisher, so I don't bother wasting any charge on it. A hose will be inside in seconds. The screech comes from upstairs. Place is a bit packed with boxes of stuff. Not necessarily hoarders, but they've got a ton of crap. This is definitely not up to code. I zap a few more small spots of fire as I make my way up the stairs past boxes and boxes of old books and magazines. Wow. Deathtrap much?

Second floor looks pretty much okay except for the back right corner. What appears to be the bedroom of an adolescent boy is thoroughly engulfed.

"Need a hose upstairs. Back right," I say into the radio. "Second floor bedroom, it's crawling up the walls."

"Copy," replies O'Keefe. "Spraying the living room wall now."

I proceed up a steep set of bare wooden steps, almost a ladder, into the loft. The ceiling's burning, as is a large lump of what appears to be random rags and such. I step off the ladder, fire a blast of the fire extinguisher at the burning patches on the roof, then give the rags a long dousing.

The blob of rags screeches at me.

"Gah!" I jump back, not at all prepared for a formless lump to sprout wings and flap into the air.

I'm face-to-beak with a bird about the size of a German shepherd. Its plumage is a mixture of black and orange, the orange coming from ember-fire burning in between charred feathers. This thing isn't *on* fire, it *is* fire. My coat is already smoking from being five feet away from it. We appear equally shocked at each other's presence.

Out of spite, I blast it with the extinguisher again. "Stop burning shit."

It squawks at me and breathes fire at me like a tiny dragon.

I duck and shoot it again. "Stop that!"

Shrieking, the bird lunges at me. Out of reflex, I bonk it upside the head with the fire extinguisher, knocking it into the wall, which promptly ignites. Dammit! As the bird bounces off the drywall, dazed, I blast the new fire patch, putting it out.

"Okay, enough of you."

It squawks at me, flapping its six-foot wings and throwing tiny embers all over the place, setting a bunch of little fires on the carpet. Grr. I advance on it, blasting the rug as best I can, then seize the bird in a telekinetic grip. The instant it feels restrained by an invisible force, the damn thing loses its little bird brain. Before it can thrash and fling burning feather-embers everywhere, I concentrate on keeping its wings immobile and stuff it down the ladder. The bird keeps screaming and thrashing around.

As soon as we reach the second floor and it spots Humberto and O'Keefe hauling a hose down the hall to the boy's room, it tries to spit fire at them. The guys respond in the best way they can. Humberto, in front, shields his face by crossing his arms and O'Keefe hoses the bird down.

Predictably, this does not go over well.

Billowing steam floods the hallway, making it impossible to see. The creature screams so damned loud I think my ears are bleeding. I still have a good sense of its mass to keep telekinetic hold of it.

"Let me get this thing outta here," I yell.

"Go, go, go!" shouts O'Keefe.

I shove the bird forward, making my way by feel to the stairs. Lamar's about halfway down, feeding hose up to the guys heading for the boy's room. He gawks at the tumbling mass of burning feathers, talons, and snapping beak.

"What the hell is that thing?"

"A giant pain in the ass," I shout while hurrying past him and out the front door.

Once outside, I pin the creature down to the sidewalk at the corner. It seems to calm somewhat as soon as we're out the door. Guessing it kinda freaked out like any bird caught in a house. The homeowners stare at it.

"Is… that something our grandson left here?" asks the man. "I heard you say his room is burning."

"Sorry. His room's a lost cause." I gesture at the bird. "But no, I don't think he was hiding this under his bed. It's a bit obvious."

"Hole in the roof," shouts Alex from the loft window. "I think it crashed into the house."

"Great." I groan and pull off my helmet and face mask. "Hey, Humberto?"

"Yo?" he shouts from inside the living room.

"Can you get on the radio and request MAC out here?"

Humberto trots out the front door. "On it."

"Mac?" asks the older woman. "You're not seriously ordering food, are you?"

I chuckle. "No, ma'am. Magical Animal Control."

"What's wrong with it?" asks the man. "Is it dying?"

"I don't think so. It's tired from being stuck in your house and panicking. Despite being huge and burny, it's still a bird and can't handle getting trapped inside a building." I adjust my telekinetic hold so the critter can stand up and not look 'squished.' "It can breathe fire. You should probably keep back at least fifty feet."

The couple makes 'oh shit' faces at me for a second or two before hurrying off to stand over by the front of our truck. A blast of water knocks out the window at the back corner on the second floor. Considering the exterior is brick, they'll probably be able to repair the house. Except for the one room, the damage didn't seem too severe.

I spend the next almost ten minutes holding the bird down while the guys deal with the flames inside. They're more or less finished and doing a final walkthrough check for embers when a large white van with city markings comes down 13th Street. It's about to turn left onto Johnston—which is a one-way—but the driver stops short upon seeing the glowing bird on the corner.

Dude hops out, nods once at me. "This the critter?"

"Nah, pet chicken got into the habaneros. The magic creature's inside the house."

He blinks at me. Not sure if he thinks I'm serious or if he's feeling pissy at me for having an attitude. Say dumb crap, expect sarcasm.

"Yeah, this is the critter." I nod at it. "You got a carrier big enough?"

"Yep." He heads around to open the van's back doors. "Fire retardant and everything."

"It can spit fire," I say.

"Firebirds do that." He drags a refrigerator-sized crate out of the van. "What'd you guys do to it?"

"Just pulled it out of the house, why?"

"Never saw one just sit there like that. They're not usually so docile." He drags the crate over and opens the door.

"He's a little tired after freaking out inside. O'Keefe blasted him with the hose. I haven't heard a shriek that loud since they told some Karen at Starbucks they'd run out of sugar-free mocha flavoring."

The animal control guy, Paul according to the name on his jumpsuit, laughs. "Hmm. Now for the tricky part."

"I got it."

"Can't touch these things. You'll burn the crap out of yourself." Paul scoots the crate closer. "Gotta try to scoop them up."

"Not a problem." I levitate the firebird into the box.

Paul screams the instant the creature shifts toward him. Not sure if it's being moved or the yelling, but something spooks the bird into blasting me full in the face with its fire breath. It's like I imagine a nice summer breeze would feel to most people. To me, every breeze is chilly. Worst part about the breath is the burned rotten meat smell. Coughing, I shove the critter into the crate then close the door. No longer concentrating on telekinesis is such a relief, I slump against the side of the fire-resistant box.

"Holy shit." Paul stares at me. "How the heck did you survive that?"

"Fire resistant enchant." I wink. "Expensive, but considering my job, it's money well spent."

Paul nods, wipes sweat from his forehead, then sighs. "I really need to find a different job. It's freakin' nuts lately. For a second there, I thought I was gonna watch you die right in front of me."

"Nuts?" I ask.

"Yeah. Yours is the third call today and it ain't even nine in the morning yet. Had a gloam rabbit on Beulah Street, a chittering crawler in FDR Park, and a freakin' shock crab in the Navy Yard."

"I'm almost afraid to ask what a gloam rabbit is." I chuckle.

Paul holds his hands about three feet apart. "Giant dark grey rabbit, looks like it's made outta shadows. Glowing red eyes. Damn things just stare at you and the longer you watch them, the more you start thinkin' random crap about how your life has gone as wrong as possible, everything sucks, and there's no point to even trying anymore. Critters themselves won't hurt ya, but stare at 'em too long and you'll end up throwing yourself off a bridge."

"So, they're basically nihilistic philosophy professors," I mutter.

He looks at me like I spoke a foreign language. "Ehh, whatever. Easy enough not to stare into their eyes. They usually do more damage to vegetable gardens than anyone's sanity. Still, crazy number of critters getting into the city. Just between you and me, the mages are up to something. That 'wall' they put up ta keep stuff out? Yeah, well, it ain't workin' so good no more."

"Sounds like it. Hope your day improves. Hey, what are you going to do with the bird?"

He grunts, dragging the crate around to the back of the van. "Drive it like an hour out of the city and let it go. I'd tag it, but any tag would melt."

I help him load the box in the van. "Take it easy."

"Yeah, you too." Paul waves and trudges around to the driver's seat, giving the finger to someone who beeps at him for parking where he did.

Heh. I love Philly.

14

PARENT-TEACHER CONFERENCE

I t's not until we arrive back at the station my thoughts jump to what Pandora said.

My kid overheard two of her teachers talking about 'letting it in' this Saturday. Taking into account the chances of a six-year-old either mis-hearing or mis-remembering, I start wondering if there's a connection between these strange glowing teachers and the increase of magical creatures slipping into Philly.

After helping the guys drain the hoses and repack them, I head to the ready room and flop at one of the general use computers. They're kinda old and don't have any decent games on them, but as far as looking stuff up goes, they work fine. Turns out, the Aether Wall runs through Rolling Hill Park. Sorta. It 'slices off' about a third of it, leaving the majority of the park property outside. The wall meets the Delaware River at the Delaware state line, then circles up and around Philadelphia to meet the river again right around Andalusia.

Everyone calls it a 'wall,' but it's a magical barrier. Invisible, too. Humans—and apparently Shaar'nath, Elestari, and half-bloods like me, can pass through it without a problem. Magical creatures are supposed to be unable to cross it. Obviously as the past few weeks have proven, there are holes. People have been complaining about critters for as long as I've lived in Philly, so the issue of things slipping in is not new. However, it does sound like more and more critters are managing to get inside the barrier.

Hmm. This one history site says a group of mages created the wall 151 years ago during a panic resulting in the wake of a dragon attack. Ugh. I almost bang my head on the desk. Just like people. Something bad happens and everyone freaks out. Humans are easily frightened creatures… says the girl who spent most of the last twenty-three years considering herself one of them. This is exactly why I'm pretending to *still* be one of them. I neither want to be worshipped nor hunted to the ends of the Earth.

Fortunately, the planet is round, so it doesn't have ends.

Yeah, society would not handle it well if we tried to tell them the truth about where humans came from. They've grown really attached to the stories they made up. I'm sure any Elestari or Shaar'nath who tried telling the truth would probably convince at least a small percentage of people to follow them, but it would almost certainly end in war somehow. Kinda makes me wonder why the idiot warmongers haven't outed themselves to humanity and sent them after me. If all of humanity wanted to destroy me, would I be more inclined to do what the jerks created me to do and destroy the mortal dimension?

Nah. Too much effort.

I'd probably find some remote region of the world where not many people lived and—nah on that, too. Gotta have TV, my PlayStation, and coffee. Doesn't have to be trendy coffee, just coffee. I get Starbucks because there happens to be one close to the station. The coffee from Kwan's is just as good. Honestly, I think it tastes better as long as it hasn't been sitting too long. Mr. Kwan isn't very methodical about dumping it after a half hour or so. Getting good coffee from the convenience store is a matter of luck and timing. I don't think he'd really care if a customer dumped out a half-pot of burned coffee and made new. Gonna try it next time. Hell, I've stopped *two* robberies. Dude owes me at least one fresh pot.

Right, back to the case of the glowing teachers. It's really curious the Aether Wall cuts through Rolling Hill Park and it's the spot they want to meet to 'let it in.' My guess is they're going to smuggle some manner of magical creature into the city, probably for a school project. I don't really care what they're doing, but it's got me curious… and I know Pandora wants to go spy on them.

Sounds like fun.

Did I mention I live in a kinda-not-nice area?

It's far from the most dangerous part of South Philadelphia. Still, it's the sort of neighborhood a person, especially a woman, doesn't want to be out alone after dark. My week is reasonably quiet, all things considered, except for Friday night. Tracy got off the bus about two blocks from our apartment building and didn't feel right. She called me to walk her home. No big deal leaving Ashley and Pandora home alone for the—at most—ten minutes it would take. Asleep, the girls wouldn't get into any trouble, and if anyone broke in, I'd most likely have to save *them* from Pandora.

Tracy having a bad feeling could mean anything from her getting some iffy weed to someone following her to a couple of warmongers in the area thinking about messing with me. Their presence tends to give off weird vibes.

Turned out, Tracy had a pair of guys waiting for her to walk away from the clearly lit bus stop area. As soon as I looked at them, I knew they intended to rob her. Didn't pick up any intention to do worse than demand money, so they got to keep their lives. They didn't have the nerve to hold up both of us, nor did they follow us down the street. Tracy started to apologize for bothering me until I explained how she would have been mugged if alone the second she left the brightly lit area. I'm happy to walk with her whenever she wants.

When Saturday finally arrives, the girls and I fly out to Rolling Hill Park. Since Ashley can't fly, I'm carrying her. It might not be the smartest thing for me to do since it's basically destroying her fear of heights. Natalie made her a protection amulet, but I'm not sure how being trapped in a magical box would save her from falling. Hopefully, Ashley is smart enough to realize she can't fly and won't do anything dumb. We'd have invited Tracy, but she's got school and work after.

Until she's done with her nursing degree, she doesn't have weekends. However, she'll be way better off once it's all behind her. Tracy won't exactly be swimming in money, but ought to have a much easier time covering the bills. Not sure cleaning up bedridden sick people who shit themselves is really a step *up* from waiting tables or slinging coffee at Starbucks, but hey, she likes the idea of being a caretaker and the pay is significantly better.

Our primary mission is to have a fun day at the park. Our side mission is spying on those teachers, if we can find them. Pandora didn't hear them talk about a specific time or where exactly in Rolling Hill Park they would gather. My guess is they probably won't be doing anything until after dark or at least close to sunset. No one does anything really fun (or illegal) in broad daylight. Ask me how I know. Another random fact: it's really scary to run away from the police in the dark after doing a few tabs of faerie dust. No, not literal faerie dust, I'm talking about the street drug. Oh, yeah… it makes sense to me now why I saw such *wild* crap when I tried that stuff. My subconscious mind knew about Shaar'nath and so on.

The trees here are nice and thick, making it easy to land without drawing attention to ourselves. Being out here in nature is kinda weird, since I'm a city girl now, but it does kinda take me back to my childhood. Lots of woods behind the trailer park where I grew up, and the creek. At Pandora's age, I'd spend hours roaming the forest. We wander the nature trails and stop by the Betty Reeves Native Wildflower Garden.

"Brook?" asks Ashley as we walk around a ring road in front of the wildflower garden.

"Hmm?" I glance at her. She's pointing at a 'no parking any time' sign a few feet away from the pavement.

"Why is there a no parking sign in a park? Isn't that kinda weird?"

Pandora giggles.

I laugh, figuring she's making a joke. She grins back at me, confirming it. Kid's pretty smart. Makes sense given her mom's doing well at nursing school. It's not a path for idiots, or lazy people. I guess you could say being a firefighter isn't for the lazy either, but I have selective motivation.

The park area isn't as large as I thought it would be from being named a park. On the other side of Rose Glen Road to the north is a residential development. We walk the hiking trails, checking out fairly dense woods, Mill Creek, as well as a number of old stone buildings. According to the signs, the buildings used to be occupied by millworkers. Seems to be a fair amount of people here, many with dogs. A few of the animals give me intense looks, like they don't quite know what to make of me.

I'm expecting the girls to get bored and want to go do something else, but they're surprisingly entertained by running around the woods. Helps I brought lunch, snacks, and plenty of bottled water. Pandora randomly gets up from our picnic spot, mutters a blasé 'gotta pee' and disappears into the foliage. Ashley gawks at me, then finds my non-reaction hilarious. Hey, when you gotta go and the nearest porta-potty is like a half mile away... The same psychic trick that keeps people from noticing us flying around or having wings is great for emergency bathroom breaks.

My concern increases after about ten minutes when she hasn't reappeared. I'm not *too* worried since no one screamed. I trail off my conversation with Ashley about stuff I used to do as a kid in the woods behind my trailer and listen.

Pandora's whispering to someone, asking them to wait their turn.

I can't think of any situation in which that request coming from her is a good thing.

Alarmed, I get up and walk toward her.

A dozen or so glowing white lights hang in the air around the kid. Three are closer to me, the rest a few feet more distant. Pandora walks up to one hovering light, grabs it, clutching it to her chest, then walks over to the small group where she releases it. Takes me a second to process what my eyes are telling me: faeries. The kid's got a matter-of-fact expression as she walks a couple feet in one direction, grabs a faerie, and carries it to the second group. Looks like she's transferring dolls from one shelf to another, except there are no shelves and the dolls are alive and hovering under their own power.

Not sure if Natalie's estimation of a faerie's size is off, but these are only about half the size of her toys, at most four inches tall.

"Pan?" I whisper.

All the faeries spin to stare at me, the closer ones seeming afraid, the more distant ones angry.

"Relax. She's cool. That's my mom," says Pandora before looking at me. "The faeries asked for help."

"Help?" I walk up to her, scratching my head.

"Yeah. They can't go past the magic here, but they can if someone carries them." The girl grabs another faerie, clutches him to her chest, and hurries to the second group. For a few seconds, the little man makes a gurgling noise like someone stepped on him. "They really want to see what's in here."

"Wow, someone's in for a serious prank. Probably many some-ones." I chuckle.

A squealing Ashley runs over to the faeries. They soak up her adoration, landing on her outstretched hand, playing with her hair, and so on. When the kid isn't drawing pentagrams on the floor with strawberry pancake syrup in hopes of summoning more 'demons,' she's painfully cute. To be fair, she's painfully cute while pretending to be a demonologist, too.

"I know someone's gonna get pranked." Pandora gives me a flat look. "I didn't want it to be me. When faeries ask for help, you say yes."

"Fair enough." I wave at the little people. "Carry on."

Not sure why Pandora is so particular about only carrying one at a time, but she does.

"Huh. So that's all it takes?" I ask. "Someone to *carry* a magical being across?"

"For them. They're so little, it's easy." Pandora waves her hand around in the air as if washing an invisible pane of glass. "The magic is here."

Ashley, futilely attempting to hug the entire group of faeries, looks up at us wild-eyed. "I wanna let *all* the faeries in! I hate they're not allowed in the city."

The area does feel a bit charged, but the sensation is barely notice-able. "Hey, guys?" I glance toward the cloud of small people as

Pandora brings the last one over. "If you go into the city, watch out for cars. Don't fly into them. It will hurt."

A tiny woman zips over to float in front of my face. "What's cars?"

I explain, as well as what happens when birds meet windshields. The faeries gasp in horror.

"People don't do it on purpose. They're going too fast to see you and can't stop in time."

The faeries appear grateful for the warning and go zooming off toward downtown. Pity I'm going to miss the show.

"They told me there's a weak spot in the magic over there." Pandora points to her left. "But they don't like trying to sneak through it because it sometimes lights them on fire and their wings burn off."

"Good reason." I nod. "Definitely a good reason."

She grins. "Think the teachers are gonna be there?"

"You know… that's a good idea. If they want to let something big in, best place to start is an existing hole."

Armed with at least an idea of a likely location, we return to our picnic site, finish eating, and resume wandering along Mill Creek and checking out the old ruined buildings. A few times, I feel watched, but see no one nearby. Probably ghosts, or maybe the faeries.

Eventually, it starts to get dark—and the girls are clearly exhausted from walking most of the afternoon. I'm about to call it a day and take them home, but Pandora insists on catching her teachers 'doing bad stuff.' No doubt in my mind she wants blackmail material. Ashley and I 'stake out' the area around where the supposed weak spot is. Pandora decides to fly around for a better view. Not only is she smaller and more difficult to spot, she knows what the teachers in question look like.

I'm shocked when she returns in less than five minutes. She swoops down from the trees, her wings, tail, and illusionary clothing vanishing the instant her toes touch the ground. Once more appearing to be an ordinary kid in a T-shirt and jeans, she rushes over, grabs my hand, and begins dragging me into the forest. She might only be six, and tiny, but the kid *is* strong enough to move me. Hey, I only weigh like 103. Cut me some slack.

"They're here!" whispers Pandora.

"Okay, okay. Stop pulling. You're making too much noise."

She lets go and stands there bouncing impatiently. Ashley scrambles upright and takes my hand. Pandora leads us into the forest, trying to be quiet. It only takes us a couple minutes to stumble upon a fortyish white dude, a somewhat younger Hispanic guy, and a woman huddled around a faint green light hanging in the air at about chest level in the shape of a rectangle. It's roughly the size of a piece of copier paper and contains a whole mess of strange symbols, as though one of them painted on thin air using glow-in-the-dark ink.

Based on what my kid told me before, I assume we've found Ms. Groves, Mr. Sandoval, and... some other man with black hair, a tall face, square jaw and heavy wrinkles on his cheeks. Dude can't be much older than forty, but he's weathered. He kinda looks like a school janitor or maintenance guy.

Going to assume the other man is Mr. Sandoval, one of the teachers Pandora mentioned. If I had to put my read on his intent into words it would be: let's hurry this the hell up and get out of here.

Pandora helps herself to my phone and starts snapping pictures.

Predictably, they hear the sound effect of the 'camera' and start looking around.

"Shit," whispers the unknown man, giving off an air of malicious indifference like he isn't specifically looking to hurt anyone but wouldn't hesitate to do so. "Someone's close. Hurry it up."

The woman also looks straight at us, though I'm unsure if she sees anything. We're about fifteen feet away and hiding behind trees, plus I'm trying not to let anyone notice us. It's a bit more effort to conceal Ashley, but she's not exactly huge. Hopefully, Pandora's hiding herself psychically as well. Not really a big deal though since we have no non-human body parts in view at present. My read on the woman is earnestness. Okay, unexpected. She doesn't feel like she's doing something dangerous and illegal, more like a resistance fighter in a movie trying to plant a bomb to destroy the evil corporation.

Now, I'm really curious. What the heck?

I drop the 'don't see me' radiance and walk over to them. "Hey. What's up?"

All three of them jump. The woman clutches her chest and bites back a scream. Mr. Sandoval nearly trips over his own feet. The other guy takes on a fighting stance, only the wideness of his eyes giving away I scared the hell out of him by seemingly appearing out of nowhere.

The man I don't like pulls a gun and points it at me. "Shit. Let's get out of here."

Ashley lets out an *eep* and jumps behind a tree.

"Vance," whisper-shouts the woman. "Put that thing away."

I keep walking up to him, acting casual. "Trying to shoot me is probably not the smartest thing you could do."

He takes a step back. "Damn, lady. You got a death wish or something?"

"No. Quite the opposite. Death wish implies I consider you any kind of threat."

Mr. Sandoval mouths WTF.

Whump.

Pandora drops straight down out of the sky onto the back of the dude pointing a gun at me. She holds her tail blade to his throat, clutching it like a knife just below the barb. She must've put her wings away in midair. The sparkle goth dress illusion makes her look beyond creepy. I think it's creepier—in a good way—than the white nightgown and hair-over-the-face thing, but I've always been a fan of wearing black.

"Gah!" yells the guy.

"Hurt my mom and I *will* cut you," says Pandora, in her best attempt at sounding like a badass.

"Pandora?" asks Ms. Groves.

She shifts her eyes to the teacher. "I see my reputation precedes me."

"Wait…" I glance at Ms. Groves. "You know my kid?"

"Ms. Groves and Mr. Sandoval are teachers from my school, just not my grade," says Pandora. "I don't know who the butthead with the gun is."

"Exactly." I gesture at the teachers. "They aren't *your* teachers. How do they know who you are?"

Pandora bites her lip. "Umm, I maybe got sent to the principal's office a few times."

"Why is this the first I'm hearing about it? And what for?"

"Refusing to be bullied."

"Oh. No worries." I'm guessing she pushed or punched some kid for teasing her. She's not wearing the same clothes all the time, but she is a little small for her age, not to mention as white as paper. Then again, some kids don't really need a reason to tease people.

Pandora smiles.

"Hey," says the nameless guy. "This kid is holding a damn knife to my throat and everyone's just standing there?"

"It's not a knife," deadpans Pandora.

Ms. Groves makes a sad face. "Don't lie, sweetie."

It amuses me the woman appears more concerned she thinks the kid is lying than she's holding a blade at a man's neck *or* the guy has a gun pointed at me. "Well, dude, you are pointing a gun at me. Having a sharp thing at your neck is kinda mild."

"Can everyone please just calm down?" Mr. Sandoval holds his hands up in a placating gesture.

"The only one here who isn't calm is this guy." I gesture at the dude holding the gun. "Don't mind us. We're just curious what's going on here."

"Vance, put the damn gun away." Ms. Groves points at him, then looks in my direction. "You might think this looks suspicious."

I smile. "Just a bit, but you shouldn't assume I give a crap. What are you planning to let in and how many people is it going to kill?"

Vance lowers his weapon, flicks the safety on, and stuffs it in the back of his jeans. He grasps Pandora's arm as if to pull the blade away from his throat, but ends up looking confused. Heh. He tried to be kinda gentle given her size and got the shock of his life when he couldn't budge her. Before he can pull harder, she relents, releasing her grip around his body and dropping to her feet behind him. She lets go of her tail, letting it swish around behind her and retracting it up into her puffy black skirt. I assume she's leaving the tail out but hiding it under the illusionary outfit so the amulet doesn't auto-shift her back into physical clothes. The teachers would start asking questions if they saw her outfit change in an instant. Questions like *why* does she have a magical necklace.

Ms. Groves appears to notice the tail retreating up under the gossamer pleats of a gauzy black 'doom faerie' dress. Surprisingly, she makes an 'oh, interesting' face, not an 'ack kill it with fire!' face.

Oops.

"We aren't trying to let any specific entity into the city." Ms. Groves faces me, hands clasped in front of herself as if she hadn't seen a six-year-old with a tail. "Our goal is to dispel the Aether Wall in its entirety to *protect* the City of Philadelphia."

Pandora walks over to stand beside me, arms folded.

"So, it's true there are people out there trying to sabotage the wall." I swipe my hair away from my right eye. "Go figure. Thought it was conspiracy nonsense."

"We're taking a risk not shooting her," says Vance.

I point my thumb at him. "Would you guys miss this dude?"

Ms. Groves goes a little pale. She glances at Pandora, then at me, and gets a little paler. Doesn't take a genius to realize she's doing the mental math regarding how alike we look. Even if she doesn't know why the kid has a bladed tail, she obviously assumes I have one, too, which makes me a bigger, meaner, nastier version of whatever the child is.

To mess with her head even more, I pace around them, obviously going through the barrier and back in. Ms. Groves gets a mild case of shaky hands, though the guys don't seem to care. I finish the circular path and stop in front of her.

"We would, yes," she mutters, then in Spanish, "Vance, don't provoke her. She's... something."

"Aye, I'm something alright," I reply in Spanish. "But right now, that something is mostly just curious how letting a bunch of magical creatures run freely into the city counts as saving it."

Ms. Groves grimaces at me understanding her, then sighs. "The barrier is building up a charge of magical energy like water gathering against a dam. Our world objects to natural energies being denied the ability to flow where they will. If we do not dispel the Aether Wall, the forces opposing it will grow and grow until something huge happens and wipes the entire city out."

"The enchantment to keep things out is having a reverse paradoxical effect," says Mr. Sandoval. "It's drawing creatures *to* the city. But it's too strong for them to get past. The longer it exists, the more force the world pushes against it."

I whistle. "Wow. That's a scary theory. So, you guys aren't trying to do like the whole 'sowing chaos and disorder' thing?"

"Certainly not," says Ms. Groves.

I get the feeling her intentions are true. At least, she believes her own story. My psychic abilities can't determine actual truth. "Okay. Cool. Good luck with it. I gotta get these two home before it gets too much darker out here."

"We cool?" asks Vance.

Ashley emerges from her hiding place and walks up behind me.

"Yeah." I nod at him. "Keep on keepin' on."

Ms. Groves steps closer and smiles at Pandora. "Well, it certainly seems you two have an interesting... tail to tell."

"Oops," deadpans Pandora. "She saw it, didn't she?"

"Huh?" asks Vance.

Mr. Sandoval raises an eyebrow.

Pandora thrusts her tail out into clear view and waves it in his face. "See! Told you I wasn't lying. It's not a knife." She dispels the tail, which dissipates into a line of black vapor. This causes her amulet to instantly shift her outfit back to her physical T-shirt, jean shorts, and sneakers. I swear, getting this kid to wear shoes is about as difficult as getting a politician to go a full day without telling any lies. Wait, no. Bad comparison. Pandora does occasionally tolerate shoes.

The men whistle.

"And it's just magic." Pandora briefly moons them. "See? No tail."

Mr. Sandoval chuckles. Vance gives me this pitying look as if to say 'you have your hands full, don't you?' Not sure exactly how we've gone from 'quick shoot her before she talks' to commiserating over parenting challenges.

Ms. Groves, on the other hand, doesn't seem to completely buy the 'evidence' of a tailless butt. She narrows her eyes ever so slightly at me.

"You don't need to hide from us. We're pro-magic. You aren't exactly human, are you?"

"Same could be said for certain defense lawyers." I smirk.

"Perhaps you can help us?" Ms. Groves smiles.

Shit. What's worse? A mage-turned-teacher's thinly veiled promise to potentially blackmail me or randomly killing three people? Yeah, it's a bit of a leap to go straight to slicing heads off, but if they are mages, they might have defenses against my charm abilities. Erasing memories is not an exact science for me. Damn. I can't really kill people in front of Ashley. At least not again. The last time I did so, the bastard deserved it and she knew it. And to be fair, I didn't tear Frank to shreds *in front of* her; she saw the carnage after the fact.

"Okay, let's talk."

15

CHEAP RENT

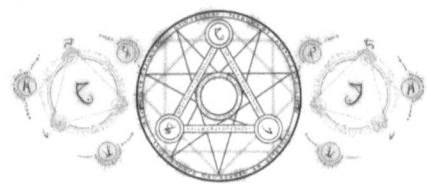

Later Saturday night, the child is monopolizing the television.

I don't mind. There are parts of Mom in my psyche, after all. I've managed to convince myself to think of Pandora as my daughter enough to where it's becoming increasingly more and more difficult to say no to her. Mom had a hard time telling me no unless whatever I asked for happened to be dangerous, wildly inappropriate, or too expensive. As a kid, I knew my limits and didn't dare ask for anything that cost money. Mostly, my 'asks' were for permission to do various things. If I *really* wanted something that cost money, I'd shoplift it.

Unfortunately—or fortunately, depending on perspective—I am more immature than my mother was at this age. Mom would certainly have told me no in response to asking permission to go spray paint random nonsense on the back of the mall. Me? If Pandora ever asks, I'd probably go with her.

Tonight, she wanted to watch a kid's movie. For a bunch of talking woodland creatures plotting a way to break into human houses and steal food, it's surprisingly funny. The writers slipped in enough adult humor to keep me snickering. My only real complaint is they made the rat speak Spanglish, and the voice actor clearly does not know Spanish. His accent is beyond fake sounding.

Pandora's cuddled up against my side, gaze laser-focused on the screen. Kid's got her horns, tail, and wings out. It's adorable watching her tail react subconsciously to her emotions from the movie, just like a cat. I can't really say one way or the other if I would have insisted on constantly showing off all my extra body parts at her age, since the truth had been hidden from me. Good chance I'd have done the same back then. We technically are the same person, after all. Mostly.

She's like a kid obsessed with their favorite superhero pajamas, wanting to wear them *all the time.* Mom would have panicked and probably asked me never to show my wings or horns, thinking the more I did, the more 'the powers of darkness' would grow inside me or some nonsense. I love my mom, but she's totally fallen for mythology.

Heck, she's not too fond of seeing my Shaar'nath bits now as an adult, though she totally made an exception when I carried her out of the maze away from those murderous little creatures. It's kinda surprising how little she flipped out when Pandora sprouted wings. Mom's a sucker for cute, and Pandora has the same slightly-too-big eyes as me. They're not so big people stare like 'what the hell is wrong with your face,' just enough to make us 'cute' to most people's sensibilities. The effect is stronger for her at the moment due to being a little kid. I exploited the hell out of it when I was younger, but it got annoying once I reached my teens. You know how freakin' frustrating it is to be seventeen, hit on a boy my age and have him blow me off because he thinks I'm fourteen? Grr. Too bad for them I wasn't the sort of girl to run off and cry into her pillow after rejection. I tended to slam heads into lockers or trip annoying people down stairs. Telekinetically, of course. Didn't want to get expelled.

Maybe Pandora will outgrow wanting to have her wings out all the time when she gets older and starts caring what people think of her. Wait, what am I saying?

I don't care what people think of me.

Natalie mentioned 'nurture vs. nature.' Different choices I make as Pandora's effective mom are going to mold her nature, and she probably won't end up being an exact copy of me in terms of personality. Good. Someday, she's going to become my sister. At least, I think so. When we both appear to be the same age, will she still think of me as mom?

The movie goes into this extended routine where the hedgehog, squirrel twins, the raccoon ringleader, and the rat nearly burn down a human house in order to steal a box of chocolate cupcakes. No sooner do the animals begin to enjoy their ill-gotten treasure back in the forest do I get a massive craving for a chocolate cupcake.

Pandora turns her head toward me with classic horror movie slowness.

We lock stares and say, "Cupcakes," simultaneously.

"Could go to Kwan's, but that would require moving… and pants."

"Not necessarily." Pandora swishes her tail around.

"Yes, necessarily." I chuckle. "Humans have weird rules. Wearing pants outside is one of them." Honestly, in this part of town, I probably *could* streak to Kwan's in plain sight and no one would bother calling the police. Still, I don't want to give the poor guy a heart attack.

"Not if no one sees you."

I twist hair around my finger. "I can't steal from Mr. Kwan. And yeah, I know I'm getting old. Used to steal from convenience stores all the time back in the day."

"Why'd you stop?" asks Pandora, in complete sincerity.

Sigh. "Well, I never stole stuff to be mean to people. It always bothered me to take things from people who also struggled with money. Nabbing a sandwich or a bag of chips from the corner store when I was ten was usually the difference between me having almost enough food in a day or going to bed hungry. Don't have to steal food now."

"You don't wanna get fired."

I laugh. "That, too. Much easier to get away with stuff as a kid."

"We are above petty mortal laws." Pandora holds her arms out to either side, extending her claws.

Is it normal for a parent to consider getting a scratching post for their kid? I'll consider myself lucky she hasn't taken to shredding the furniture yet.

"While you are technically right, if we keep abusing it, it'll become impossible for us to blend in."

"Oh. Poop." She huffs. "Okay."

A battle between craving and laziness rages inside me. Well, the opposite of rages. What's the lazy version of war? Craving and laziness are like little cartoon characters in my head, both slumped on sofas, staring at each other, lacking the motivation to fight.

Pandora climbs up onto her knees and leans her face into mine, so we're almost touching noses. Less than an inch separates our eyes. "Cupcaaaaakes."

"Okay." I pause the movie. "Be right back."

"Yay!" She flops over.

I get up and go to my bedroom for a pair of jeans. This T-shirt is enough to lounge around the house in without pants on and not embarrass any surprise guests. It's a little long to wear over jeans, but changing it for a ten-minute trip down the street is too much effort. So is putting on shoes. It's tempting to just go naked from the waist down and hope I don't have to bend even slightly in any direction so nothing peeks out from under my shirt, but I'd rather not taunt fate. Also, this isn't exactly the best part of town. Walking around like that might be considered an experiment in Darwinism. Heh. I should do it purely to make myself the equivalent of a bug-zapper for creeps. Nah. Too much work dealing with bodies. It's less effort to put pants on. After grabbing my purse, I toss my hair over my shoulder with a nod and head for the door.

Pandora, still sprawled on the sofa, watches me go by.

"Don't burn the place down."

She twists around and drapes herself over the sofa back, looking at me. "Are you going to leave a six-year-old version of you home alone?"

"Poor impulse control..." I mutter.

"Yeah, that." She grins.

"Good point." I pause at the front door. "Put something on and let's go."

"You know I won't do anything. I like having a home." She grins.

"Yes, but you know I'd know you'd know that, so you only said it because you wanted to go with me."

She blinks at my purposefully confusing sentence, then cracks up giggling. Pandora vaults the sofa back and glides to land beside me, flaring her wings. As soon as her toes hit the carpet, she pats her amulet. The goth dress appears, but she puts her wings and tail away.

I tap my finger on one of her cute little horns. "Shouldn't leave these out."

"Oops." She glances up and her horns dissipate into wisps of black vapor.

The kid stands there wearing illusions and smiling at me. Should I insist she put something real on? Meh. Screw it. We're only going down the block. Would've been lazier of me to use my amulet, but I've been a functional adult too long. The concept of getting in trouble for streaking has taken deep enough hold on my brain. I open the door and head out.

"You don't use the amulet at school, do you?"

"No. The seats are too cold." She hugs herself. "Our couch is soft and warm."

I get the bizarre thought a solid stone sofa heated to 500 degrees would be even more comfortable. It's fleeting, though. Probably have to be a full-blooded Shaar'nath to consider sitting on a hot rock better than a cushion.

Because it's only a block and a half, and out of habit, I walk down the stairs and exit the apartment building on foot. Flying is cool and all, but it's more work. Not only do we need to go up to the roof, it's a mental drain to keep making people not see me. For such a short trip, it's less work to just walk.

Pandora trots along at my side, grinning.

I really ought to go have my head examined for contemplating giving a six-year-old chocolate cake less than an hour before bedtime. Whatever. Mutual cravings must be obeyed. If the craving is enough to get me off my ass, it's serious business. We'll split a two-pack, anyway. She's a lot more tired than she lets on after we spent all day walking around the park. We reach the end of the block my apartment's on, cross the street, and start down the block Kwan's Market occupies. Annoyingly, it's all the way at the opposite corner.

Two guys emerge from behind a porch in front of us, both in hoodies, one grey, one black. Grey-hoodie points a glowing red wand at me... or kind of a wand. The ones I've seen at Natalie's shop are all between ten and fourteen inches. Dude's packing about half that. Also, I recognize these two as the same guys who almost robbed Tracy the other night.

"Cash. Phone. Jewelry," says Wand Guy.

"Pff. Seriously? Put that thing away before you get hurt."

He takes a step closer, wand in my face. "I'm serious, bitch."

"Mommy? Why is that guy's wand so tiny?" asks Pandora.

"Bad genetic luck," I deadpan.

Guy's face reddens. He swings his arm over to aim the wand at Pandora—or starts to. The instant my brain processes what he's doing, I telekinetically swing his arm around so he stabs the wand a few inches deep into his chest, then grab his hand in both of mine and shove. The wand emits a sharp *crack* as the force of my push breaks it off inside him. Dude flies off his feet, lands on his back, and slides about fifteen feet away from us. Only about two inches of wand is visible sticking out of his chest, probably impaled into his lung. Painful, but he'll live.

"Holy shit," rasps black hoodie guy, gawking at me.

The other guy scrambles upright, stares in horror at the wand bit sticking out of him, screams, and runs off. He doesn't make it three full steps before he explodes into a fine red mist from the middle of his chest upward. One of his arms smashes through a fourth-story window on the other side of the street. No idea where the left arm went. Head's probably in orbit if it didn't disintegrate. From about bellybutton down, the rest of him remains upright for a little more than a second, then collapses.

"Eww," says Pandora.

Black hoodie doubles over and vomits.

"Are you going to kill him, too?" Pandora peers up at me.

"Nah." I take her hand and walk around the puking guy. "And I didn't kill the other one. A broken wand did. Enchanted items really don't like to be broken."

A woman in a fourth-floor apartment screams.

"Disappear," I whisper.

We both concentrate on not being seen and resume walking to Kwan's, stepping carefully around the half-mugger.

"Is this a dangerous place?" asks Pandora.

"Most people think it's a bad part of town, yeah. Not the worst, but far from 'nice.'"

She nods once, then looks down where she steps to avoid bloody bits. "Why do we live here?"

"The rent's cheap."

"Oh."

"Hey, I did my part to clean the area up." I wink. "One unregistered wand off the street."

16

ACCEPTANCE

Operation Cupcake went off without any other complications.

Casual nudity or drug deals might not be enough to make the locals call the police, but dudes exploding does. No one paid any attention to the kid and I as we walked home. As long as we don't physically touch anyone, make sound, or do something to attract attention, our little mind trick is fairly potent.

It's a few hours later and I'm in bed, staring at the ceiling. Pandora's curled up on her side, tucked against me. It didn't freak her out to watch a guy explode. She's not frightened at all, merely wanted cuddles. In spite of eating a cupcake two and a half hours ago, she fell asleep pretty quick. Not sure what's keeping me up. Maybe I'm trying to savor having this quiet time with her while she's still tiny and—relatively—innocent. Compared to the amount of time we're both going to live, childhood's going to disappear in basically an instant and be gone forever.

She's going to be the only person to stay with me. Maybe Natalie will, too, if she ever figures out immortality, but people have been chasing it for... well, as long as people have existed. If anyone's managed to pull it off, they haven't advertised. She teases me all the time about how she needs to unlock the secrets before she gets too much older. As soon as she looks like an 'old woman' (meaning past thirty-five) she's going to be jealous of me. Yeah, she's kidding about the jealousy part. It's going to be sadness and fear, really. Watching me stay the same as she ages is going to terrify her. She won't know what to do with herself in wherever humans go after death without me.

Maybe she'll end up sticking around as a ghost or trapping her mind in an enchanted item.

But Pandora? She's going to be here.

A sudden fit of clingy possessiveness comes over me. I squish her like a teddy bear. She stirs a little, emitting a soft grunt, but doesn't wake. It's not an unhappy grunt. Maybe in her dream, someone hugged her. I lay there brushing my fingers through her hair, and thinking about Melisandre. I'm sure giving me an emotional support demonling was the *last* thing he expected when trying to make another world-destroyer. No, I'm not really worried about becoming emotionally attached to her. Melisandre is a dickhead, but he's not (completely) an idiot. If he knows how I feel about the kid, he won't harm her, fearing I'd blow myself up out of spite.

Can't call it suicide really, since there is at least a seventy percent chance I'd wake up in Imbreleth as a full-blooded Shaar'nath. Not in any hurry to be 'reborn' though. But if I shed my human side, I'll no longer be any threat to the Armistice... meaning no chance of destroying the physical world and thus, useless to his plans.

He's kinda screwed either way. Forced to watch me being happy while unable to take any sort of revenge. Piss him off enough, he won't care and simply wait another few hundred years to try again. I am not unique or irreplaceable. It's just a crapton of work. Human women aren't terribly receptive to mating with Elestari or Shaar'nath. Biologically, I mean. The average Elestari could easily charm his way into any woman's bedroom. They're all pretty much unbelievably gorgeous. Take Laniah, for example. I've never been romantically drawn toward women, but if she looked at me the right way, I'd be open to experimentation. What can I say? I have poor impulse control. Probably wouldn't work with a human woman, though. Elestari are so *ridicu-*

lously pretty it has to be a supernatural charm effect. One could even use the word 'pretty' to describe their men.

Anyway, on average, it would probably take a couple centuries of repeated attempts before anyone got pregnant with another half-human. Male human with a female Elestari or Shaar'nath doesn't work. The mother has to be native to the Armistice—that means Earth, or more accurately, the physical dimension.

No, it's likely Melisandre is going to be hounding me for the next several centuries, trying to figure out some way to convince me to end reality. Ironically, creating Pandora might make it harder for him. Two of us to resist. Or… what if he's biding his time until she grows up so he can kill me and hope she rages enough to destroy everything. Ugh. I hate where my brain goes when I'm sleep deprived.

Need a new topic.

Pandora's tail's coiled around my leg again. It's like being hugged by a garter snake. Hmm. Should I try to discourage her from sleeping like this, with her wings and tail out? My worry is she might become too comfortable with what we are. If the extra parts become normalized, it's easier for us to forget ourselves and get caught. Would it even be a problem if someone caught us? What would happen if we embraced it?

I'm already convinced human society couldn't possibly handle the truth of what we are. They lose their minds and kill each other over mythology already. Humans have been doing it for as long as they've existed. Gods people used to murder each other over are now considered myths because they came up with new gods. Like that Zeus guy. No one thinks he's real anymore. Go back in time far enough, people killed in his name.

Sigh.

They might accept us as 'beings from another plane,' but it's still going to be a pain in the ass. Lots of work and effort for no real advantage. It's easier to hide and not be interrogated by every police mage we see. Oh, damn. I know what's keeping me awake. Ms. Groves. The number of people who know I'm *something* has increased by one. Lieutenant Sims got the real truth, as did Lawrence and Detective Zheng. None of them took it very well, but at least they're not freaking out. As far as the fourth-grade teacher knows, my mother is a luminare who invited 'some kind of planar spirit' into her bedroom. I lied—shocking, right?—and told her I had no idea who or what my father was. A chance exists she might report me as a 'magical creature.' Then again, I have photos of her trying to destroy the Aether Wall. The woman also didn't threaten me at all. Didn't even get the feeling she intended to imply threat. All my senses tell me she's sincere in her belief Philadelphia will be destroyed by some giant magical beast if the wall isn't disenchanted.

Also, no idea what 'being reported as a magical creature' means. Maybe nothing. Depends on if they declare me a non-sentient animal. Doubt that since I can speak.

Anyway, Ms. Groves thinks my supernatural nature could somehow let me help them shatter the Aether Wall. She's put me up to stealing something called a nyctus crystal from an Academy guild downtown. I have a few problems with this. Stealing in general, not so much. Stealing from *mages* could be a pain. No idea if human mages can do that bullshit green forcefield crap Melisandre trapped me in. I suppose mages have spells to trap humans, too. However, breaking into an Academy building is almost certainly going to require me to kill—or at least knock the shit out of—a few people. Playing chicken with mages when they think you're an intruder is like juggling loaded handguns. I could pull it off if I get lucky enough, but more than likely, people are going to end up dead.

By the way, total metaphor. I couldn't juggle tennis balls, much less loaded guns.

Every time in my life where I've stolen something or broken the law, I've done so purely for fun. Sure, joyriding in a stolen car—which someone else actually stole, by the way—*could* have easily ended in tragedy if a high-speed police chase came to a stop at a crash site. We got lucky. Point being, I've never misbehaved for malicious reasons. Boredom, desire, discontent... giving the middle-finger to society that wanted me to be all sorts of things I didn't want to be, society that kept my mother poor, that made fun of me for being poor... society that sent me home from school for 'showing too much shoulder' but ignored it when my friends complained about boys snapping our bras.

Well, *their* bras. I hate them. Stupid tit prisons. Never wore 'em, except for the occasional racerback sports bra. Those aren't too bad. Gotta deal with them for work since our polo shirts are a bit on the thin side. Another bit of double standard that pisses me off. No one cares if a guy's nipples poke out their shirt. Me? I get 'talked to.'

Anyway, before I keep myself up even longer from being angry...

Stealing a crystal from mages wouldn't bother me if it hit me on a whim as a fun thing to do or if necessary to protect Pandora, Ashley, or Natalie. Some weird little part of me is actually resisting the notion of crime. Probably because this would be actual crime with consequences an 'oops' or an innocent look can't fix. I've broken into places before, but they'd always been abandoned. Old malls, old stores, abandoned houses, crap like that. Just looking around. Trying to break into a place that's still in use—not to mention full of mages—is out of my comfort zone. Also, I'm not sure if helping Ms. Groves take down the Aether Wall is a good idea. Her theory of magical forces building up to critical mass sounds reasonable to me, but remember, I don't know much about magic. Wouldn't, you know, the *mages* have figured this out by now? Also, the last time some people wanted me to help them destroy a 'wall,' it turned out to be a super bad idea.

Maybe I can ask for a second opinion before doing anything.

Mm. My bed really is comfortable.

In what feels like an instant, my alarm starts screaming at me.

Somehow, it went from 2:13 a.m. to 7:00 a.m.

Ugh.

One thing no amount of growing up or maturity will ever fix for me is how *not* a morning person I am. Left to my own devices, I'd stay in bed until somewhere between nine and ten.

Pandora stretches, squeaks, and emits a huge sigh. "I hate that thing. Why does morning have to get here so early?"

"Seriously." I groan.

The almost five-hour instant jump of time means I got *some* sleep. Small favors.

17

A HIGHER ORDER

Despite what most people say, I have matured noticeably compared to my teenage self.

'Most people' can also go screw themselves. Not so many years ago, I'd probably have thought taking down the Aether Wall the most epic of epic pranks. What could be more hilarious than letting a whole bunch of magical creatures run loose into the city? It wouldn't have taken much more than seeing a teacher encouraging 'misbehavior' to make it the most awesome thing ever.

I probably would have also adored sneaking into an Academy building and messing with mages. Most of them are aloof, self-important assholes. At least, it's what most people say. I haven't really spent much time around them except for my mother and Natalie, and neither of them really count as mages. For one thing, they don't parade around in robes acting better than everyone. For another, neither are true mages. Nat's an enchanter and my mother's a luminare.

Anyway, I have a lot more to lose now for getting in serious trouble than as a kid, so if there's a way for me to avoid having to rile up a bunch of mages at an Academy campus, I'm going to go for it. The Philadelphia Academy house is no small thing either. It's one of the oldest and largest mage guilds in the US. There's gotta be over a hundred uptight 'mancers' of various persuasions in a giant old building. Guessing. I haven't researched it because, you know, me. If I'm going to do something, I'm going to jump straight in without much thought.

Except for the slight bit of maturity I've gained.

I land atop the Comcast Center a little past noon. This is the tallest building downtown, which makes for a great vantage point and an even better meeting location. Another upside to illusionary clothing: it's not my fire department uniform... as much as a white polo shirt and black Army pants can be called a uniform. Anyone who happens to slip through my psychic defenses and sees me isn't going to see a firefighter. They'll see a crazy goth. Did I mention the 'dress' Natalie made me is super frilly?

No point retracting my wings after landing. This shouldn't take long, and I need to be back to the station fast enough to seem like nothing more than a long line at Starbucks got in my way. What I keep referring to in terms of having increased maturity is getting a second opinion *before* breaking into the Academy. It doesn't track that the entire mage community of Philadelphia has somehow failed to realize an imminent catastrophe with the barrier spell. Either the story is nonsense, or the mages are covering it up. Because I suspect they might be covering up the truth, even if they tell me it's nonsense, my brain won't fully believe them.

It's good to have a healthy distrust of authority. Alas, I happen to have an *un*healthy distrust of authority. So, I've appealed to a higher authority... well 'authority' in the sense of knowledge, not legal power.

Laniah.

One could say the Elestari invented magic. If they're like Rembrandt, human mages are still learning to finger paint. And sure, some of those 'finger paintings' are pretty damn impressive, but bear with me here. I'm being comparative.

A blur of yellowish-golden light crosses the sky in front of me, growing into the shape of a gold-winged Elestari woman. She's wearing her usual physics-defying 'dress,' basically a long strip of white fabric wrapped around her. No natural force explains how it stays on her without unraveling.

She alights beside me, tucks her wings up and gives me a huge hug.

Yeah, she's the touchy-feely type. Looks like a twenty-year-old blonde, blue-eyed airhead cheerleader with feathery wings. She's way smarter than she looks, but a total hippie star child. I'm not a total grump. Honest.

"Hi!" chirps Laniah.

"Thanks for coming. Got a question for you."

She nods, eyes widening. "You said the city might be in danger?"

"That's basically what I wanted to ask you." I explain what Ms. Groves told me about the Aether Wall. "Do you know if there's any truth there? Will magical forces build up until something massive stomps all over Philly?"

Laniah gazes off to the west. Hmm. Wonder if she can see the 'wall'. "Yes."

"Yes?"

"The woman you spoke with is correct, though she is not entirely accurate in her estimation of time." Laniah turns back to face me. "It will likely be sixty to eighty years before an event of catastrophic proportions takes place."

I raise both eyebrows. "So… it *is* going to happen?"

"Almost certainly. Over the next several decades, the instability in this region will attract more and more powerful beings until the Earth balances itself out once more."

"Damn. Guess I steal a crystal."

"Crystal?" She chuckles. "How is a crystal going to be of any help?"

"The teachers thought I could use a nyctus crystal somehow to destroy the spell."

Laniah covers her mouth to hold in a giggle. "Sorry. I shouldn't laugh."

"What's funny about it?"

"It's like a little child putting a sticky bandage on a car to fix a dent. Adorable, but won't help."

I slouch. "Oh. Suppose it means she doesn't really know what I am then. Plan-B time."

"What is that?" Laniah tilts her head at me. "Plan-B?"

"Means my best option is to convince the Academy mages to dispel the Aether Wall before something huge crushes it."

She shakes her head. "You won't be able to. The humans are aware of the possibility of an energy backlash. Some do not believe it while others are certain they will die before it becomes an issue, so they can't be bothered with it."

"Grr. Politicians." I scowl. "Leave it for the next guy is *not* the way to do anything."

She scrunches her nose in confusion. "Aren't we talking about mages? What do politicians have to do with this?"

"Mages, politicians… bureaucrats. Same thing." I scoff. "Damn. This is going to be a pain in the—" I blink. "Hey, wait. Can the Elestari get rid of it? Leave the Academy out completely."

She shrugs. "Sure. I could get rid of it myself, but I can't."

My turn to flash cavewoman eyebrows. "Huh? You just contradicted yourself. You can, but you can't."

"It's not too difficult for me to do, but I'm not really allowed." She sighs, patting me on the back as if comforting a kid being given bad news. "We're not supposed to get involved with humans."

"Umm… why not? Melisandre and his idiots want to *destroy* all humans… and all anything else that might be alive out there on other planets. The Armistice is this entire plane, not merely Earth. That's 'getting involved,' isn't it?" I thrust my arms out to either side.

She bites her lip, shifting her gaze from me to the greenery in the west, and back to me several times. The fairly strong wind up here keeps throwing our hair around and making feathers in her wings ruffle. Mine don't have feathers, just a leathery membrane. 'Course, mine also catch more of the air like parachutes, making it a chore to remain upright whenever it gusts.

"Umm," says Laniah.

"Preventing one city of humans from destroying itself through stupidity can't be too big a deal, right? Why can't you get involved?" I go to put my arm around her, but wings… so I end up resting my hand on her shoulder.

"I guess they think if we get involved, we'll start to feel sorry for humans and not want to wipe them out." Laniah looks down, kicking her toe at the roof.

"But… you already don't want to wipe them out."

"Yeah, I know." She glances down, making this sad, pouty face like a little girl at a pet store who got told no when she asked to take the kitten home. "When they made the rule not to get involved, humans were still basically advanced monkeys. Back then, more Elestari were expecting the Armistice to be temporary and the war to resume. Now, though… support for continued war is fairly low. It's only like fifteen percent of *us*. Hate to say it, but it's twenty-two percent on your side."

"Grr. Well, my kind are a bit less given to thinking things through before acting." I chuckle. "Speaking of which, let's blow up the wall."

"Hah."

"I'm serious. I know you like helping humans. You were pissed at me when you thought I hurt Lawrence."

She gives me an apologetic grimace of a smile. "Yeah… I assumed. Saw what I thought was a Shaar'nath carrying a mangled human and—"

"Forget it. Old news. I can't carry a couple hundred thousand people after whatever smashes the city gets done with it."

We stand there in silence for a few minutes. Finally, she nods once.

"I can disenchant this barrier spell. However, it will cause chaos."

"Are you talking about toddlers in Ikea chaos or yelling 'fire' in a crowded movie theater chaos? Or… Black Friday at Walmart chaos?"

She cringes. "Not that dangerous. The sooner it's done, the less severe the ripples will be. Know that when the spell falls, pent up energy will rush over the area it had been excluded from. You'll most likely see several months of various magical beings and phenomenon being attracted to the area without knowing why."

"So, not specifically malicious?"

"No. Some of the creatures will be dangerous, but it's not as if any of them would be coming to the city specifically to cause damage. Think of it like animals trapped in a flowing tide, being pulled into the city by forces beyond their control."

I shrug. "Considering the other option is do nothing and eventually the city is destroyed, it's really not a choice. Better to deal with a bunch of small fires than having the entire city get smashed. The longer we wait, the worse it will be, so do it as soon as you can."

"True."

"C'mon." I pat her arm. "Consider it saving the city from future destruction. You think humans are adorable, right?"

She huffs. "Fine. Okay."

"Are you going to get in trouble with the Elestari for it?"

She smirks. "Not really. Worst anyone will do is whine at me. It's not like I'm showing myself and teaching them magic or anything capable of drastically affecting the balance of power between humans and Elestari. That's what they're really worried about. They like thinking of humans as weak and trivial. No real threat."

"Oh, the same way our politicians think about people."

Laniah laughs.

"Thanks. I owe you one."

She raises an eyebrow. "One what?"

"It's just a saying. You're helping me, so I'm saying if you need me to help you with anything sometime in the future, you got it."

"Oh." She smacks herself in the forehead. "I do not understand why humans sometimes say things so different in meaning from what they intend."

"Huh?"

"For example, they often refer to things as 'cool,' even when those things are incapable of having a temperature."

I laugh. "Yeah. We have a lot of words with multiple meanings."

"Confusing."

"Can't argue that."

She hugs me again. "I better let you return to your work before you face consequences for being away too long."

"Yeah. I should get back. Talk to you soon."

Laniah waves, then leaps into the air.

Hope there isn't too much of a line at Starbucks. I stand at the edge of the building, spread my wings out, and let gravity take me over the side.

18

CURTAIN CALL

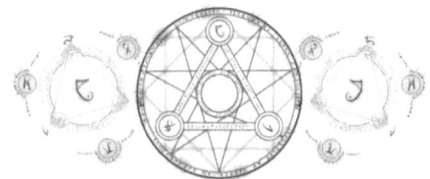

The remainder of my day is fairly uneventful.

Except for one brief moment of hilarity when I stumble into the garage to find Alex Edison tapping the pole and muttering Brian's ridiculous chant when he doesn't think anyone is watching. He doesn't see me enter, so I rush over to hide behind one of the trucks. It's impossible to resist an opportunity like this. The next time he babbles nonsense, I telekinetically fling him up the pole. Due to the angle—I can't see upstairs from here—it requires giving him enough force to send him flying through the hole out of sight.

Seconds after his boots vanish into the upstairs, a loud, metallic clattering *thud* shakes the ceiling.

"Oops," I whisper.

No way he hit the roof. I didn't chuck him *that* hard. It totally sounded like he hit lockers. Alex probably landed weird, lost his balance, and stumbled a couple paces into the lockers. No serious injury, so I resume finding it hilarious. Poor guy is either going to believe the pole is magic until he dies, or come after me for some epic prank revenge when he learns the truth. Speaking of guys and magic poles, I slip off to the ready room to call Jason.

Ugh, this trip of his to Germany feels like it's taking forever. As soon as he's back, Pandora—and maybe Ashley, too—will be spending a whole weekend at my mother's. I try to call him but get voicemail. At least he updated the announcement to say they're in the middle of an exercise and his cell phone's sitting in a locker while he's dangling off giant ladders.

"Hey, It's me. Call me when you can. Bye."

Long, rambling, sappy, romantic drivel is not my style.

Natalie went out with a guy named Tito for a while. Whenever she tried to call him and got voicemail, she'd invariably leave a twenty-minute-long monologue. I'd be shocked if the poor guy actually listened to any of it.

An old feeling I know all too well haunts me for the rest of the day. Ever break into an abandoned store, smoke a bunch of weed with your friends, then leave… but not be entirely sure you didn't drop a still-lit joint in the wrong place? No? Just me then? Ugh. It kinda sucked, wondering if I'd accidentally started a serious fire. Doubt it would've hurt anyone considering the old department store hadn't seen an active customer since my mom was a little kid. Still, if anyone figured out we were in there, Logan, Aiden, Gina, Jose, and I *all* would've gone to jail for arson.

Took me two days to set aside the worry. By then, I figured the joint had burned out.

The same dread hangs over me now. Only this time instead of dropping a joint, I've lit off a fire-and-forget Elestari. Laniah is going to dispel the Aether Wall—or maybe already has. I'm not worried about getting in trouble for it. There's no way anyone could connect me to the spell collapsing… without being psychic, and psychic stuff doesn't work in courtrooms. Also, no one would believe a person claiming I put an 'angel' up to doing it.

There's something I will *never* understand about humans. Tell me if this makes sense: a large portion of humans believe in a god, angels, and demons… but if someone claims to have seen or spoken to an angel or demon, everyone thinks they're crazy. How does that follow any sort of logic?

So, yeah. The rest of my day went by quiet and boring. I like quiet. Boring, not so much, but I'd rather be bored on the job than busy. Once

I'm off work, then boredom is bad. When my shift ends, I fly to Natalie's. Sometimes I envy her for living and working in the same building. No commute. Must be awesome.

"Hey." Natalie grins at me from behind the counter. "How'd it go today?"

"Oh... fairly quiet."

"What did you do?"

"Nothing."

"Oh, come on." She winks. "You've got that tone and look. Something serious went down."

I lean on the counter and tell her about the situation with the Aether Wall.

She gawks. "Wow. You know I've seen some posts on the enchanter boards about the energy dam theory. People are pretty divided over it. You know how stupid some people are. Tell them not to jump in a tank full of sharks for their own safety, and a scary number of people would jump in to spite you for telling them what not to do. Lots of cities have wards and it's not a problem there."

"You know I'm no mage, but I read other cities use repelling spells, not walls."

Natalie holds up a finger. "True. That helps. When the resistance builds up too much it pushes past the repelling field, then stabilizes. Much smarter to do it that way than try to keep *everything* out."

"Where are the girls?"

"Watch where you step. They shrank themselves with the dollhouse and are driving toy cars around the store." Natalie leans forward, peering left down the aisle of shelves. "Ashley? Pandora?"

I hop up to sit on the counter. "How safe is the shrink enchant?"

"Totally fine. I'd never have incorporated it into a kid's toy if I wasn't totally certain of its safety. Only real danger is them getting stuck somewhere or maybe mistaken for enchanted toy dolls and someone trying to buy or shoplift them."

"Pandora would bite."

Natalie laughs.

Two small cars, both made mostly of wood, skid around a corner and come zooming down the aisle toward me. They're about twelve inches long and a little big for the girls, but somehow, they work. Ashley and Pandora race by me and swerve into the toy area. They ditch the toy cars in front of the dollhouse, run up onto the porch, and ring the doorbell before dashing back down the steps and waiting.

Ten seconds later, they expand back to normal size.

I've never asked her what the price of the dollhouse is. It's been here seemingly forever. Gotta cost more than the unicorn. Or, maybe she has no plans to sell it. The dollhouse does kind of serve as the centerpiece for the play area.

We decide to hang at Natalie's tonight for dinner and cartoons. Tracy texts me a little after eight to say she's home. I invite her here, but she declines, citing homework. She's okay with Ashley staying a little longer, but wants her home by nine—bedtime. Not a problem. The girls are tired anyway.

Every so often, life feels good.

Which only means something's about to bite me in the ass.

THURSDAYS ARE UNASSUMING, RIGHT?

Nothing bad ever happens on a Thursday. In fact, the worst thing about Thursdays is when they impersonate Fridays. Like, ever think all morning it's Friday then learn the truth it's only Thursday? At least, assuming a person who has weekends off. Spent my first year in the department on the worst shift… Thursday-Sunday, ten-hour overnight shifts. Yeah, I'm a night owl, but staying up *all* night is rough. At least we got to sleep if we wanted until or unless an alarm went off.

I wake up Thursday morning, which is already a good sign. Waking up, that is. I'll take the lack of screaming and explosions to mean Godzilla hasn't arrived. Pandora rushes into my bedroom two minutes before my alarm clock goes off. She proceeds to go in circles around the bed, bouncing like a kangaroo.

"You are far too excited for a Thursday morning," I mutter past the arm draped over my face, which, by the way, isn't doing much to shield my eyes from the sun.

"We get to use the new rune oven!" Pandora leaps onto the bed and continues bouncing.

She's referring to the one Natalie sent me home with last night. Talk about messed up. I feel more guilty accepting a gifted rune oven from her than I ever did over stealing a PlayStation as a kid. I'd feel less guilty if I stole a brand-new rune oven from some other enchanter. Considering Natalie just sold a toy unicorn that cost her about one grand to make for six and a half, it's probably not as big a deal as I think it is. By the way, she's making another unicorn because kids loved to play with it in the store.

"You're way too little to be excited about new kitchen appliances."

Pandora sticks out her tongue. "I'm excited about not having break-fast trying to eat me."

"Fair." I move my arm off my face, groan, and sit up. "What do you want?"

"Waffles!" cheers Pandora, thrusting both hands over her head.

I throw on a long T-shirt and trudge to the kitchen by way of a quick stop at the bathroom. The new rune oven has a place of honor on the kitchen counter. It's freestanding, unlike the one belonging to the apartment, which is mounted to the cabinets above the stove. If-slash-when the day ever comes we move out of this place, Natalie's oven is coming with me. I grab some freezer waffles and toss them in. Controls look pretty much the same, so I hit the purple gem.

A 'hologram' screen appears in front of the panel asking me if I want to 'enhance' the food. Sure, why not? I haven't fully woken up yet. Nothing like a life-and-death battle with cheap frozen pastry to get the blood flowing in the morning.

As soon as I tap the glowing green 'y' gem, the rune oven whirrs to life. A previously unnoticed tank on the right side bubbles a little. It's about the size of a one-liter soda bottle, upside down, and connected to a narrow copper tube leading into the oven. The bottle contains a dark amber liquid similar in appearance to apple juice, though it's much thicker.

Why does the rune oven have a reserve of maple syrup? That's oddly specific.

Pandora stands next to me, swishing her tail back and forth like an impatient cat.

We both stare at the new rune oven as it hums away. It's much more a work of art than the other one, made mostly of wood, brass, and gems. Except for having glowing gems on the control panel, the cursed rune oven resembles an ordinary black microwave, if a bit dated looking. Hell, they did make it in 1918 after all. That's another sign, according to Natalie, of it being made cheaply. Assembly line enchantments suck. Of course, a new 'mass-produced' rune oven would probably cost about $900. The one she gave me retails for $3,500. Yeah. I feel bad accepting it.

Ping.

Pandora holds her breath.

I open the door and almost yelp in surprise. Not because food attacks me, but because the freezer waffles have turned into *real* waffles complete with whip cream and strawberries. The kid stares in awe as I move the plate to the table.

"That is *way* too much for me," she whispers. "But it smells sooo good."

True, the little five-inch toaster waffles are now nine inches across and at least an inch thick—and there are two of them stacked on top of each other under a mountain of cream and berries.

"You eat half." She whips her tail up and slices the waffle stack in half… then licks the whip cream from the blade.

"Works for me. That does smell amazing."

I HAVE QUESTIONS.

So many questions.

But they'll have to wait for a bit.

Once we finish the *amazing* breakfast, we go up to the roof and jump into the air. The more people in an area, the more draining it is to project the 'don't see me' psychic energy. Pandora's school has a ton of people (mostly kids) running around in the morning. So, we've gotten into the habit of landing about a block or two down the street. Gives us a chance to hide the wings and not let anyone see a sudden change of outfit. We walk the rest of the way there.

Today, though, I go inside while Pandora zooms off to join her fellow first-graders in the recess yard before the official start of school. The inside is eerily quiet, no surprise as the bulk of the children are outside or in the cafeteria. Even though the hall kinda smells like scrambled eggs and bacon, it doesn't tempt me in the least. Waffles are ridiculously filling.

I make my way down the hall, peering into each classroom. A few school staff give me odd looks, but the fire department uniform buys me some leeway. Schools aren't too keen on random people walking into the building. Eventually, I spot Ms. Groves sitting at the desk of a room marked 4B.

As soon as I walk into the otherwise empty classroom, she jumps to her feet, as wide-eyed as a kid on their birthday. "Did you get it?"

I smile at her. "Not exactly, but I did something even better."

"Brooklyn, without the nyctus crystal, there's little chance of creating a large enough fissure in the spell matrix to—"

"Wait." I hold up a hand. "Let me explain."

She folds her arms.

"I have a friend. Let's just say she confirmed what you told me about the barrier eventually leading to the city's destruction. It's more like sixty to eighty years away, but still going to happen. Anyway, she's agreed to get rid of it."

Ms. Groves laughs.

"What?"

She pats herself on the chest and clears her throat a few times until she regains her composure. "One person? You're telling me this *single* friend of yours is going to simply 'get rid of it' like it's some runaway enchanted broom?"

"Yeah, basically."

Ms. Groves stares at me like I've lost my mind. "Every mage in Philadelphia worked together to erect it over 150 years ago. My associates and I—and others before us—have been chipping away at it for years, getting nowhere. Do you honestly think *one* person is going to be able to control the amount of power necessary to dispel it"—she snaps her fingers—"just like that?"

"Yep."

My confidence makes her right eye twitch... twice.

"Trust me. Give it a couple days, and you'll see. If I'm wrong, it'll be obvious. No rush, right? We've got anywhere from forty to eighty years, so a couple days is nothing."

"Mmm. You will understand if I am skeptical."

"Yeah. Fair." I smile a little wider than necessary. Sure, I *could* tell her my friend is an 'angel,' but Lieutenant Sims would kill me if I spent the entire day here talking to this teacher. "Give her a day or two. She's not exactly an ordinary mage."

Ms. Groves glances away from me to the window. "I don't know how you can be so confident. If it works, everyone in Philadelphia will owe you a debt."

"Nah. They'll owe her... and they'll probably be pissed off at her for at least the next few years until they get used to random critters."

She chuckles. "True, but mild inconveniences are better than the city being wiped out."

"Yeah. Some creatures are dangerous, though."

"Correct." Ms. Groves rubs her forehead. "I can't believe I'm daring to hope you're not delusional. If this really happens, we will need to do what the rest of the world does."

I tilt my head. "Which is what? Repelling field?"

"I'm talking about establishing an agency or some such thing to deal with creature incursions. Simply walling areas off is not the answer. The easy fix is never the best one and often creates unseen problems."

Ugh. My easy fix is sitting on my ass and simply *not* destroying the world. Hope I'm not creating different problems. "Yeah. We'll figure something out. If something goes wrong with my friend's plan and the spell doesn't drop, I'll be back in a few days. I ought to run. Need to be at the station soon."

"All right." Ms. Groves sits at her desk as I start walking out. "Oh, Brooklyn?"

I pause, glancing back at her. "Yeah?"

"If you don't mind me asking, what exactly are you?"

"Umm." I scratch at the back of my head. "Still trying to work that out."

She nods. "Anything I should expect from your daughter when she's in my class three years from now?"

"Heh. Yeah. Poor impulse control. But, she's a good kid. Won't give you any trouble unless she feels singled out. Also, she's not going to tolerate being teased or bullied. I don't expect it will happen, but if it does, you'll save yourself and the school a giant headache if you squash it before she takes matters into her own hands."

Ms. Groves gives me a sad smile. "Speaking from experience?"

"A little, yeah. But I'm going to make sure she doesn't have the same issues I did as a kid."

"Oh, good. Take care, dear."

I sigh to myself. No, Pandora's going to have *all new* issues.

Note to self: do not teach her how to call Imbreleth fire until she's at least in high school.

19

BUTTERFLIES

A few minutes after I arrive at the station, Alex the probie asks me if I want anything from Starbucks.

Takes me a moment to process not being the most junior person here. Traditionally, the probationary firefighter makes the coffee run. Going to get coffee never bothered me, even if some people might have laughed at the only woman here being the coffee gopher. However, it appears the time has come for me to hand off the title of official coffee bitch to Alex. I put in an order for a venti redeye, pat him on the arm, and proceed with the start of my day.

We have a quick briefing with Lieutenant Sims, during which he goes over what we'll be doing today, assuming we don't have any fire calls. Maintenance and cleaning, mostly. An hour and two coffees later, I'm out front on the driveway with O'Keefe and Alex cleaning our high-ladder truck. Any minute now, I'm expecting a barrage of crazy. As soon as Laniah disenchants the barrier, will thousands of magical creatures invade Philadelphia? Some might accuse me of being callous by not warning 'the proper authorities' it's coming... but I have no way to do it and not end up being scapegoated as a 'magical terrorist.'

Got a feeling the punishment for that would be worse than getting caught spray-painting penises on the police chief's car.

A white SUV with red emergency lights pulls into the driveway nearby. It's got fire department markings with a little 'arson investigations unit' under the door emblem. Lawrence is here. Oh, goody. What manner of nonsense is afoot this time?

I jump down off the ladder truck and wait for him.

Lawrence smiles on the way over to me. "Good morning. Got a minute?"

"For you? Of course." I wink. "What's up?"

"Not great news, I'm afraid. The police haven't been able to identify or locate the man who gave Mrs. Underhill the owl statuette."

Ugh. I roll my eyes. Cops sure could 'detective' the crap out of everything I did as a teenager. You'd think they could catch a real criminal once or twice. "There isn't enough of a link in the owl for me to locate him. If you find some blood, let me know."

"There's something else maybe you could help with." Lawrence scratches at his eyebrow. "The police released the composite sketch of the suspect you described and also put it out on the news that the fire started from a small figurine. Word's going around the locals as well. Had a little girl tell her mother a strange man walked up to her and randomly gave her a butterfly necklace. Her mother then called the police. One of their aethermancers determined the pendant was a firebomb."

"Grr." I narrow my eyes.

Lawrence nods as if to say 'I know, right?' "Hoping you might be able to use your psychic talents to find the guy before he gives something like this to a kid whose parents haven't heard about a similar arson."

"If it's the same as the owl, he's not going to leave enough of a psychic imprint. I... don't know how to track people from a vision. Need blood."

"Well..." He exhales. "It's not exactly the same."

"Yeah, amulet compared to statuette."

Lawrence chuckles. "More than that. This one hasn't gone off yet. It's still primed. I got to thinking about what Miss Diaz told us regarding an alchemist's connection to active talismans."

"Miss Diaz?" I blink.

"Your friend?"

I laugh. "Oh, right. Natalie! Sounds weird hearing anyone call her 'Miss Diaz.' Makes her sound like a grade school teacher."

"Shall we do the usual and talk to your lieutenant?"

"Yep."

The sky flashes to an intense, glowing white, so brilliant it washes most of the color out of the world. It's painfully bright, but gives off no heat. Tires squeal from every direction. Hundreds of fender bender accidents happen close enough to hear the metal-on-metal *whuds* of bumpers kissing. Swearing starts before the glare goes out. The ghost of a domelike shape over Philadelphia hangs on my retinas, appearing every time I blink.

Everyone involved in a minor traffic accident on the road in front of the fire station jumps out of their cars, blinking and waving their arms around like they can't see. Lawrence has a hand over his eyes. O'Keefe and Alex the probie both blink and flail around like someone snuck up on them in a dark room and snapped a camera flash in their faces.

A barrage of pink and purple lightning bolts rain down all over Philadelphia from a visible ghost of a dome for several seconds... I'm no mage, but at a guess, it's probably uncontained magical energy dissipating back into the fabric of reality.

Two cars change color. Clothing flies off six random people seemingly for no reason, leaping into nearby trees. Faerie giggles echo from everywhere around me. The covers blow off a hydrant at the end of our block, turning it into a pair of horizontal geysers. A parking meter across the street begins to cry. Two passing pigeons laugh like humans as they cruise overhead. Several firehoses fling themselves off the ladder truck like boa constrictors and wrap around O'Keefe and Alex the probie. My hair decides to stand on end, every strand sticking pin straight out from my scalp—which is impressive considering how long it is. I look like I've got a giant black puffball for a head. Screaming draws my attention to an elderly woman on an electric scooter thing. She's gotta be doing forty miles an hour down the street, barely hanging on.

As she zooms past the fire station, I grab hold of the scooter with telekinesis, dragging it gently to a stop so she doesn't go flying over the handlebars. The wheels start smoking, so I lift it a few inches into the air. Alex the probie fights his way free of the serpentine hoses and runs over to fight with the console, trying to turn the electric scooter off, but the machine's not having it. He even removes the little key and the wheels continue spinning.

"What on Earth?" asks Lawrence. "Are we being attacked?"

"Attacked?" I ask in a dazed tone, since I'm still concentrating on the scooter.

Static electricity type sparks dance over my scalp... and my hair drops back to normal.

Alex helps the old woman off the runaway scooter. As soon as she's safely on her feet, he finally notices the thing's hovering in midair. Also, the instant she's no longer sitting on it, the electric motor stops... so I set it down. He looks around, making a WTF face. The old woman starts thanking him and apologizing for losing control of her 'runabout.'

Various screams, bangs, screeches, inexplicable 'magic' sound effects, and something like the noise a 400-pound startled rooster might make go off in the distance, growing progressively quieter and less frequent over the next few minutes. O'Keefe runs to turn the crazy hydrant off. I run around checking on people who had minor car accidents. A pair of tween boys nimble enough to climb trees help recover clothing the faeries tossed, except for a few pieces *way* up near the top.

Doesn't look like anyone in immediate sight from the station is hurt. At the flash, everyone more or less slammed on the brakes at the same time, so all the hits occurred at relatively low speed. I walk back over to Lawrence.

"What the hell is going on?" he whispers.

I scratch my head. "Not sure. Looks like it might be magical in nature."

He smirks. "No kidding."

"If I'm going to help you at the police station, we better just go right now before the calls start pouring in." I chuckle and start toward the SUV. "Let me text Sims."

Lawrence, still blinking away the aftereffects of the flash, follows me. "Your motto is 'easier to ask for forgiveness than permission?'"

"Nah. More like 'don't get caught.'" I chuckle. "Didn't work too well for me though, so your suggestion is probably better."

20

THE OPPOSITE OF HARMLESS

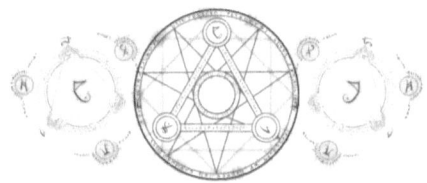

Traffic is an absolute mess.

People are naturally freaking out at the large flash overhead, not knowing what happened. This is Philly after all, so only a small handful of drivers who hit something bother trading insurance information. Almost everyone involved in a bumper tap just keeps on going once they can see again. I would not want to work for a car insurance place or a garage over the next few days. At a guess, there had to be half a million accidents in the span of a minute.

Sims replies to my text with an ‹Ok› and nothing more. Maybe we won't get slammed with calls from weird bits of magical chaos unless people end up stranded in odd places. Cops are probably hating life about now. If the Pomeranian dog floating down the sidewalk is any indication, they're going to be fielding some *weird* calls.

On the way there, Lawrence tells me the woman who called the police about the amulet, Divya Patel, didn't see the man who gave the talisman to her daughter, Amy. The girl described him as 'an old white man, but not super old.' She also said he 'kinda looks like him' when shown the police sketch. If the butterfly necklace is a similar talisman, we don't need a good description to know where it came from, though it will complicate a trial.

The police station isn't too far away, but it's a madhouse. We make our way inside, past a bunch of cops zooming all over the place. Once in the detective area, things calm down a little. Lawrence heads straight for a stairwell to the basement level. Hmm. This is making me nervous. Going into the basement of a police station is setting off all kinds of alarms in my head. Every other time I've ever been led downstairs in a cop shop, I've ended up being processed and locked in a cell. I'm tempted to re-penis the police chief's car out of spite. What kind of power-tripping asshole leaves a fifteen-year-old in an isolation cell for six hours with handcuffs on her wrists *and* ankles? Oh, so I mouthed off to him. Big tough guy trying to scare a kid.

I'm kinda out of it from nerves, just sorta reflexively following Lawrence around as he stops and talks to a few people, including a seriously athletic black guy he calls Detective Watts. We eventually stop in a small room with no furniture, only an armored door on the opposite wall next to a reinforced square window looking on an equally small room containing a cheap folding table. Atop said folding table is a bit of gold jewelry.

"It's in the blast room," says Lawrence.

"Since when do the police have a blast room?" I whistle. "Don't they usually get rid of bombs outside?"

The detective and two cops who've escorted us in here chuckle.

"It's a secure evidence storage area, specifically for unknown magical items used in crimes," says Detective Watts. He's an intense-looking guy in his late thirties. Makes me feel like I'm in an action movie and he's the former special forces guy turned cop. "Ellis here says you're some kind of psychic, but I have to warn you… it's not safe. Magic Division said it's a ticking bomb. Could blow up at any second. You psychic enough to see it coming and get the hell out?"

"Not that kind of psychic. I don't see the future." I approach the glass for a better look at the pendant. Seems to be a two-inch butterfly made of gold with pearls at the tips of its antenna. Pretty, but deadly. "When you say explode, do you mean like a bomb or just make a bunch of fire?"

"Bunch of fire," says the detective. "Mage looked at it for like twenty seconds, threw it in there and got the hell away from it. She said the thing's liable to go off without warning."

"Alchemist's talisman?" I ask.

The detective gives me the look cops give people when they decide to move them into the 'suspect' column. "How do you know that?"

"My friend's an enchanter and she studied the first device this guy used." I gesture at the window. "If this is the same thing, it's not going to go off now. If he thinks the kid kept the necklace and brought it inside, he's going to be lurking somewhere near the property after dark when he believes the building is at its most full. This guy loves to watch. He won't set it off in the middle of the day. Even if he knows it wound up here, he won't set it off."

The cops still seem wary of going near the inner door.

When I reach for the knob on the armored door, Detective Watts and both cops retreat into the hallway. It's not locked, so I open it and go in. The storage room feels *weird*. It's as if an invisible energy radiates out from the walls, pushing in on me. In a moment of uncertainty, I back out of the room. Okay, not trapped. My sudden retreat spooks the cops into flinching. Lawrence takes one step back.

"Weird energy in the air. I think it's the room," I whisper.

Detective Watts, out of sight in the corridor, clears his throat. "Yes, it's protected by defensive enchantments in case something inside releases magic."

I grin. "You guys don't seem to have much trust in the wards."

Lawrence chuckles.

Once again, I enter the storage room and pull the door shut behind me. On the off chance this thing goes off, best to be safe. To be extra cautious, I activate the amulet and swap my uniform for the illusion. Fire doesn't bother me at all, but can't say the same for fabric.

Okay, here goes.

I gently pick up the delicate butterfly pendant and open my mind to whatever imprints it holds.

My vision changes in an instant to a view as if standing on the sidewalk somewhere in the city looking at an eight-story apartment. Doesn't appear to be the most well-kept building, slightly more run-down than the one I live in. A sense of anticipation and excitement washes over me. People are going to die in agony and it will be exquisite. He can't wait to hear the screaming. A brief flash. He spots a cluster of children playing. Since he's got a butterfly amulet, he picks the only girl among them. She's maybe nine, sitting on the steps of a concrete porch by herself, watching the boys kick a ball back and forth on the street. Her dress is immaculate and pink. Long, thick black hair frames a narrow face. She also has big eyes and seems sad or worried about something. Maybe it's just the way she looks. 'Resting bitch face' is apparently a thing, why not 'resting sad face?' The girl shies away from the strange man, but he rushes over to her before she can get up and run. The poor girl is about ready to scream or pass out. When he extends an arm toward her, dangling the necklace from his fingers, she freezes.

Just a gift. You don't have to do anything for it.

The girl holds up a hand.

He rests the amulet on her palm and walks away, grumbling to himself in disappointment because the girl will be near the talisman when it activates. She'll die too fast to feel any pain. Disgust at this man overpowers the psychic vision and kicks me back to reality. I tap my necklace, putting my uniform back in place, then storm out of the warded evidence room, slamming the door hard enough to make the cops jump.

"That bad?" asks Lawrence.

"Bastard," I whisper.

"Are you all right?"

"Sick bastard." I scowl. "Guy was upset the girl he gave the necklace to would die too fast to feel anything."

Lawrence looks down. "Cops have their hands full with an invasion of magical creatures. While you were in there, things got kinda crazy. Word is, the barrier spell completely failed."

"That would be… interesting." I shrug. "Critters have been getting in for a while now. Spell's pretty old. It probably just collapsed."

"Whatever the reason, I'm concerned the police might not be able to dedicate the appropriate resources to deal with this guy before he kills again."

"They won't have to," I whisper.

21

NOT MY JOB

Detective Watts seemed eager to get us out of the building. His captain probably wanted to send him into the city, some 'all hands on deck' situation to deal with the invasion. From where Lawrence and I sit in his SUV, parked outside the police station, the city appears calm. The only visible sign anything unusual is going on to us is the stark emptiness of the lot. Almost all the patrol cars are out.

In good news, Lieutenant Sims hasn't texted me about any emergencies I need to rush off to.

"Did you mean what I think you meant?" asks Lawrence.

"Hmm?"

"About the cops not having to find the guy?"

"Oh." I shrug. "The man gave a firebomb to a child and the strongest emotion he felt doing it was being disappointed she wouldn't feel any pain when she died."

Lawrence closes his eyes. "I can't know about anything like what you're implying you intend to do. Hell, you shouldn't be thinking anything like what you're implying you're going to do."

"What are you talking about? Our arsonist is going to be an unfortunate victim to an unexplained creature attack."

"Mm hmm." Lawrence makes a 'not buying it' face.

I twist my hair around my finger absentmindedly. "How many people do you think this guy's killed we don't know about?"

"It's not our job to take the life of anyone who breaks the law." He glances at me. "Didn't you say you're one of the good guys? Not a demon?"

I half smile. "I never claimed to be a good guy. I said I'm not evil. Also, not saying everyone who breaks the law deserves death. This dude is batshit crazy and dangerous. He's not shoplifting Twinkies from a corner store. The only emotions he feels over murdering people is literal sexual gratification at their screaming and extreme disappointment if someone dies too fast to suffer."

He sits there in silence.

The quiet disapproval gnaws at me. I tolerate it only for a minute and a half. "Fine. I'll see what happens. Won't plan on tearing the guy apart, but if he so much as twitches wrong…"

"That's fair." Lawrence smiles. "Did you get anything about where to find him?"

"No. Nothing useful. Same as always. His sick gratification over killing people overpowers every other psychic imprint on the item."

"Damn." Lawrence shakes his head, then starts the engine. "He's going to realize pretty quick something went wrong as soon as he tries to light the building where the Patels live on fire and nothing happens. Cops aren't going to have the resources to stake it out, but I will ask."

I bite my lip. It's my fault the cops are overextended. Sure, the alternative is the complete destruction of Philadelphia, but my timing could've been better. Not like the big bad monster had an appointment for next Tuesday. Five to eight decades is a bit of wiggle room.

"I can keep an eye on the place tonight."

Lawrence raises an eyebrow. "What are you planning to do?"

"If I see him, I'll call the police to come pick him up… and make sure he's still there when the cops arrive." It's almost painful to say that. *Me* call the cops on someone else? Ugh. What's happened to me?

"I will, of course, deny suggesting you do it. Tracking down and apprehending dangerous suspects is outside our job description."

"Good, because you didn't suggest it. This is my idea." I wink.

A DAY IN THE PARK

Figure the guy would strike at an hour he assumes everyone would be sleeping to maximize kills.

His past fires broke out between two and three in the morning, so no reason to expect he'd do anything different here. I haven't stayed up this late since college. I'm not a morning person, and being awake past 2:00 a.m. is not a problem for me—except when my alarm is set for six.

Alas, Operation Gargoyle—e.g. me sitting like a creature on the edge of a building for two hours—doesn't accomplish much but keeping me awake when I want to be sleeping. Dad was kind enough to pop in and keep an eye on my apartment (and Pandora). The psycho alchemist didn't show up at the apartment where Divya Patel and her daughter live. Not sure if he knows the talisman didn't make it into the place or he's spacing it out a few days in case anyone saw him talking to Amy.

I give up at 3:45 a.m. and go home.

Friday sucks.

Not for being Friday, but for me getting little sleep the night before. A zombie firefighter is no use to anyone, so I crash in the barracks for a few hours. Thank the powers of fate, nothing blows up.

We get two calls late in the afternoon, neither of which involves fire. One's a woman caught in the webbing of an enormous spider that got into her basement, the other's a routine multi-car accident on the Pennsylvania Turnpike. I'm in such a surly mood over lack of sleep and not finding the arsonist, I don't even care who sees me tear the car door open and break the steering wheel. Much faster than setting up the jaws of life. Excuses roll around my brain: strength potion, one-shot strength enchant from Natalie, telekinesis... whatever. Getting people out is more important than me keeping my cover. So what if people discover I'm 'special'? Extraplanar being. Half-dragon. People won't believe the truth anyway, so what's the point of telling them?

The scene's chaotic enough, plus the guys kinda know I'm a lot stronger than I look–though they have no idea *how* strong. It's strange to think about having this strength all my life and never using it because I didn't know about it. Had the Elestari cast a spell on me to force me to act within human limits, or did my brain do it? Can't use abilities if I'm unaware of them. Pandora's tiny but supernaturally strong, too. She can't flip a car over yet, but she's probably already slightly stronger than a human can be. When she kicked Melisandre between the legs, I swear his testicles bounced off the inside of his skull.

Lawrence and I trade some texts throughout the day. He tells me Detective Watts will be staking the Patel's apartment building out for the next few days in an unmarked car. Takes some pressure off me. The crazy influx of magical creatures is starting to subside. Ms. Groves analogy of the Aether Wall working like a dam is apt. When a dam falls over, a surge of water floods in, but eventually goes back to normal. They're going to be hauling cockatrices out of bus stop awnings for a few weeks, but the storm is showing signs of abating.

Naturally, the news has been going crazy about it. All the pundits and opinion idiots are screaming various theories about what happened, everything from the spell simply failing from age, to divine punishment, to terrorists. In a weird sort of way, all of those theories are partially correct—if anyone counts Laniah as 'divine' and Ms. Groves and her friends as 'terrorists.'

Saturday happens. I shouldn't be surprised considering yesterday was Friday. This is my last free weekend before it's my rotation to work Saturday and Sunday. I ought to be relaxing and having fun over the next three days as much as possible while trying to prevent a child from suffering a premature death, but I haven't been able to stop thinking about the sick bastard ever since my read on the butterfly amulet. Mom calls it 'raising a child.' Honestly, parenting is more like following around an oblivious, short, impulsive drunk person and making sure they don't stray into traffic or light themselves on fire. Pandora's a lot more resilient than most kids, so my job's easier.

I also happen to *still* be a child inside, so when she wants to do stupid shit, I'm right there with her. Yes, I am mature. That means I don't get quite as many ideas to go out and do dumb things. It does not, however, mean I've developed the ability to resist someone else's suggestion of going out to do dumb things.

You know how kids find something they think is fun then become obsessed with it nonstop? Yeah, my kid's into the creepy girl with the hair covering her face thing. We spend a couple hours abusing Natalie's amulets. Sure, we get weird looks running around in goth dresses, but the amulets allow us to easily smuggle the 'creepy white night-gown' costumes into random hotels, apartments, and the mall.

Scaring the hell out of people is hilarious. Watching these big, muscle-bound dudes stop short at little Pandora simply standing there in the middle of a hallway, not wanting to go anywhere near her is ridiculous. One guy who could've been a pro wrestler by size shrieked when she took a step toward him. So funny. The best reaction was when I telekinetically levitated Pandora so it appeared she crawled toward someone on the ceiling. It might have been a bit *too* much. The poor guy loaded his pants.

Anyway, we eventually had to stop when Tracy needed to go to work, so we traded the scary nightgowns for normal outfits, picked Ashley up, and met Natalie at FDR Park. Within minutes of us picking a spot to relax, the kids rush off to join a group of other children around their age who are tossing a Frisbee around. Natalie and I relax in the shade, watching them play. She right away hits me where it hurts and asks about Jason. Well, at least it's a distraction from thinking about the alchemist or the magical barrier coming down. In the midst of telling her how frustrated I am at not seeing Jason for so long, it occurs to me I haven't thought about the warmongers using me to end all creation in at least a week.

And shit. I just thought about it.

Our conversation soon shifts gears to the butterfly talisman, then enchanting in general, and me thanking her for the new rune oven.

"Oh, speaking of which..." I glance sideways at her. "Why does it have a reservoir of maple syrup? You know I don't make waffles or pancakes *that* often."

She laughs. "It's not maple syrup. Just looks like it. Just a dense starch solution."

"Explains everything." I puff at a strand of hair hanging over my right eye.

Natalie grins. "It's basically extra matter the enchantment can use to enhance whatever you're reheating. Like if you put in some cheap frozen thing, it can add to it and make it come out like real food."

I blink. "Those waffles..."

"You thought it only worked on waffles?" She pokes me.

"I haven't put anything in it other than frozen waffles yet. Now I'm going to have to try other stuff and see what happens."

"You can get more of the stuff from any apothecary shop. It's not too expensive. The cost of enchanting is front-loaded. Once you have the item, upkeep is almost nil."

I bite my lip at her. "You know how guilty I feel about you just giving me the oven."

"Pff. Don't worry about it." She waves dismissively. "You know most of the cost of enchanted items is labor and artistry."

"You're too good to me." I fidget at my amulet, laughing at the little chibi succubus pendant. "Like this thing. Such a lifesafer."

"Saving your shirts and sweaters from being ripped apart when you sprout wings is hardly a life-saving matter." She smirks at me.

"Not that." I chuckle. "Pan's just like me at the same age as far as clothing goes. Not like she hates it, just has more important stuff to do than waste time getting dressed. She uses the amulet, though. You are saving me *so* many headaches with CPS. I used to give my mother two heart attacks a week, and that's still with us living in a semi-rural trailer park. No one there really cared if I ran around bare-assed when I was little. Course, no one there really cared if people sold drugs out of their trailers or chopped up stolen cars either…"

She chuckles. "Think she'll grow out of it?"

"Nah. I didn't."

Natalie pinches my shirt as if examining the material. "What's this then?"

"Dealing with something out of fear of punishment isn't the same as doing it because you like it." I wink. "At least I have an explanation now. It's instinct to us. Do you think cats enjoy being put in sweaters?"

She snarfs her iced tea and half chokes while giggling.

"Our home plane is full of fire. Fabric wouldn't last two seconds."

Some little boy about seven or eight running after the Frisbee abruptly falls flat on his chest then zips feet-first into the bushes, dragged by a green tentacle wrapped around his ankles. Before I can even get to my feet, Pandora—who happened to be right there—dives headfirst into the same bush. Like something straight out of a cartoon, the whole bush shakes amid a bunch of growling and splat noises. The boy comes flying out into view two seconds later. He scrambles to his feet, as do I. Pandora emerges from the bushes after him, wiping her hands on her jeans. The boy stares at her, making this 'holy shit' face as she calmly walks past him to pick the Frisbee up from the grass.

None of the other kids appear to notice anything strange happened. Based on their reactions, it seems they believe the boy simply tripped and went sliding into the bushes.

"The heck?" asks Natalie.

"Something grabbed that kid… and I think Pan just shredded it."

The boy continues staring at Pandora. She tosses the Frisbee toward the pack of kids, then grabs the boy by a fistful of his shirt collar, pulling him nose to nose. She stares into his eyes for a moment, then smiles at him and lets go. He appears bewildered, then shakes it off and runs back to join the kids like nothing happened.

I snicker.

"Wow, she's doing the memory wipe thing already," says Natalie. "That's really scary."

"Nah. Doesn't work on me." I wink. "She can't use it to get away with stuff."

"Except… you *let* her get away with a lot of stuff."

"Guilty." I hold up a hand. "Be right back."

"Oh, heck no. I wanna see, too."

Natalie follows me across the grass to the bushes, where we find something resembling an octopus that crawled onto a highway and had a close encounter with a large truck… with snow chains on the tires. It's not exactly an octopus, though. The tentacles don't have suction cups and there's a pseudopod sticking out of the main body with a mouth like a large dog's snout, only it doesn't have eyes… or fur. Eww. The creature is *clearly* dead. Pandora tore it apart. Death to a thousand paper cuts. Her claws aren't huge, but they're sharp. Also, the thing looks pretty squishy, basically a fleshy balloon full of gelatinous muck. I'm honestly impressed she splattered it without getting herself covered in red gloop.

"Eww," deadpans Natalie.

I look around to make sure no one is watching us, then blast the remains with a bolt of Imbreleth fire, cremating it. "Any idea what it was?"

"Not a damn clue."

"So, when's Jason coming back?" asks Natalie.

"Whoa. Topic shift without a clutch."

"What the heck is a clutch?"

I stare at her. "Something from old cars. Like really old cars."

"Oh." She rolls her eyes. "The roads would be so much safer if everyone had Scarabs. Or other enchanted cars. Let the car do the driving."

"Right…" I glance at the ashes. "He'll be back next week. Went to Germany with Lancaster and a bunch of firefighters from other stations, a team repping Philly in an international firefighting competition."

"Oh, neat. So, how serious are you guys?"

I start walking back to where we sat before. "I love him for now."

She follows, waiting for a pack of Frisbee-chasing kids to run past us before asking, "For now?"

"Yeah. I'll love him for as long as we love each other. Might be months, years, the rest of his life. I dunno. However long it lasts, cool."

"Aww." She looks down. "Guess it's kinda rough since you're going to live forever."

"Assuming nothing kills me… and I'm pretty sure my half-human state *does* have a time limit even it if it is a few thousand years. I'll eventually die, then most likely wake up in Imbreleth."

She makes a comically serious face. "Brook, when they say 'go to hell,' they're not being literal."

"Weak." I shake my head. "So, any luck making yourself immortal yet?"

"Working on it."

I flop back on the bench and glance over at Natalie as she sits beside me. "That sounded way too serious. Are you messing with me?"

"Nope. Can't leave my best friend alone in the world. There are numerous ways to go about extending life." She flashes an innocent smile. "I'm trying to find one that doesn't require sacrificing an elf or something."

"Good call. Murdering the innocent is bad."

A few kids jogging past us skid to a stop, stare at us, and scream.

"What?" I whisper. "Are my horns out?"

Natalie shakes her head. "No. You look normal."

"What are you guys screaming about?" I yell.

The kids point as if to say 'look behind you.'

I turn and lock stares with a decent sized black panther. The giant cat somehow gives off a sense of annoyance.

"This is going to sting, isn't it?" I ease myself standing. "Can't be worse than an angry Shaar'nath trying to kill me."

"Oh, calm down," says the panther in an almost aristocratic tone of voice. "Can't a cat enjoy the park in peace?"

It occurs to me it has huge batlike wings tucked against the sides of its body.

"You're not here to eat anyone?" asks Natalie.

"Heavens, no. Humans are *far* too fattening these days. So many chemicals and preservatives. It would be healthier to eat plastic trash."

He pads around the concrete picnic table and stretches out in the grass maybe fifteen feet away from us. "I'm merely here for the sun. Do be a dear and ask your cubs to cease screaming so shrilly. It hurts my ears."

"Wow," whispers Natalie.

I wave at the kids to resume playing. "He's not going to hurt anyone."

Most of the children give me 'yeah right' looks, though they *do* stop screaming.

"Looks like the cracks in the Aether Wall are getting big," says Natalie.

I give her side eye. "Yeah. Real big. Remember what I mentioned the other day?"

"Oh... Wow. Really?"

"Remember when everything in your store went bonkers? The weird lightning?"

She gazes at the sky. "Ugh. Yeah."

"That energy surge came from the shield spell collapsing entirely," I whisper. "Don't tell anyone yet. Not until the mages officially figure it out or you'll end up having to answer questions you can't."

She makes a zipper gesture over her lips.

"About time," says the panther... or manticore. Whatever it is. Pretty sure manticores look more like lions with human faces. Panthicore? Bleh. "I've been wondering if you lot would figure out the error of your ways before it killed you."

Natalie blinks at me. "Umm, is Magical Animal Control going to give him a hard time?"

"No. They don't deal with anything capable of talking." I fold my arms, glance at the panther, then at my friend. "The city's going to get interesting."

23

DONALD HUXLEY

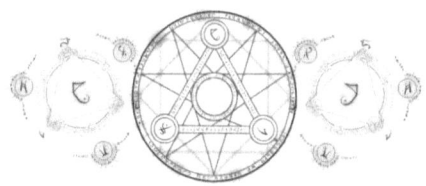

On the ride home, Pandora casually tells me the 'blob monster' was about to bite the boy.

"He won't remember." She beams with pride. "I told him to forget."

"Nice. You worked out the short wipe already?"

She nods.

"Amazing." Natalie turns to look into the back seat. No big deal since her car is driving. "Did you just know you could do it?"

"No. I used it before." She bites her lip.

"Oh?" I flash a sly grin. "Details."

"Got sent to the principal's office. She said 'I'm tired of seeing you walk in here,' so I said, 'then tell the teachers to stop sending me.'"

Natalie bursts out laughing.

Ashley gasps in shock.

I might have kept a straight face if not for Natalie laughing.

"She got mad," says Pandora. "Yells, how dare I talk back to her. You need to be taught a lesson. I said 'duh! That's why I'm in school.'"

Oh-emm-gee. I'm dead.

Ashley makes a face at her like she just confessed to murder.

"Principal got mad. Said I just earned detention. I said 'no, you're giving it away for free.'" Pandora examines her fingernails. "Her face turned like bright red. I thought she was maybe gonna hit me, so I just wanted to make her forget I said anything. My head felt fuzzy and the principal got a stupid look on her face. Umm, I mean a more stupid look than normal. She forgot what I said."

Natalie seems mildly horrified but continues snickering.

I'm all in. I high-five the kid. "Nice."

Ashley gawks at me. "She's not in trouble?"

"No. That's awesome!" I wipe tears from my eyes. "I met the woman once. Total power trip."

"What's that mean?" asks Ashley.

"Means she loves having power over other people, and she uses it wrong." I frown. "Hate people like that."

Natalie whistles. "Guess we should consider ourselves lucky she didn't throw the principal out a window."

"Tempting," says Pandora, "But the school's only a one-story building. Also, I'm not allowed to kill anyone unless they try to kill me first. Or have super icky stuff in their head when they look at me."

"I don't want you hunting creeps until you're at least ten. If you can run, run."

"Yes, Mom," says Pandora in a mildly sarcastic tone. She's teasing me a little about the 'mom' part, not mocking what I'm telling her to do.

Natalie finally gets control of her laughter. "Oh, wow… impressive, you're so good at it so fast."

"She's basically me." I shrug. "Maybe she has some subconscious memories."

Pandora smiles innocently. "I am the queen of sarcasm. Every time my mouth gets me detention, the teachers forget what I said. And the man with the brooms caught me writing on the wall, so he couldn't remember."

"Hah!"

Natalie elbows me. "You shouldn't encourage her."

"Oh, I should." I wink. "Giving a kid detention for a sarcastic comeback is lame. The teacher's admitting they got owned by a little kid."

The car jams on the brakes. My face bounces off the dashboard. Natalie ends up on the floor under the steering wheel. Ashley bounces off the back of Natalie's seat, and Pandora winds up inverted between the front seats with her butt against the radio console.

"What the hell!" shouts Natalie.

I peer up at the windshield. A terrified centaur is standing in the road in front of us. His human half looks about twelve, maybe eleven. "Kid ran into traffic."

"Oof," deadpans Pandora. She rights herself and crawls back to her seat.

The adolescent centaur snaps out of his deer-in-the-headlights paralysis and zooms off.

"Car's got good reflexes," I say. "Wonder if the police would treat that as a wildlife encounter or hitting a person."

"I'd rather not find out." Natalie climbs into her seat.

"Yeah… so, in less sad topics… do you know any way to trace a talisman back to its alchemist?"

We spend the rest of the ride to her shop talking about it. Unfortunately, she doesn't have an easy way to trace the guy without making an enchanted 'detector' item. Sounds costly and time consuming, so I tell her to hold off for now. We have more immediate concerns, like what we're going to do for dinner.

THE KNOT IN MY GUT OVER THE ARSONIST CAME BACK SUNDAY AFTERNOON.

It persisted through Monday into Tuesday. I did spend a few hours on the phone with Jason Sunday night after Pandora went to sleep. He's still having a blast over there, but he's gone over the vacation hump and is fully in the 'I can't wait to be home' phase. Unfortunately, he's sharing a hotel room with Lancaster, so we couldn't do anything sexy over a video call.

Neither Lawrence nor the police contact me, which I take to mean the arsonist hasn't struck again. It also means they haven't found him. At least, I'm guessing. The cops wouldn't need to involve me if they find him, but Lawrence would let me know. Speaking of him, he shows up at my fire station a little after ten in the morning on Tuesday. I don't like his facial expression. Too grim. I also don't like the read coming off him. He's going to give me some bad news.

"Another fire?" I ask as soon as he's close enough not to require yelling.

"I'm afraid so." Lawrence spots the coffee machine in our ready room and heads toward it.

"Don't do that to yourself, man." I jump up from the sofa and grab him like he's about to jump off a cliff. "Starbucks is just down the block."

"That may be, but this is right here. I'm old school, Brooklyn. Coffee is better when it tastes like the scorched remains of failed dreams."

I shiver. "That's gas station coffee. This is worse."

He chuckles and pours himself a cup. "A suspicious fire broke out at a large home in Bryn Mawr. Two people died."

"Damn." I look down. "Same guy?"

"We haven't been able to determine. Strange coincidence, though." He sips the coffee—which has been sitting there for at least forty-five minutes—and doesn't flinch at all. "The man who died was involved in a legal battle over various properties... including the Stedman Building."

I tilt my head. "What kind of legal battle? Charles Maxwell didn't say anything about being sued."

"The deceased, Donald Huxley, was a wealthy land developer. He's been trying to buy up a bunch—"

"Wait." I point at him. "Huxley?"

"You know him?" Lawrence raises both eyebrows as he takes another sip of death sludge.

"No... but Maxwell thought about someone named Donald Huxley when you asked him who might want to burn down the Stedman Building. He didn't really think the guy would do it, just an 'if anyone would' situation. I didn't say anything because we already knew the psycho was responsible."

Lawrence nods. "Huxley was buying up a bunch of property in the area around the Stedman Building. Maxwell initially refused to sell to him, so Huxley tried to get the city to intervene and force the sale. He wanted to develop the area and 'improve' the city."

"Meaning, replace apartments normal people can afford with places for the rich."

"Something like that, I suspect." Lawrence swishes his coffee around in the cup.

"Weird coincidence his house burned down, too."

Lawrence nods. "Yes. I think it is more than a simple coincidence."

"I'm guessing he didn't torch his McMansion to make way for a luxury apartment building."

"Not exactly." He chuckles. "I'm working off a theory that Huxley may be involved in the Stedman fire."

"So, Maxwell's gut instinct was right?" I shift my jaw side to side, thinking. "How, though? Huxley somehow finds this psychopathic alchemist in Henchman Weekly and hires him to torch the Stedman Building? Something goes south so the guy burns Huxley out?"

"Not so sure about the Henchman Weekly part, but essentially, yes." He drains the last of the coffee.

"Gah. How can you drink that?"

"By tilting the cup backward." Lawrence refills the cup. Hey, they're small.

"Does this sound like anything the guy's done before? You—or at least your office—has been investigating this firebug for years."

"Yep. As far as we know, the man doesn't work for hire. He's an opportunistic killer. However, a 'McMansion' as you say out in Bryn Mawr is definitely outside his usual MO. We think his initial fires targeted mostly empty or abandoned large industrial properties, but he soon graduated to row houses or multi-story apartments in poorer areas."

"Think the guy has a problem with minorities or the poor?" I raise an eyebrow.

"It's more likely he targets those buildings due to assuming they will have maintenance problems, not be up to code, missing fire-suppression or alarm systems. Anything to increase the body count."

"Grr." I fold my arms. "You're starting to un-convince me to let the legal system handle this guy."

He gives me this 'you aren't that person' stare. Maybe. Maybe not. Frank would disagree. I gleefully tore him to pieces. Then again, I *did* walk in on him trying to molest Ashley. Maybe I'd need the emotional shock of the guy being about to kill someone to just walk up and tear his head off. Or maybe not. Guess I'll burn that bridge when I cross it.

"It's worth looking into the possibility Huxley somehow made contact with our firebug and arranged the Stedman Building fire. It's also a possibility this is a coincidence."

"You said yourself a fancy house in a nice area is outside the guy's MO. Doesn't feel right to me." I tap my foot. "Let's assume Huxley did somehow convince this guy to torch the Stedman Building. What reason would he have to go fry Huxley?"

"Dispute over payment seems the most likely." Lawrence drains half his cup in one gulp.

"Maybe a blackmail situation."

"Or the guy didn't want anyone knowing who he is." Lawrence toasts me and finishes the coffee.

"That sounds more likely." I frown. "You said two people died... who's the other casualty?"

"Huxley's wife. Their daughter survived."

"Kid got out in time?"

He shakes his head. "Wasn't there. Snuck out to go to a party her parents forbid her from going to. Probably the only reason she's still with us."

I offer a solemn nod. "Partying saves lives."

Lawrence tosses the empty cup in the wastebasket. "Kid's a little guilty."

"Are you here to ask me to check out the scene?"

"Not yet. Bryn Mawr is outside my territory. Locals are handling the investigation. I've sent a few emails. They might be in contact. Wanted to let you know about it."

I fold my arms. Doesn't take psychic intuition to know he's trying to let me know he wants me to see if I can find and stop the guy unofficially. Good chance he wouldn't be too upset with me for tearing the dude's head off. However, it might make him permanently afraid of me. Oddly, the idea of scaring Lawrence bothers me more than killing the arsonist. Okay, fine. I'll put in *some* effort to not kill the guy.

24

BEAR

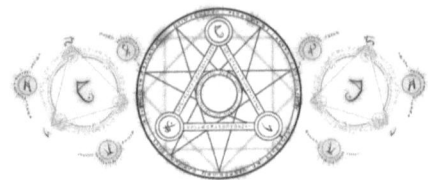

Tuesday night is unusually cold.

Doesn't say much. I'm always chilly. It's not as much the actual temperature as it's a howl in the wind making me feel colder. Pandora's asleep at home. Thinking about bed bothers me at the realization it feels cozy. No amount of clothing I wear from none at all to a heavy winter coat changes my thermal reality. I'm always 'a little chilly.' But... in bed? I feel cozy and snug. Maybe my perception of comfort is more of a mental thing? I expect to be snug in bed, but cold everywhere else.

Meh. I can experiment later.

Dad's housesitting for me again. Yeah, I have weak impulse control and Pandora's a bit tougher than an ordinary child, but it still seems wrong to leave a kid her age alone, even asleep in the middle of the night. Besides, my father *adores* babysitting.

I cruise in over Bryn Mawr, circling the approximate area where the Huxley's lived. Obviously, the daughter is not sleeping in the burned-out ruin of the former home. I've already managed to 'sweet talk' some information out of the local police detective investigating the case. The daughter, Leigh, is sixteen, so not a 'little kid'. She's presently staying with the grandparents who also live in Bryn Mawr.

There's no one around the ruined house, so I land right on the collapsed porch. After shifting up into my armored form, I duck under the top of the doorway. Still feels weird to get taller, but it comes in handy sometimes. Makes it easier to carry people in the air for one. Also, leverage. At the moment, the armor is mostly for stopping splinters. Recently burned houses, even big ones like this, have a nasty habit of collapsing when poked. I'd prefer not to be impaled by a giant stake, thank you.

The place is a total mess. In this form, my eyes act almost like flashlights, projecting blue light wherever I look. Neat. I am a multipurpose demihuman. After a little exploration, I guess the fire started on the second floor, probably in the part of the house where the walls and roof are entirely gone. Some seriously intense fire ripped across the upstairs. Only the skeletal remains of a few beams and struts suggest the outline of the former upper story. The right half of the building is also largely gutted, which tells me the flames ate their way down through the floor before the fire department got here. On the left, the downstairs is stained black from soot, but the ceiling isn't gone.

Gives me the impression of the fire starting in a room on the right side second floor, burning across the entire upstairs and about half the downstairs before people started throwing water on the house. Well, this is Bryn Mawr. Bit of money around here. They probably had hydromancers or even pyromancers respond to the fire call right away. Even in Philly, the mages only come out once the traditional fire crews realize we've got a big problem on our hands... except for like chemical warehouses or anywhere the chief thinks might explode huge if the fire isn't contained as fast as possible. Nice houses like this only get immediate magery in well-to-do areas.

Plenty of signs of water damage and black ash muck, so traditional fire crews definitely participated. Unfortunately, walking around the ruins while psychically sending out sonar pings doesn't do anything. I grab a few random objects, hoping for a read. Nothing useful. Some old guy died in a chair I touch, consumed by anger his family wanted nothing to do with him. A large metal candlestick got thrown at the wall. Wow. I think Mr. Huxley may have cheated on his wife and she found out. The emotion she imprinted in the candlestick is hurt, not rage. Probably why she threw it at the wall, not his head.

I don't find any trace of an alchemist talisman. Maybe the mages found it already, or it destroyed itself in the fire. This one appears to have burned exceptionally hot. Likely because whoever set it knew the local fire department—being smaller and much better funded than Philly—had hydromancers riding on the trucks as a matter of routine. Whoever set this fire wanted to ensure full casualties before mitigation efforts could begin. The lack of anything even remotely identifiable as a bedroom makes me think the 'origin area' on the right used to be the bedrooms.

Welp. Nothing more for me to do here.

I tromp back outside, shift down out of my armored form—while keeping the wings and tail out—then leap into the air. You'd think ten minutes of staring at an internet map aerial view would be enough for me to find the grandparents' place easily. Flying over actual Bryn Mawr doesn't look anything like what I saw online before leaving my apartment—for about five minutes. I finally spot the 'fan' shape of a baseball field on the ground and recognize it. The grandparents live on Fishers Road, northeast of downtown. I memorized the shape of their pool. Easy to find from the air.

Gotcha.

It's not *too* late, so people ought to still be awake. I descend, concentrating on my psychic 'invisibility' and land on the street near the house. The second my extra body parts dissipate into smoky vapors, my real clothes jump back from the pocket dimension inside my amulet. Leather jacket, blue T-shirt, jeans, and black boots. Yeah, I'm somewhere between poser biker chick and grunge metal fan, but whatever. Not here to fit into the social scene.

Gotta admit, flying is cool. Also have to admit, I am super lucky *not* to have known about it as a kid. I would've gotten in so much more trouble. Wow. Hope I can do even half the job my mother did. Pandora's gonna be a handful. Probably don't have to worry how many times the police will bring her home to me. The same psychic trick that lets us fly and not be noticed also works for 'mischief.' If I knew how to do it as a teen, I wouldn't have every cop in the Quakertown area knowing me by name.

Nah. No need to worry about Pandora. We'll be just fine. Everyone else around us, not so much.

I walk up a curvy footpath to the door of a seriously large house. It's no McMansion, but it's at least four of my apartment in terms of space. Good thing materialism is not one of my flaws. Otherwise, I'd be jealous as hell. It's a lot easier to shoplift a video game console than a house.

An older man answers the doorbell and gives me this 'who the hell are you' stare.

Been a while since I faked being upset and teary, but here goes. "Hi, Mr. Huxley. I'm Leigh's friend Marissa." Sniffle. "They told me she's staying here. I just heard about what happened... and she's not answering her phone. Wanted to make sure she's okay."

My charm seeps into his brain, none-too-gradually forcing his 'Leigh's friends don't dress like you' into a neutral-slash-welcoming demeanor. He does at least buy me being a teenager. Another point for the eyes. Also helps it's kinda dark out here. Half of coming off as a teenager is in voice and body language. Yeah, I have a young face, too, which doesn't hurt.

Mr. Huxley (Donald's father) stammers, his brain going in a loop thanks to my psychic influence shorting out his logic circuits. "Yes. She's in her room."

Wow. Fast. Already has 'her' room here. Not surprising... she's going to be living here from now on.

I dab my fake tears and walk in. He shuts the door behind me, then heads left into a living room. Okay... guess he expects I know the layout of his house being 'Leigh's friend.' It's two stories, so good chance the bedrooms are upstairs. I head up and make my way along the hall, peeking into rooms one after the next. The third door on the left is closed. It's quiet in there, but all the other doors are open.

Not wanting to be rude—well, more so than forcing my way into the house—I knock twice. "Leigh?"

"The heck?" asks a young woman. A moment later, the door pops open a few inches to reveal a teenager. She's the quintessential 'popular' type. Blonde, blue-eyes, knockout. Some humans inherit more Elestari influence than others. Girl looks sad but not devastated. "Who the hell are you?"

"Your friend, Marissa." I smile, then whisper, "At least, that's what your grandparents think."

"Cop?"

I shake my head. "No. Can we talk?"

Her defenses go up.

"Promise nothing I can do will get you in any trouble. I'm here to help." I give her a slight nudge of charm.

She backs up. "Okay."

I step in and close the door behind me. The room looks more or less exactly like I'd expect the 'seldom-used guest bedroom' in an old person's house to look, except for a few plush animals on the bed and a hot pink laptop on a little writing desk that looks stolen from a motel. Yeah, this probably *was* a little-used guest room in an old person's home. Leigh hasn't been here long. Three days at most. Everything she owned is ash, and her grandparents haven't had the time to buy her new furniture yet.

Leigh backs up to the bed and sits on the end, giving me this look like I'm a cop who just caught her with a little weed and she's hoping I let her go.

I sit on the chair by the desk. "Okay, real talk?"

"Or what?"

"Psychic stuff." I wink. "I'm going to be totally legit with you, okay?"

"You're seriously not a cop? You aren't a high school kid."

"Wow. Thanks. Most people mistake me for a teenager."

She blinks. "You're no teenager, but you can't be older than twenty-two."

"I am, but by one year."

"Close enough." She smirks. "You super overdid it with the goth face paint. Not every kid does that."

I hold up my arm. "Not paint. I'm just pale."

Leigh grasps my hand, feeling the back of my wrist with her thumb. "Wow. Damn, girl. You need to put in some salon time."

"Won't help."

"I've never seen you before. Why are you here?"

"The fire. I'm trying to catch the guy who started it."

Leigh folds her arms. "You said you're not a cop. So much for 'real talk.'"

"I'm not a cop. I work for the fire department. I'm sorry you lost your parents."

She looks away, shrugs one shoulder. "It happens."

Not as much emotional damage as I expected. She's giving off a reasonable amount of sadness, but also a bit of 'whatever.' "Didn't get along with them?"

"We got along okay. Just… didn't agree on a lot of stuff. Sucks they died, but I'm not going to collapse over it."

"The fire was set intentionally to take your father's life. Did you ever see him meeting with anyone unusual or creepy?"

She rolls her eyes. "Like all the time. I didn't pay attention. My dad used to do horrible crap."

"Bad stuff?"

"Yeah. He'd always evict poor people from their apartments or houses so he could take the land and make malls or crap. Didn't care what happened to anyone his construction projects made homeless. He believed we were better than other people because we had money." Leigh looks down. "We, umm… didn't really get along too well once I realized what he did for a living. Been kinda fighting with him since I was twelve."

"Sorry."

"He thought I was going through some stupid 'woke' phase and I'd 'come around' and see how the world works, eventually." She overacts rolling her eyes. "Guess he's not going to realize I'm always gonna think screwing people over is wrong. Mom didn't deserve to die. She didn't hurt anyone."

I nod.

"Ugh." Leigh buries her face in her hands and sighs hard. "I should be dead, too."

"No, you shouldn't be dead. Neither should your parents. Someone did this to your family. I'm hunting them. He's hurt a lot of other people by starting fires."

She rambles about some girl named Tara and her boyfriend Jimmy having a house party, but her father didn't want her going because he assumed drugs would be involved and possibly sex. Surprisingly, it doesn't sound like Leigh got into a screaming match with her parents over the party... probably because she'd already made up her mind to sneak out.

"... climbed out my window like a movie or something. Almost broke my neck jumping off the garage. Jessica gave me a ride home after the party. As we're going up the long driveway, I'm trying to figure out how the heck to get inside without waking them up—and all we see is flashing lights and flames."

A pulse of sorrow radiates from her. I get the feeling she's mostly upset over her mother. The emotion tied to her father comes off as the frustration of unfinished business. This girl desperately wanted her father to stop being the jackass who threw poor people out on the street to make fancy shopping centers, and now, she'll never convince him to change. Gonna guess a lot more angst existed there than she's admitting. Maybe she's hiding her grief, but it doesn't seem like his death hit her hard. Totally a 'I almost thought I could save him, oh well' vibe. Mom's a slightly different story, but there's still some ice hanging in the air between them. None of my business why.

"Like I told my colleague. Partying saves lives." I wink.

She half smiles.

"One more question. Did anyone approach you with a package or give you a strange curio recently?"

"Umm... my boyfriend gave me a gold teddy bear a couple days ago."

"Do you still have it?"

"No... they told me everything's gone. Granddad went to the house the morning after the fire and said my whole room is, like, totally missing. The bear probably melted." She looks up from the floor, scrunching her nose a little. "Why are you asking about a figurine?"

"Just covering all angles." She doesn't need to know she brought the incendiary device into the house.

"You said real talk. Tell me the truth."

Fine. Screw it.

"The arsonist is a kind of mage who puts fire spells inside little curios. It's possible the golden teddy bear started the fire."

She gawks.

"It's not your fault. You had no way to know."

Leigh scoots back on the bed, crosses her legs, and buries her head in her hands. "Holy shit. Cayden... he used to joke about how happy I'd be if my dad wasn't a cartoon villain."

"Hey." I lean forward. "I sincerely doubt your boyfriend knowingly gave you something like this to hurt your parents. He couldn't have known what it was."

She sniffles. "You think so?"

"Yeah. Not to be painfully blunt here, but he'd expect you to keep it in your bedroom. You'd be the first one to die, so it doesn't make any sense for him to do it if his goal was to get rid of your dad."

Leigh shudders. "Okay, I'm legit not okay now. Stupid party... if it hadn't been that night. Or I decided not to go or had too much homework or listened to my parents..."

I move to sit on the bed next to her and offer a shoulder to cry on. She takes advantage. I've never had anyone weep on me like this before. But hey, Shaar'nath are beings of emotion, right? I can help a sixteen-year-old deal with the 'holy shitballs' feeling of narrowly avoiding death. In the midst of her meltdown, grandma pokes her head in. I pretend to be crying, too.

"Are you all right, dear?" asks Grandma.

"I almost died," sobs Leigh. "If I didn't sneak out and go to that party, the bear would have killed me."

Grandma stares at her like she spoke Latin backward. "Bear? Are you sure you're feeling okay?"

"Not an actual bear," I say. "Some of the cops said the device responsible for the fire was shaped like a miniature bear."

"Who are you?" Grandma looks me over, giving off judgy vibes over my clothes. I'm a little too 'wrong side of the tracks' for this area.

Not wearing a cute (expensive) dress or something from Aeropostale or whatever.

"Marissa."

"It's okay, Gram. She's a friend." Leigh exhales hard, her breath shuddering. "I had no idea the bear was…"

"Neither did he. Cayden?"

Leigh nods.

"Mind if I talk to him?"

"Sure, I guess." Leigh wipes her eyes. "Let me give you his messenger."

Grandma seems to think we're okay and walks off, leaving the door open.

"Ugh. They hate it when I shut the door."

"My mother was the same way when I lived at home." I roll my eyes. "She'd always walk over and open it whenever I closed it. 'Course, she stopped doing that after the Charlie incident."

Something in my tone makes Leigh look up from her phone screen with an impish smile. "What happened?"

"We were both fourteen, me and Charlie. Totally at random, I brought him home figuring what the heck, we'll do it."

Leigh gasps.

"We're in my room. We both get naked. I flop on the bed. He climbs on top of me, sorta hovering, not really touching me anywhere yet. And we're just kinda looking at each other, I guess wondering how it's supposed to work. We didn't know a damn thing."

She giggles. "Oh, my god. Really?"

"Yeah, totally serious." I snicker. "Anyway, my mom picks that moment to open the door. Sees us like that and yells my name. I tilt my head back, looking at her upside down and all I can think to say is, "What, are we doing it wrong? Should I be on top?'"

Leigh squeals, falls over backward, and dies laughing. I haven't seen someone turn this red in the face since, well, Charlie. "Wow. What did she do?"

"Not much. Charlie grabbed his clothes and ran. Mom spent the rest of the day telling me how disappointed she was in me."

"Lucky. I think my parents would have kicked me out of the

house." She sighs at the ceiling, no longer laughing. "Thanks. I really needed that."

"No problem."

"Real story?"

"Swear. Totally."

"Wow."

I wag my eyebrows. "Charlie could never look me in the eye again."

"Ugh. So embarrassing. I'm blushing just thinking about it." Leigh sits up and shows me her phone screen. "This is Cayden's IM."

"Thanks." I pull my phone out, open messenger, and send him a quick note telling him I'm from the Philadelphia Fire Department, looking into the fire at the Huxley residence and asking if he has a few minutes to chat.

Leigh sends him a text confirming it's okay to talk to me. "Think you're going to find him?"

"Hopefully. Don't know for sure yet. Hey..." I give her my number. "If you need someone to talk to, feel free to shoot me a message anytime."

"Cool. Thanks. So, umm, what's your real name?" whispers Leigh.

"Brooklyn."

"Hi, Brooklyn." Leigh holds out a hand. "Nice to meet you."

I shake. "Same."

Ping. A message arrives from Cayden.

‹Uhh, yeah. I guess. What do you need me for?›

I reply, ‹A few routine questions about something the arson investigators missed. Would it be okay to speak in person?›

He sends back a 'sure' followed by an address.

"Cayden's a couple streets over on Gatcombe Lane," says Leigh. "Don't steal him."

"Hah. No chance of that. Some people might think I look it, but I'm not sixteen. Also, have a boyfriend." I wink.

"How psychic are you?"

"A little."

Leigh looks over at me. "Can you do something for me?"

"As long as it doesn't involve farm animals and excessive quantities of whipped cream."

"Umm, eww." She snickers. "No, not at all. Can you like read minds? Is Cayden really interested in me like seriously, or just trying to get in my pants."

"Hmm. I should be able to get a read on that. Consider it done."

"Thanks."

I stand. "Okay. Better get moving. Just try to keep in mind it's not your fault."

"I know. More freaked out at how random my survival was." She shivers again. "I'll be okay. Please catch the son of a bitch."

"Trying…" I stuff my phone in my pocket.

She gets off the bed. "I'll walk you out. It'll look weird to my grandparents if I don't."

We head downstairs, do the 'friend' thing for a moment, then part ways.

Not sure exactly what I'm expecting from her boyfriend, but it's not like I have any other leads.

25

THE SOURCE

Cayden Kinney meets me on the porch of his parents' house. He's a fairly normal looking affluent high school kid. Probably plays football or... what is it the rich kids play? Lacrosse? I dunno. Never paid attention to varsity jackets, so I've got no idea what the hell sport he's into. Maybe hockey.

"Wow," says Cayden as I walk up to him.

"What?"

"Are you really with the fire department or is this some kinda prank?"

"Legit, promise."

"C'mon. You're a senior."

"Thanks, kid. Little older than I look."

"No uniform?"

"Off duty right now and technically out of my 'jurisdiction.' Not a cop, so I'm not really sure if that applies." I wave dismissively. "Philly FD, remember?"

"Umm. Okay. So, what are you doing out here in Bryn Mawr?"

I lean on the column at the top of the porch steps. "The fire at Leigh's house was arson, set by a man we have been hunting for years. Burning a house like the one where your girlfriend used to live is outside his usual MO. Leigh told me you gave her a gold teddy bear figurine recently."

Cayden makes a face at me like I asked him if he ever farted and had a literal duck fly out of his ass. "Huh? What the hell does that have to do with her house burning down?"

"The arsonist uses magic to start the fires. He puts this magic into little figurines... like gold teddy bears. Did some weird guy come out of nowhere and give you the figurine?"

"Uhh, no. I got an email ad for it. Dammit." He stomps. "I knew it."

"Knew what?"

"It sounded way too cheap to be real gold. Figured it was a scam. It looked real when it arrived. Figured a little gold teddy bear like that ought to cost at least a grand, right? Email ad sold it for $399. Leigh *loves* teddy bear stuff. It's like her thing."

Opportunity knocks. "You really like her, don't you?"

As soon as a question is asked, the answer forms in the mind. Cayden is... a typical sixteen-year-old. He thinks he loves her. Definitely not merely trying to get her in bed, then leave. Whether or not he's going to wind up marrying her, who knows, but I feel safe telling Leigh he's sincere... as sincere as a kid his age can be about 'being in love'.

"Yeah." He nods. "Shit. Are you telling me I blew up her house?"

"I'm telling you that a really sick bastard might have used you to attack her father. Do you still have the box the bear arrived in? Maybe the email?"

"No on the box, but the email's still on my computer. Wait here a sec. Let me go print it out for you."

"Great. Thank you." I nod.

Cayden runs inside.

I take my phone out and send Leigh a text. ‹As sincere as can be for sixteen. Not lying to you.›

Sure, maybe unethical, but heck. I'd want to know in her position, too. 'Are you lying to take advantage of me' isn't as invasive as looking for some deep, personal thing about him to exploit. Doesn't bother me at all.

A few minutes later, Cayden pauses in the living room to talk to—I assume—his parents. Can't hear much from out here, but he's probably updating them on the situation with me. He soon emerges from the house and hands me two pieces of paper. His parents hover in the doorway, watching us.

"That's the email. Website and everything is on it." Cayden stuffs his hands in his pockets. "Weird. The bear showed up the next day. Real fast."

"She looks so young," whispers the father.

I lean to my side, peering around the boy at his parents. "Thanks. Might as well say this. I'm FD, not PD. No one thinks Cayden's involved as anything other than another victim."

"What exactly is going on here?" asks the father.

Sigh. "We think Mr. Huxley was targeted by an arsonist who uses magical trinkets to initiate fires. Just following up on the theory he might have tricked your son into facilitating the incendiary device making its way into the house." I explain the alchemy talismans, the golden bear, the suspiciously cheap sale price, and the fire.

A little charm keeps his parents calm and convinced no one's trying to come after their son as an accessory. I thank them for their time, tuck the printed email into my jacket pocket, and walk off down the street. As soon as they're back inside, I spread my wings.

26

LAZY AND INDIFFERENT

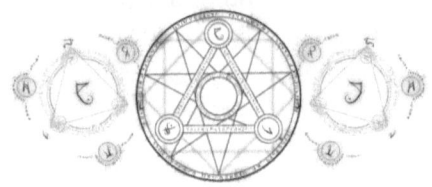

So, I'm cruising toward home while tossing around the new facts in my head.

Knowing a golden teddy bear figurine of some form started the fire at Donald Huxley's McMansion isn't exactly a revelation. It *does* confirm my suspicion, but brings me no closer to finding the alchemist. A printout of the fake email ad isn't going to do me any good either, but maybe the detectives can use it.

"Damn queers!" shouts a man below, to my right.

I glance toward the voice.

A group of six dudes brandishing baseball bats, a pipe, and police style batons stalk toward two other men in an alley. They all look to be roughly in their mid-twenties. The two being threatened are wearing nice-ish clothes, like middle-managers from a 'cool' office, definitely not part of the same social crowd as the other guys, who really love denim. It's like a motorcycle gang and a local labor union had a fashion baby. Soon-to-be-victim number one has snow white hair and a raspberry button-down shirt, the other guy's Hispanic and wearing an expensive looking suit.

Got the feeling either an ass-kicking or a shitload of running is on someone's agenda for tonight. Meh. This is *so* not my problem. I flap my wings again.

"Let's get out of here," says the Hispanic guy.

"You queermos try to run, you get shot," barks a deep voice.

… and they're gonna kill those guys.

I look down again. The six dudes have backed the two men into a space between a pair of dumpsters, blocking them in against a filthy brick wall. Can't I just go back to saving the entire world by sitting on my ass? As soon as I really look at the guy in the middle with the bat, I know he wants to kill them. Grr. Screw it. I roll into a dive for the alley. The raspberry button-down shirt guy snaps a collapsible baton out to length. Guess he's used to having to defend himself. He's scared, but intent on protecting the other man… who's more frightened, but worried only about his partner's health.

It's tempting to land right on top of the assholes so they see the wings. Nothing like a weird monster dropping out of the night sky to make a dude shit his pants. Problem is, if I do that, they'd just run away screaming. Kinda wanna hurt a bitch, so I land at the intersection where the alley meets the street and collapse my wings. The illusion of a super frilly goth dress vanishes as my real clothing returns to the physical world.

"Well, well," says a silky voice slightly behind me to the left.

I glance back—and my heart nearly stops at the sight of Melisandre. The beige business suit is seriously pretentious. Or maybe it's his long blond hair. Perhaps his Adonis-like face, making himself six-foot-four, or giving himself a Greek god physique. Nah. The pretentiousness is everything. He's an asshole.

"Did anyone ever tell you that you look like the entitled corporate douchebag bad guy from every semi-serious movie made between 1980 and 1998?"

"What'cha gonna do with that rod, gay boy?" barks a man brandishing a pipe.

Melisandre frowns at me.

"I don't have time for your ego right now." I start walking toward the imminent beat down.

He grasps my arm. "Look at what humans do."

I glare at him.

Melisandre gestures at the men—they seemingly freeze in time as the ringleader raises his baseball bat as if to swing at the guy holding the baton. "Have you yet realized that half of them would happily kill the other half if they could do so without consequence? It does not take much. Wrong color skin, wrong mythology, wrong choice of who to love, wrong choice of footwear. The humans are feral, my dear. Some of them would even start a fight over an incorrect selection of condiment on a meat tube."

I stop, face him, and blink. "One—no one kills people for wearing the wrong shoes. That's simply robbery. They're not murdering the person for what the shoes mean. It's greed. Two—what the hell is a meat tube?"

"Some manner of crude sustenance." He holds his fingers about six inches apart. "Often placed upon an oblong bit of bread?"

"Oh. Normal people call them hot dogs."

He cringes. "I hadn't realized where the meat came from. Repulsive."

I sigh. "They're not made out of dogs. They just call them dogs for some reason. And you're not serious about the fighting over condiments on hot dogs. That's ridiculous."

"Visit the place the humans call Chicago and attempt to put the red paste instead of the yellow paste on a meat tube. You will, at best, be screamed at. At worst, someone will try to punch you."

"You're no better. Violent."

Melisandre scoffs. "Hardly."

"Oh? You want to destroy the Armistice, annihilating thousands of individual species including humans, plus any life on however many other planets exist out there, purely so the Elestari and Shaar'nath can resume killing each other for no reason anyone even remembers. How is that any better than what you're criticizing humans for? It's pointless violence for the sake of violence."

"Elestari and Shaar'nath are not the same." He gestures derisively at the eight men still standing still as statues. "Humans are killing their own kind."

I jab a finger at him. "You and the warmongers are trying to start a war that *will* result in hundreds of thousands of Elestari—your kind—dying. There is no reason the two sides *need* to go to war. You just want to. Blind hatred. If you ever succeed in destroying the Armistice, *you* will be responsible for every Elestari death since they wouldn't have happened if the human world remained intact. You also think Elestari are *so* much better than humans, which makes you murdering hundreds of thousands of your own kind far worse than anything humans have done."

He blinks, mouth slightly open.

I start to stomp toward the humans again, but Melisandre grabs my arm… again.

"What?" I roar, glaring at him.

"So, you are a vigilante now? I thought you only wanted to sit on your backside doing nothing. What happened to being lazy and indifferent?"

"Sitting on my ass—in your case—*is* saving the world. I am lazy and indifferent, but I'm not a damn monster. Can't let these morons murder two guys just because they love each other."

"You threw a man into a speeding bus, Brooklyn." Melisandre frowns.

"So? He survived… *and* he shot me first."

Grumbling, I stomp toward the guys.

27

SELF-CONTROL

Time resumes for the humans in front of me as Melisandre gives a bored sigh.

A dude with a red bandanna on his head swings a baseball bat at the guy in the raspberry colored shirt. The guy ducks, then pops up and baton-whacks Bandana Man in the face, knocking him backward two steps, bleeding from the nose.

"You got some moves, *Lance*," says another guy.

A big man holding a pipe overacts a 'gay' tone of voice. "I think his name is *Bruce*."

Three of the guys laugh.

Bat guy grabs his face, lowers his hand, and glares at blood. "Goddamned fag!"

I telekinetically yank the asshole back before he can swing at baton guy's head, hard enough to put him on his ass. The Hispanic man looks at his partner, gob smacked. The other thugs appear to blame baton guy for somehow shoving their buddy over.

"Hey!" I yell, then jump over the fallen idiot to put myself between the two groups. The gay men as well as the six guys about to jump them all look at me like I'm crazy. "You idiots have two seconds to get out of here. I know you guys are too stupid to leave, and don't expect you to. But, I at least said it so I won't feel guilty about what's going to happen to you."

The guys chuckle.

"Is this girl for real, Delbert," whispers the Hispanic guy behind me in Spanish.

I hold a hand up to the six idiots. "Wait one second."

Bat dude snarls as he picks himself up, but for some crazy reason actually waits.

I look at the guy in the raspberry shirt. "Your name is Delbert? Like, seriously?"

"Yes, why?" asks the white-haired guy. He's not too old, so either dye or way premature grey.

The high school I attended, any kid named 'Delbert' would have had his head flushed in the toilet at least twice a week, gay or not. Given the present situation unfolding around me, it's probably not the most tactful thing to comment about. Still, feel sorry for the guy.

"No reason, just making sure I heard him right." I look back at the six 'tough guys.'

"Fag boy's name is *Delbert?*" A skinny guy with a neckbeard laughs. "Ho-lee-shit."

"Look, lady… just get out of here. They're not going to hurt you," says not-Delbert.

A short but muscular Hispanic guy on the right end of the horseshoe formation suggests in Spanish to his buddies they force the two gay men to 'prove their manliness' by making them have sex with me at gunpoint, right here in the alley. One of the guys makes a shocked, 'dude, wrong' face at him, but the others don't seem to mind. I glare at him. The only reason he's still breathing is he's not serious. Just saying crazy shit to impress his buddies.

I point at Mr. Suggestion Box and say in Spanish, "Tonight is your last night to participate in the gene pool."

The guys laugh.

I hold my hands out to the side. "Well, come on. Who wants to learn what his own nuts taste like first?" Hmm. Tempting to say it's only been a couple days since I killed someone, but they'll either think I'm psycho or just talking smack. Not sure if saying it would scare them off or goad them into taking a swing. Better to just stay quiet and wait for some idiot to take the first move.

They keep staring at me.

I look at the guy who suggested they force the gay men to rape me. "You first. I really want to twist your head off. C'mon, tough guy. What are you waiting for? Afraid of me?" I switch to Spanish. "Bet you wanted to watch because your dick's so small you're jealous of cockroaches."

He gets pissed off and lunges at me, swinging a police baton for my ribs.

I catch it in my left hand since he's a rightie. Stings the palm a little, but his attack stops cold. I stare into his eyes and casually overpower his arm, pushing the weapon back. When he's thoroughly distracted by the WTF factor of my strength and staring in disbelief at his weapon, I slug him in the jaw, knocking him off his feet. The police baton remains in my grip. I toss it up and catch it by the handle.

"What the hell?" whispers Delbert.

"Last chance." I point the baton to the right. "Go away while you can still all walk."

Melisandre saunters up behind them. "You are wasting your time, dear. These cretins aren't going to listen to reason. You may as well get started on your mission and kill them. Six down, a billion or two to go."

Maybe I'm hallucinating but the Elestari's tone is odd. Wonder if he's thinking about what I said before and having doubts.

The five remaining dudes jump, startled, and spin toward him. Their horseshoe formation splits into a group of three and two on either side, so Melisandre is no longer behind any of them. Guy I punched is still on the ground. Pretty sure I pulled the shot enough *not* to disintegrate his jaw. Might have cracked it. He's moving but doesn't look fully conscious.

"Get a load of this guy." Red Bandana looks Melisandre up and down. "Who are you supposed to be?"

The Elestari ignores him, continuing to give me a patronizing smile.

"You guys are being stupid. Delbert and..." I look back at the Hispanic guy. "What's your name?"

"Trent."

I face the idiots again. "Delbert and Trent having a relationship with each other has no effect on you. Go home."

The men shift wary glances from me to Melisandre and back.

"Dumbass with the bat." I point at Red Bandana Guy. "What food do you hate the most?" The answer leaps into his head. "Do you feel the need to randomly beat up anyone who likes sushi? Does someone eating sushi affect your life in any way at all? Also, you hate sushi because it's 'foreign,' not because you don't like the taste. You've never even had it. Try it sometime."

He blinks. "You some kinda mage using dark-ass magic on us? I didn't say a damn thing. She knows."

"Cretins," whispers Melisandre, pinching the bridge of his nose like he's gotten a sudden migraine.

"No. I haven't even started using ass magic yet." I pat myself on the butt. "You couldn't handle it."

The moron stares at me like 'that's not what I meant'. Wow, these guys are so dumb I can't even be sarcastic effectively.

"You know, dear," says Melisandre, "killing these fools would be the simplest solution. It is, after all, what you have in mind for your arsonist, correct?"

I exhale hard. "Mel, I am exercising an extraordinary amount of self-control right now. These guys are just a bunch of hateful morons."

"Bitch!" yells Bandanna Guy. He swings his bat at me.

I swing the police baton into the bat, shattering it and sending the top half flying into the air, then smash the baton into the dude's left thigh. From the sound of the crunch, his femur snapped. He goes down screaming. "Like I said. Morons."

The four idiots still standing all take a step back from me. Bandana Guy begins weaving in every conceivable word he can think of to insult women between screams: bitch, whore, skank, and so on. He even drops a few C-bombs when I start laughing at him.

Melisandre clucks his tongue. "These *astounding* examples of human advancement are likely to harm some other random talking monkey at some point. You are doing a disservice by allowing them to live."

"Dude, I'm gonna rip that million dollar smile right off your face and shove it up your ass," bellows the one black guy among the group of idiots.

"How... colorful." Melisandre frowns at him.

"He doesn't mean it like that. He refers to all humans as 'talking monkeys.'" I hold a 'don't do it' hand up at the guy before glancing at Mel. "Maybe I'm toying with the idea of sparing the cops the need to deal with the arsonist, but he's killed a lot of people and intends to kill more people. He's also completely deranged."

"And these fools *aren't* intending to hurt anyone else?" Melisandre gestures at Delbert and Trent. "They desire to kill those two men. If they see other people like them, they'll feel inclined to harm them, too."

"Who do you think you're talkin' to?" barks a tall guy wielding a crowbar. He sneers at the Elestari. "You're probably one of *them*. You look like you're into guys."

Melisandre scoffs again. Gawd, that sound is so damn annoying.

Crowbar guy appears increasingly angry the longer he glares at Melisandre. Guessing he's having certain thoughts. Elestari are *ridiculously* pretty. I'm not the least bit attracted to women and looking at Laniah makes me question myself. No doubt Mel is having the same effect on these guys. Anyone who's attracted to men and unaware of how much of a complete egotistical asshole Mel is would be weak in the knees from seeing him. It's true what they say about how personality affects attractiveness. I *know* the kind of monster Melisandre is, so he's not affecting me at all. I'd sooner have sex with Laniah than him, and that's not happening any time soon.

"You might as well get on with it," says Melisandre. "Kenneth Walters is about to employ a firearm. Kill the one you punched first. He's about to run away."

Bandana guy stops screaming curses and gawks at him. "What the shit is going on here? How's he know what we all thinking?"

"He's an angel," I deadpan.

Melisandre rolls his eyes. "I do wish you would cease using the term."

"I'll stop calling you an angel when you stop trying to destroy the world." I trace an X over my chest. "Cross my heart. I'll never call you guys angels ever again if you give up the plan to break the world."

He smirks.

I snap my fingers. "Idea. Why don't you just stage battles here? No one dies permanently. Work out your frustrations all you want. Keep score, even. Have rematches every fifty or sixty years once everyone can get back in. What even is the point of invading Imbreleth? You guys would never want to live there with all the fire and black rock and lava monsters."

"What the heck did we stumble into?" whispers Trent.

"I have no idea." Delbert puts a protective arm around him.

I gesture at the black guy, who still looks about ready to swing a length of pipe at Melisandre. "All you want is the same as these morons. Mindless violence."

"Morons? You Bitch!" He swings the pipe for me.

For the second time tonight, I catch a weapon and stop it. Ow. My hand is going to be sore for a day. We lock stares. The anger in his eyes melts to worried confusion.

"I know what you're thinking. How is this chick who's half my size not laying on the ground with a cracked-open skull right now?" I squeeze the pipe, crimping it a little. "Remember what I said about self-control? I've never really had much of it. Don't push me."

"Look at you, pretty man." Crowbar guy reaches to pat Melisandre on the cheek.

In a flash of silver and gold, the Elestari pulls his sword into reality straight into a swing, slicing the guy's hand off before it can make contact with his face, sending it flying across the alley. It hits the pavement with a sorta-splat noise like dropping a raw hamburger patty.

"… and he has less self-control than me," I deadpan.

Smoke peels from the cauterized—mostly—stump. A little arterial blood spritzes out of the imperfect burn, but far from the amount that ought to be spraying. Crowbar dude shrieks a few times, then sprints off. The other guys scream, running after him. Kenneth—a.k.a. Bandana Guy—hobbles upright but realizes his left leg is broken at the femur and falls again, howling in agony. Lost to panic, he drags himself away down the alley like the idiot blonde girl from every slasher movie.

The guy I punched remains oblivious to everything and simply lays where he fell, partially conscious. I toss the police baton into one of the dumpsters next to me.

"What just happened?" asks Delbert.

"Nothing. You'll be happier and saner forgetting tonight," I say.

Melisandre stretches his perfect white wings out and smiles at the two men. "Why… your prayers for assistance were answered."

I sigh at the sky and start walking away down the alley—in the opposite direction from where the morons fled. "Drama queen."

Melisandre tucks his wings away and falls in step at my side. "Relax. They think I'm an illusionist."

We walk together for a minute or so in silence. Okay, this is weird. What's he playing at?

"Seriously." I glance at him. "Think about it. Destroying the world and starting a war is every bit as stupid as you accuse humans of being. No one on either side even remembers why our people fight each other. Pick a desolate space of land—or better yet, do it on the Moon. No witnesses up there. Two teams of a thousand. Last one standing wins. Make a giant trophy the winning side holds until the next fight."

He doesn't react.

"Do you know why the war started?"

He continues staring into space.

"Didn't think so." I let my wings out. "It's just a bigger dick contest. Staged fights and a trophy would scratch the same itch without murdering billions of living beings."

Melisandre gives me a weird look as my outfit changes. "Illusions? Since when do you know shame?"

"I don't. It's for the humans' benefit. They're super uptight about nudity, but you know that. You guys did that to them for laughs with all the religion stuff."

He chuckles. "Humans are woefully gullible."

"Well, nice chat, but I need to get home. Think about what I said." I leap into the air and don't look back.

28

PSYCHIC DREAMS

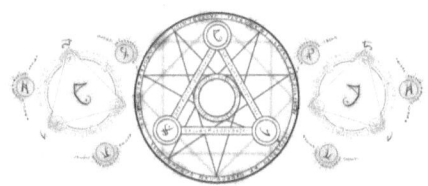

I t's weird the best thing to be said about my night is, "I didn't commit murder in front of witnesses."

I land on the patio, collapse the wings, and walk into my apartment to find my dad's discovered late-night television. Pandora's curled up on the sofa next to him like a cat, asleep. He's munching cookies and channel-flipping between two different talk shows and a home shopping channel. How are those still even a thing? The internet exists. Amazon exists.

"Please tell me you haven't ordered like a shitload of things you don't need?"

Dad doesn't take his eyes off the screen. "Nope. Not ordering anything. Merely curious."

"Home shopping channel? Seriously? Use Amazon."

"They don't ship to Imbreleth."

"Get a PO Box in Alabama. That's close enough. Might even be warmer there."

Dad bites his lip to stop himself from laughing loud enough to wake Pandora. Seeing her cuddled up beside him using his leg for a pillow kicks me in the feels. Can't *really* call it jealousy since it doesn't give me any negative emotions toward the kid... merely gets me angrier at Melisandre and the shitheads who threatened to kill me if Dad showed himself. This could have been us. Me having a father in my life.

Grr. Thinking about it won't change a damn thing. I go to my bedroom and change into a long T-shirt, then flop at my computer and check out the printout Cayden gave me. Predictably, the website to order the bear from no longer exists. Whatever. I'll give it to the cops in the morning. I stare at the URL on the screen and the 404 error for about five minutes before inexplicably getting up and going to the living room.

I sit on the couch beside my father, lean over sideways, and curl up with my head on his other leg. Without missing a beat, he brushes a hand over my hair. Pandora's curled up on his left, me on the other side. Screw it. Who cares if I'm grown up and it looks kinda weird? I have a father and never got to do this as a kid. Doesn't take long for the rambling voices from the TV to blur into a haze of oncoming sleep.

I'M FLYING IN LAZY CIRCLES OVER PHILLY.

No idea how I ended up in the air, which must mean this is a dream. They say if you find yourself in a situation and can't remember how you got there, it's a dream. Could also be old age or mushrooms, but neither of those apply to me now. Damn. Haven't had shrooms in a while. For that matter, haven't touched any drugs in a long time. The job kinda frowns on it. 'Course, when I was younger, the world felt like a place I had to escape from, and not all of it came from being poor. Used to be, an anxiety goblin lived in my head. Some part of my brain knew the truth about my mixed blood while my conscious mind didn't. That sense of not belonging here needled at me constantly, to the point where I legit had PTSD from sitting still. Meaning, if I didn't distract myself or occupy my mind with something constantly, I'd start to get anxious and freak out, not understanding why. The best way to describe the feeling to someone who didn't grow up as a half Shaar'-nath and not know it is to be a CIA spy in the middle of Russia during the height of the Cold War and suspect at least one in five people knows the truth… and an enemy spy is following me just waiting for the perfect moment to pounce.

Probably why I had such little care about getting in trouble with the cops. My entire life felt like being somewhere I didn't belong with serious consequences looming over my head. Getting busted for graffiti didn't compare. Being stuck in a juvenile detention cell alone for a weekend with no drugs and nothing to distract me *sucked*.

But here I am cruising over dream-Philly. Never had a flying dream before. I'm naked, which isn't surprising. No idea if it means something since I'm in a dream. Could just be my brain on lazy mode and not filling in details. Whatever. It's pretty rare for me to feel in control of a dream. Usually, dreaming is kinda like watching a movie where it keeps jump cutting to new scenes without warning. This dream is more like a video game. I'm in control. I swerve back and forth, going nowhere in particular… until I spot a woman in a grey skirt suit waving at me from the roof of an apartment building.

Whatever. I'll bite. I pull around in a diving turn, swing my legs forward, and land next to her. Oh, shit… it's George from *Dead Like Me*. She's wearing the outfit she had on when she died in the first episode. Well, it's obviously *not* her. For one thing, she's a fictional character from a television show and doesn't really exist. For another, I'm obviously dreaming so it isn't even Ellen Muth, the actress who played her. I'm looking at something my brain is creating.

"What the heck are you doing here?" I ask.

"This is your dream, Brooklyn. How should I know why I'm here? Probably because of how often you watch my show."

"Yeah. Makes sense." I smile. "Weird to sorta meet you. I expected you to be taller."

"I get that a lot. Oh, here." She hands me a yellow Post-it note.

"My assignment?" I take it, then glance down at black sharpie marker writing: 'Go that way.'

I look up at her.

She points.

"Okay. Thanks."

George nods once.

I jump back into the air, flying in the direction she pointed. No idea what I'm looking for, so I keep scanning the ground while going in as straight a line as possible. Feels like it's pretty straight. Time's kinda mushy in a dream, so it's hard to say how long it takes before a weird pop noise comes from the Post-it note in my hand. I look down at it. The writing has changed.

Land here, and by the way, this is a psychic vision, not a dream.

Neat.

I dive into a tight spiral, corkscrewing around to lose altitude without covering much ground. Soon, I touch down near the outer edge of a massive parking lot. A fair distance away in front of me is a ten-story tower-like building with weird narrow windows. Lettering on the top says Keystone. It appears to be on the other side of or part of a mall complex. An odd urge pulls me around to look at the building behind me. The right side is only a single story, but the left half is two. Out-of-control trees and bushes growing in front of it makes it seem abandoned. Can't really see much of the building's face due to all the greenery, but I think it might have been like one of those places with a bunch of unrelated offices in it. Red brick swaths separate banks of large, square windows blocked off by damaged blinds. The upper part of the roof is decorated by a band of vertical grey wooden slats.

The same weird urge pulls me forward. I walk out of the mini parking lot belonging to this building and follow a small sidewalk to a door. To my left, two giant stone cubes act like flowerpots for little trees. There's no signage identifying the building above or near the door, only a white one on the glass informing me that 'all deliveries must be made at this door Monday to Friday between 8:00 a.m. and 5:00 p.m.

Oops. I'm a bit late.

My fingers pass through the door handle without contact. Fine. Makes it easy. I go full ghost and simply walk in, not bothering to open the door. It's a small reception area with a counter and a table. Doesn't look like it's served as an actual office for quite some time. The smell of freezer entrees hangs in the air… vaguely Asian with a hint of pizza rolls. I make my way left down a little hallway and through another door into a corridor leading west into the two-story part of the building.

Light spills out of a room up ahead on the left, really showing off the filth of grey office carpet no one's bothered to clean in years. I approach the seemingly occupied room, silent as a phantom. Gee, wonder why. George told me this is a psychic vision, not a dream. Well, my brain is sending me the messages. George doesn't exist. Irrelevant point, though. Does that mean I am seeing reality? Maybe it does.

Can't say I've ever experienced anything like this before. Psychic dreams.

The door's only open a few inches. Like a moron, I try to push it out of my way. Hand goes through the wood. Duh. Ignoring the door entirely, I step forward. The room is like a crazy Santa workshop. Looks like it used to be some manner of IT lab. Shelves of old computer parts stand against the walls, arranged between huge tables where someone used to set up computers to be worked on. No computers here at the moment. The tables are full of random bronze, brass, and gold junk. Boxes of gears, springs, coils, metal scrap, jeweler's tools, and a vast assortment of colored powders and other random stuff in jars cover every scrap of usable surface space.

A man sits on an old office chair at the innermost part of the room, working on something. Can't see much other than shoulder-length light brown hair from behind. I step closer, trying to get a better look at him.

I'm about ten feet away when he abruptly swivels around in the chair and stares at me.

It's the guy. The fake UPS dude who gave Joyce Underhill the owl. The same guy who felt depressed Amy Patel wouldn't experience pain when she burned to death too fast... and he's staring at me. Like seriously *at* me.

The shock of him seeing me knocks me straight out of the dream.

I'm in bed.

Pandora's curled up at my side. My heart's racing, pounding in my ears. Holy shit, that freaked me out. I slide an arm around the kid and hold her like a teddy bear. She emits a soft, approving moan out of her nose. Still dark out. I partially sit up, peering down the hall. Apartment's dark and empty. Guess Dad needed to go. Nice of him to carry us to bed.

I let my head fall back on the pillow.

Should try to sleep.

Yeah, right.

29

ADULTING IS A PAIN

I lay there for not quite an hour before my bladder forces me out of bed.

Pandora doesn't stir much as I get up and trudge to the bathroom. My apartment feels strange, hyper-real. It's like I'd been playing a video game for months on a first-gen PlayStation and jumped straight to a PS4. The psychic vision/dream thing had kinda been blurry and blank in spots. I guess stuff not relevant to my focus had the bare minimum of details.

Sirens wail in the distance. Not an unusual sound for Philly. It's far enough away not to worry me. Surprisingly, I don't have a flinch reaction to sirens as much as I do to cops coming out of nowhere. They rarely used sirens when coming after me since it's pretty rare to end up in a high-speed chase while under eighteen. Most of the time, we'd be doing some crazy shit and *bam*, cops outta nowhere.

A reptilian shriek-roar cuts across the sky. It's loud and close enough to make me jump. Thanks to video games, I know what the sound of a dragon or wyvern roaring is… and the noise that *just* came from the real world above me sounded exactly like one. I mean, everyone knows dragons exist… they just don't often bother with cities. World War II kinda pissed them off. After the dragons collectively smacked humanity on the hand for being naughty, they kinda retreated into more sparsely populated areas. I think what really did it was a whole bunch of CIA pyromancers casting a massive ritual and flattening the entire town of Hiroshima. According to history class, the dragons hadn't realized humans could wield magic so powerful and had a similar reaction a person does when a giant spider sneaks up on them in the bathroom. No, not screaming and fainting, smashing it before thinking.

I prepare myself for the painful coldness, clench my jaw, and sit on the toilet.

My mother always teased me for complaining how cold the seat was. I have an excuse now. Everything feels cold to me. See, Mom? Not a drama queen. Yes, as a kid, I'd scream sometimes. Sit bare-assed on a giant block of ice and tell me if I'm overreacting.

I sit there with my face in my hands, elbows on my knees, waiting to finish so I can crawl back to bed. Everything's foggy. Guessing the psychic vision took a lot out of me. Feels like I've been awake for three days without sleep.

In fact, I nod off on the bowl.

Fortunately, nearly falling off wakes me up. I finish up, flush, and head back to my room.

Whispering comes from Pandora's room.

Okay, odd.

I back up and poke my head in.

The child kneels on the floor beside her bed, horns, wings, and tail out. She's arranged a bunch of toys and crayons to form a ritual circle, and she's trying to pronounce what appears to be Latin words from the screen of my e-tablet. Operative word being 'trying.' Note to aspiring occultists… Latin is not a magical language. It just *sounds cool.* I could say 'I just took a wicked long piss' in Latin and some hipster occultist would think I'm calling Beelzebub into the world.

Also note: Beelzebub isn't real.

"Pan?" I ask, my voice raspy from fatigue. "What are you doing?"

"Trying to summon stuff."

"Why?" I rub my right eye.

"You told me I should try to make some friends… so I'm trying to make some."

The *smack* of me facepalming makes her twist around to look at me. "What?" asks Pandora.

"One—we can't summon creatures. We're not 'demons' or mages. Two—I didn't mean *literally* make as in create friends. You might like having a few more friends to play with… but you don't *need* to. Let it happen naturally. I really only have Natalie now as a best friend. You and Ashley are tight like us."

She grins. "Okay."

"C'mon. Go to sleep. Your bed, my bed. Don't care. Just go to sleep."

"Why?"

"Because you're six and it's three in the morning." I half turn toward the door and grab the wall to keep myself from falling over.

"Are you okay?"

"Yeah, just tired."

Pandora stands. "Did you go to bed every time your mom told you to?"

"Honestly?"

She nods eagerly, her smile getting bigger.

"I did. She's the only person who I ever listened to all the time without arguing."

"Wow, really?"

"Yeah. You know how we can tell what a person's intention is just by looking at them?"

"Uh huh."

I pick the kid up and carry her into my room. "Every time I looked at Mom, I knew she loved me and only wanted what's best for me. She also busted her ass"—I fall into bed, still holding Pandora—"working multiple jobs, doing everything she could for me. So… she didn't deserve the headache of dealing with my attitude on top of it all."

"Okay." She curls up next to me, coiling her tail around my leg.

I close my eyes and hope sleep grabs me. So damn exhausted. It's unnatural. Don't think the alchemist did anything to me. My ass vanished in an instant. Did he really see me or did the vision represent my brain trying to tell me he knows I discovered his location? Did I use 'distant seeing' or do some weird astral projection type thing? Also, there's a possibility everything came from a weird dream. Just because I had a dream and saw a Post-it note claiming it's a vision doesn't prove anything.

No, finding the mall and that building looking exactly as I saw it would prove the vision was a genuine psychic distant seeing. If the guy *did* see me, here's hoping he doesn't get spooked and go into hiding.

The wyvern (hopefully not a dragon) screeches again. At least it sounds like it's flying away from here. Ugh. Laniah told me leaving the Aether Wall up would have resulted in Philadelphia being destroyed, but knowing that doesn't make me worry any less about if removing it was a good idea. Magical creatures are like cats. A door opens they don't usually get to go through, and they rush to see what's in there. Something big could wander in and cause a lot of damage. What if a basilisk decides to slam dance on Pandora's school building?

Crap. I have a kid.

Yeah, not a surprise, but really thinking about her now... I can't just do whatever whenever I want anymore... only most of the time. Heh. Teasing myself. Having her to look after isn't a cramp on my style. Truth be told, teenage me would consider 'now-me' kinda lame, at least in terms of my day-to-day. Teenage me would probably be totes jealous of the demi-human stuff.

Wow, Melisandre cut a dude's hand off. Sure, he did it because the guy tried to pat him on the cheek—seriously disrespectful to an Elestari, especially him. Not being touched in general, mostly a human being condescending or mocking. So weird to think an 'angel' did more murder-type-stuff than me there. Slicing a dude's hand off is worse than breaking a femur, right? Is a broken jaw plus a busted femur equivalent to a severed hand?

Wow, I'm tired. My brain's going in random directions.

Got a kid to protect. I squeeze her close. They say people need to take care of themselves. Probably not intended to be so literal. I'm gonna protect her. I have to protect her. I've got someone who won't grow old and die on me. Before I know it, tears sneak out of my eyes. Dammit. When did I turn into a wimp?

"Mom," whispers Pandora. "Air please."

I loosen my hold.

"Thanks. Is something gonna fight us?"

"Not that I know of. Why?"

"You're getting super clingy." Pandora yawns.

"Sorry."

"It's okay. Just wanna know if we need to cut a bitch." She holds her tail blade up and waves it around.

I chuckle. "Nothing specific, but keep your eyes open."

"Right now? You told me to sleep."

"You know what I mean." I kiss her atop the head. "Stop teasing me."

She sticks her tongue out, closes her eyes, and snuggles in again.

Come on, sleep. Any minute now...

30

THE WORKSHOP

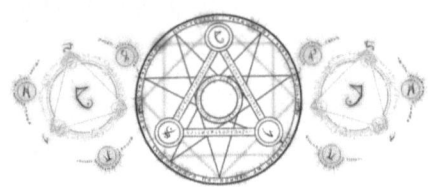

Wednesday morning sucks like no morning has ever sucked before.

At least, in my experience. Without a doubt, an uncountable number of people have had worse Wednesday mornings than me in history. I'm being melodramatic due to fatigue... and wrong. I've had a worse morning than this. The Sunday I woke up in a holding cell at age eleven. I'm *still* traumatized by that. Being trapped anywhere I can't get out of freaks me out. Today's issue is mere exhaustion. Any day that doesn't start off with giving me lifetime PTSD is not my worst morning ever.

I wake up to small hands patting me on the cheek.

Pandora's kneeling on my chest. I open my eyes to her grinning at me. She's wearing an off-white dress and ballet flats. Hmm. Kid's been awake long enough to get ready for school. Why do I smell eggs and coffee?

"Wha?"

"Alarm didn't wake you up." Pandora grabs my arm and pulls me into a seated position. "I made breakfast and got you coffee."

"You got me coffee?"

She nods.

"They sold coffee to you?"

"Yep. Told them it's for my mom. Not lying."

I drag myself out of bed. "What time is it?"

"Six-four-five."

Shit.

Screw it.

I stumble to the kitchen. Two Starbucks cups stand guard on either side of a plate holding a serious breakfast burrito. Looks like something from a sit-down Mexican restaurant. Guess she hit the enhance button. Pandora sits there watching me wolf down the—amazing—egg, chorizo, and cheese. She got me two redeyes. This *might* be enough coffee to keep me awake, at least until noon.

We're running late thanks to me oversleeping by forty-five minutes. As good as this burrito is, there's no choice but to rush it. Not savoring it is better than letting it get cold or tossing it. Once it's gone, I chug one of the coffees as fast as I'm capable of swallowing liquid. No human could drink coffee this hot so fast, but fortunately, I'm not fully human. I chuck the plate in the sink, run to throw on my uniform, then grab the remaining coffee. One's for waking up, the other one's for tasting… and more waking up. We rush to the roof and jump onto our wings.

I'm so damn tired, it escapes me to even concentrate on not wanting to be seen. Pandora must be doing it for both of us as no one screams, points, or gawks. Maybe having a wyvern cruising around last night has desensitized people to catching a glimpse of a flying being. Meh. Whatever. We land about two blocks from her school and walk the rest of the way to seem normal. Such a zombie right now. Ugh. At the entrance to the schoolyard, Pandora stops and looks around.

"What?"

"Something's not right." She peers up at me, her eyes narrowed in suspicion. "Just feels weird."

I glance around at the area. Rowhouses across the street, cars going by, kids, teachers, and parents rushing around in a chaotic dance of irritating morning energy. How anyone can be smiling this early in the day is a mystery to me. An older green Volvo stands out to me for no particular reason. It's parked across the street from the school and apparently empty. Pandora's also staring at it.

"I'm gonna be late." She hugs me. "Can I yoink a cell phone later?"

"You're six. You don't need a cell phone yet. And they're too annoying to steal. If the place marks it stolen, they can brick it remotely."

"Huh?"

I pat her on the head. "We'll talk after school. Go on before you get marked late."

"Okay." She scrambles off to join her classmates as they're forming up into lines in the yard.

We made it here barely a minute to spare. Due to the odd feeling of unease, I stand there watching the teachers and kids until everyone's safely inside the building, then walk over to the Volvo. No one's in it or hiding behind it. The weird feeling it gave me earlier is gone, too. Thinking there might be a creep staring at kids, I search the area a little more thoroughly, probing around mentally... but it makes my brain feel like lukewarm tapioca. Psychic exhaustion. Ugh.

I snap some pictures of the green Volvo, making sure to catch the license plate. It might not be related to anything. My odd sense of unease could have come from a person near the car. Whatever. I'm too tired and whoever it is left. For all I know, it might've been a mischievous gremlin or some other magical creature running amok in the city since it can.

After walking far enough away from the school to get out of anyone's direct sight, I focus on making people ignore me and fly to the station. Not even going to ask the Universe to go easy on me today. It'll totally spite me and go nuts for me having the temerity to ask for leniency. Whatever happens is gonna happen.

An hour of sitting in the ready room doing and thinking about nothing helps my fatigue.

Wouldn't call it 'meditation' per se, but it does make me consider my 'dream' the previous night in a new way. If quiet calm recharged my proverbial batteries more than sleep, it must mean I did some serious psychic shit. I've moved cars—and heavy concrete debris—using telekinesis and never felt anywhere near as burned out as I did this morning. Any 'exertion' from forcing people not to notice me flying doesn't even register. Whoa. Probably a good idea for me to talk to Dad about it as soon as possible. At a guess, psychic 'visioning' is either way advanced for my level of practice using psychic abilities, or it's somehow more 'expensive' to use.

I went to sleep fixated on finding this guy after staring at the useless email printout. Speaking of which, I call Lawrence and fill him in on the golden teddy bear situation as well as the vision. Time had a strange quality during the dream/vision, so it's not really clear how long I flew before landing at the mall. I'm certain I'd gone generally northwest from Philly, though. Thankfully, there aren't a ton of places northwest of Philadelphia likely to have a giant mall. Much past fifteen miles, it's all forest and small towns.

Couldn't have gone *too* far. The alchemist is also not going to put himself too far away from his hunting ground, so to speak. Small towns and open land don't have the kind of high-density, high-body-count apartment buildings he favors. This is the kind of monster who thinks in terms of fire economy. The more people he can kill with one device, the better.

I try to zen myself as much as possible. Lawrence asked me not to kill this dude. Gonna give the legal system a chance first... or at least try to. After what this man did, being locked up is a more fitting punishment than death. Could be it's my experience talking there, but I can't *stand* captivity. Used to seriously freak me out when the cops got into the habit of putting cuffs on me every time they detained me. That didn't really start until past age twelve, though. Maybe it worked out for the best I didn't know what I was back then. No way would I have been able to control myself and *not* break handcuffs off. Still not sure how simply not knowing I had the strength to do it stopped me from doing it. I damn sure tried to back then. Oh, it had to be some bullshit Elestari magic nerfing me.

Bleh.

I'm about to hit a computer to look at malls in the surrounding area, hoping to find one matching my dream when the alarms go off. Figures. The alchemist knows someone saw him. It's not a giant leap to assume he's going to do *something*, either clear out and leave the state or maybe try to come after me to keep his secret... if, in fact, he saw *me* and not merely became aware of some random person looking at him. I still don't know what happened between a vision or astral projection. Maybe being so close to Dad while sleeping somehow boosted my power?

Anyway, alarm.

It's a small one at least. We roll one truck to an apartment building on Vollmer street. No smoke... just a fritzy alarm system. Humberto, Alex the probie, and I do a basic inspection of the area while Baker heads for the control panel to shut the system off and reset the alarm. We're unable to find any cause for it going off, so it gets chalked up to a wiring fault. Baker suggests the building super call an electrician to check the system out.

On the way back to the station, we're sitting at a red light when the wail of a siren comes from behind us. Next thing I know, a little black car shoots past us on the left in the oncoming traffic lane, dodging the cars waiting for the signal change. He doesn't make it through the intersection. A big, white plumber's truck coming in from the left T-bones the guy, throwing the tiny black car like a kickball across the intersection and into another head-on collision with a red sedan.

Six police cars come from behind us and flood the intersection. This is the exact end of high-speed police chases that scared the crap out of me when joyriding. As a teen, I carried a knife most of the time, and damn straight I'd have held that bitch to the driver's neck and ordered him to stop if he didn't pull over.

The plumber's van is out one headlight and will probably need a new bumper. Little black car comes to a halt upside down on the opposite right corner sidewalk, having smashed a few tables in an outdoor café. A woman's voice screams from behind (or under) it. The red Honda no longer has a front end. The whole thing crimpled in like a stepped-on soda can. All the airbags are deployed, but there doesn't appear to be any damage in the passenger cabin.

Both the little black car and the red one are giving off a scary amount of smoke.

Baker turns on our emergency lights and blares the horn along with a few pips of siren.

The rest of us don't wait for the truck to be free of stopped traffic. Humberto, Alex the probie, and I jump out and hoof it. Cops are already rushing over to the damaged cars. Some of them give us a 'holy shit' look like they're baffled how the FD got here so fast. Alex starts following me toward the little black car. I wave him to go with Humberto and check on the sedan.

Two cops are trying to lift the teeny car off an almost-elderly woman who'd been sitting at one of the tables. It's pinned her up against the wall of the café, more pressing against her than sitting on top of her. One cop has his gun pointed sorta at the driver side door, but his facial expression is a mix of confusion and disgust. What I can see of the windows looks like a bucket of green slime exploded inside the car.

I grab the car and help the guys shove it away from the woman. Really, it's a tiny damn thing. I could lift it over my head alone. Two-seater. Basically, a high-performance golf cart. The cops could have moved it around easily if it hadn't been all tangled up in iron fence and tables. Speaking of tables, a steel one is wrapped halfway around the woman like a human taco. Blood's seeping out of her mouth.

"You guys got jaws?" asks a cop, futilely trying to bend the table away from her.

"Yeah." I throw off a bit of disorientating charm while peeling back the relatively thin sheet metal. Thanks to the brain massage, neither the cops nor the woman think it's at all unusual to watch me treat the table like a giant piece of aluminum foil. "Her leg looks like it's broken below the knee."

The cops snap out of the fog and help me free her from the remains of the chair. We position her flat on her back. By now, the truck's pulled closer. The guys are hosing down the smoldering cars with chemical extinguishers. A middle-aged couple from the red sedan appears shaken up but mostly unhurt. Only a few scratches from glass.

Since there's nothing more for me to do with the old lady, I walk around and rip the driver side door off the little car. Green and teal gloop is everywhere inside. A small, mostly humanoid skeleton lays in a congealed puddle of slime on the roof (which is now the floor). Looks like someone dropped chicken bones in a huge glob of noseblow and food coloring. Dark smudges on the deflated airbag pique my curiosity. I gingerly pinch the fabric in both hands, pulling it out like a curtain to reveal a splat mark in the approximate shape of a small creature with long ears, large head, and a spindly body.

Ugh, a gremlin.

Looks like the airbag blew it to pieces. Little bastard must've been clinging to the steering wheel at the time of impact. I drop the bag and back away from the car to find a cop standing next to me.

"Driver didn't make it," I say.

He peers into the vehicle. "Yeah, it looks a bit late for CPR."

We remain at the scene as a precaution until the damaged vehicles are loaded onto flatbeds and carted off. By the time we get back to the station, it's 1:36 p.m. The four of us head down the street to grab lunch from this little falafel joint. It's close, cheap, and tasty. Can't go wrong spending two bucks on a hummus sandwich. For whatever reason, the dude who owns this place gives everyone a hockey puck of sweet potato with every order as like a side or something. Weird, but it works.

I call Lawrence again while eating. He tells me he's passed the info on the fake website over to the detectives investigating both recent fires. Obviously, it's too soon to know if it helped, but he's not sounding optimistic. It's really easy to set up a website using fake names and addresses.

Another call comes in around two, but it's also small and I don't end up going on the truck this time. We try to rotate. Sounds like a little backyard grass fire. Nothing a resident couldn't have handled using a garden hose, but hey, never hurts to call in the professionals just to be safe.

The more I sit around, the more restless I get.

Grr.

I head to Sims' office. "Hey, LT, got a sec?"

Lieutenant Sims gestures at me to wait as he's on the phone.

Sounds like he's talking to his boss, so I back out of the room and ease the door closed. A few minutes later, he calls, "Amari? What's on your mind?"

I go back in. "Would it be okay with you if I ran a quick errand? It's for Lawrence, related to the arson case."

"Is he here?"

"No. This might sound a bit strange. We've been trying to track down an arsonist responsible for multiple deaths. A real sick bastard. He's apparently an alchemist." I explain the teddy bear, website, and my dream vision. "Got this weird feeling I really need to get moving and do something now. Can't explain it, but the feeling I need to do something fast or bad shit's gonna go down is starting to become impossible to ignore."

He leans back in his chair, clasping his hands in his lap. "For anyone else, it would sound a little nuts, but for you, it's Wednesday."

I chuckle.

"Well." He pats the desk. "As long as you keep your phone on you and can show up if we need you."

"Totally. You know I can get around fast."

Lieutenant Sims gives me this weird, long stare. I still don't think he's completely sure how to process knowing I can fly. Telling him the truth could've been risky, but it's nice to have the ability to talk level and not need to lie to him about the paranormal stuff. If nothing else, it's job security for me having my commander understand my capabilities.

"All right," says Sims. "Things are kinda off the hook lately. I might end up asking you to swing by a minor incident or two solo since you're so, uhh, mobile. Trick will be how to fill out the reports."

"No problem, LT. Thanks. I'll be back as fast as I can."

He nods.

I head out the rear door, make sure no one pays any attention to me, then spread my wings. Since the amulet 'eats' all my clothes as soon as it senses my wings coming out, I've gotten into the habit of extending my tail, too, as it helps me fly. Like some kind of oversized goth faerie, I zoom more or less straight up to about 1,500 feet. Every single time I see the illusionary dress Natalie gave me, I chuckle at how extra it is. She's totally clowning on me. I've never worn anything this frilly by choice.

A moment or two of flying in circles later, I spot the building where George handed me the Post-it note. Obviously, my dream phantom isn't there now. After orienting myself in the same direction I flew in the vision, I accelerate to the equivalent of a brisk jog, which translates to around the low 300-MPH range give or take a bit. Shifting up the rest of the way into my armored form is a good idea, too. Keeps my boobs from giving me black eyes in the high-speed wind. Okay, I'm exaggerating. My girls aren't that big. Still, it's not fun to feel like the wind is trying to rip them off. Another reason armor's a good idea for longer flights than zipping around the city: random creature attacks.

Granted, if I'm hauling ass, a wyvern, dragon, or some other monstrous bird can't catch me. No non-magical aircraft can either. Almost everything humanity has made capable of flying is some form of helicopter or balloon, either a mechanical or magical. I've heard people in some places out in super rural areas like Ireland or Wales tame giant birds as flying horses. A couple scientists experimented making various other sorts of flying machines, but the few that survived wyvern attacks or horny drakes ultimately failed due to money issues. Who'd spend millions on an airplane when a teleportation portal ticket costs thirty bucks no matter how far away you go, has no risk of crashing, and is instant?

Anyway, I fly. The scenery below—except for being the middle of the afternoon—looks the same as the dream/vision. Good sign. I don't have a magic Post-it note this time, so it's important to pay attention to the ground. A giant mall ought to be easy enough to spot from the air. My primary landmark is the weird tower-like building with the narrow windows. I cruise out over Northwest Philadelphia, Chestnut Hill, Roxborough, and a whole shitload of trees.

I'm not quite four minutes away from downtown when I spot the pale grey of developed area where forest isn't. Kinda looks familiar, so I veer toward it... and aha! Right next to a highway with some loopy bits is a massive swath of paved lot. Time to go down for a closer look.

Bingo! I spot the narrow-window building. Oh, hmm. It's a rectangle, not a square 'castle tower.' At the southernmost end of the mall parking lot, closest to the highway, there's a building that, from above, kinda looks like a stubby rocket capsule with an engine sticking out the west side. Or a fat arrow pointing to the northeast. The roof is mottled in brown and grey, all the HVAC equipment rusted to heck. It looks as decrepit as it did from the ground. Gotcha, bitch!

I glide down to land in the trees by the narrow part on the west side and shift back to normal. As soon as my uniform reappears on me, I grab my phone and check the map application. I'm at Plymouth Meeting Mall. I send Lawrence a geotag with a text saying 'found the bastard,' stuff my phone back on the belt holder, and hurry around to the door I entered in my dream.

When I get within ten feet of the building, a bizarre 'walked through a cobweb' sensation washes over me. Confusion and fear follow, but only last for an instant. Aha. He's got an enchantment on the place, some manner of repelling magic to make people go away. The confusion part gets me wondering if there's also a memory fog curse, too. Whatever it is, it didn't have any effect on me more than a momentary disorientation. Thanks for the supernatural genes, Dad.

The door is predictably, locked.

I laugh at your aluminum door frame, puny mortal. Just kidding. I don't actually laugh. I do, however, pop it open with a forceful tug. So much for the stealthy approach. The *clank* of breaking aluminum probably startled a mall security guard on the other side of the parking lot. Psycho boy definitely knows I'm here. Gonna assume he's not interested in talking. Hmm. What works to my advantage better? Armor up in case he gets the drop on me, or save shifting forms as a possible psychological tool to catch him by surprise if things take a bad turn? He might be a normal human, but he's still a mage… kind of. Could be dangerous. Natalie said alchemists tend to carry a ton of talismans. Means he could potentially throw a 'handful of spells' at me in an instant, not like a mage who'd need to take a few seconds to concentrate on each spell.

Meh.

I go in appearing human. Much easier to navigate a junked-up building without wings in the way. One problem with my armored form is it's an all-or-nothing situation. I can selectively sprout wings, tail, horns, or claws while my body remains normal, but pulling out the armor plates is pushing the proverbial lever all the way up. Getting two feet taller can come in handy for intimidation, too.

Anyway…

The building looks exactly as I saw it, which makes it easy for me to go straight to the man's workshop. I'm not a total dumbass and resist the urge to run down the hall and kick the door in. Keeping an eye open for traps or whatever, I creep down the corridor expecting something to explode at any second. The guy likes fire. Hopefully he uses it here. I'm kinda chilly.

I ease the workshop door open and peek in at the same arrangement of old information technology work tables, bins of dusty computer parts, and enough jewelry supplies to keep a clocksmith going for forty years. I step into the room, expecting a sudden explosion or blast of flames at any second. Hope that he'll use fire keeps me calm. It's like expecting a kid to sneak up on me and make a loud noise for laughs. Sure, flames might torch my clothes, but I'd rather enjoy a blast of warm. However, just because he loves burning places down doesn't prove he *only* uses fire. I don't know if alchemists tend to focus on magic the way mages do. Like, is he a pyromancer or a generalist?

Whatever he is magically, one thing he is *not* is… here.

At least, if he is in the room with me, he's crawled under a table. I crouch down to look. Nope. Just boxes. These tables aren't like cabinets or anything. No doors, only built-in power strips and network plugs. From the looks of things, whatever business existed here before abandonment went full technology. I don't see any magical workstations. They aren't too common, really. But some people insist on using them for art, video, and graphic design. Can't beat the graphics when they are basically generating reality out of magic inside their 'screens.' Took a long time for electronics to catch up, but they had the advantage of being cheaper to make. Five hundred bucks for a basic computer vs like three grand for the low end magical one? Besides, no decent game developers publish for magic computers.

Okay, so he isn't here. However, this *is* definitely his workshop of horrors.

I head over to the spot he seems to have been using as a desk in hopes of finding something to tell me where he went. Guessing he's not here because he's either grabbing food or planting another bomb. Even though I'm alone, my nerves are still on edge. Feels like there's a guy sneaking up behind me with a sword... but every time I look, no one there. Something is wrong. Just can't put my finger on it.

A small digital voice recorder sticks out from under some papers. I pick it up and check out the screen. It's got one file titled 'hux.' I push play. Two men discuss an agreement to 'start off' with the Stedman Building and see how things go from there. One voice reminds me of the fake UPS driver I saw talking to Joyce Underhill. The other voice is unfamiliar, but the arsonist refers to him as 'Huckster,' which seems to annoy the guy. My guess, the arsonist is talking to Donald Huxley. Wow, so Henchman Weekly really is a thing. How the heck did these two meet? Donald makes an offhanded comment about doing him a favor if fewer people die in the fire since it will cut down on lawsuits, which could complicate and extend the time needed to buy the property. Damn. The guy's only concern with life is lawsuits. Leigh is better off without him, hate to say. No, I don't hate to say it. She is. Hopefully, Donald turned into a greedy jackass on his own and his parents aren't going to have the same effect on the daughter. Then again, if living with him for sixteen years didn't turn her into a spoiled princess, she can handle the grands.

I tuck the recorder into my pocket. As they say in the biz, this is evidence.

Most of the papers are design sketches of figurines and jewelry. There's the butterfly, the owl, the bear, a unicorn, some kind of large mushroom with a cartoony face. He's done at least a dozen drawings per figure to show details of various parts, how the pieces interconnect. I'd be impressed at the complexity of the workmanship if the guy wasn't such a disgusting psycho. Touching any of these papers fills me with nauseating emotional memories. The guy was perpetually aroused while working on the drawings due to thinking about killing people. While rifling through the papers, I bump into a digital camera hidden under a mountain of drawings. Whoa. People still actually use cameras?

It's not too big, only about the size of a pack of playing cards with a lens sticking out of it. Wonder what he's taking photos of...

The instant my fingertips touch the camera, my surroundings change. I'm outside, down on one knee behind a green Volvo—pointing a camera at Pandora. Time freezes in a series of quick pauses, suggesting he's taking photos of my kid. Once she runs off to join the children in the recess yard, he takes a pic or two of me.

Shit.

Scenery changes again. I'm walking down the street among a light crowd of pedestrian traffic. Twenty feet ahead, Pandora and Ashley walk hand-in-hand. They don't know someone's following them. The girls walk toward our apartment in no big hurry. My view shifts upward, off the girls, to the building.

My head fills with imagined screaming... ecstasy. The guy's practically getting himself off by daydreaming about people burning to death.

Disgust and rage kick me out of the vision.

He definitely saw me during the vision. How the hell did he find me so fast? I stand there for a few seconds in horrified silence as my brain chews on the psychic read from the camera. I know what his next target is going to be...

My place.

My kid.

And yeah, I'm not worried about him burning Pandora to death, but Ashley and Tracy aren't immune to fire—nor is anyone else living in our building. However, I'm also irrational at the moment and worrying he's figured out what I am and has a special non-fiery surprise in store for my child.

31

WRATH

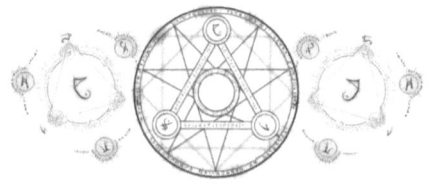

M y heart is practically in my throat as I run out of the workshop.

I shift up into my full armored form on my way across the reception/shipping room, and nearly tear the door off its hinges. The instant I'm outside, I'm airborne and rushing home, wings tucked in close to my body to minimize drag. Don't even give a shit if anyone sees me. Not wasting time or energy concentrating on psychic stealth. Every ounce of power I have goes to speed. Not breaking the sound barrier, but I've gotta be teasing at 400 MPH. This is me sprinting as hard as I can.

My scattered brain has no capability to worry in the little over a minute it takes me to get back to South Philly. Once I'm a half mile away from home, I slow down enough to actually steer. Upon seeing my building *not* on fire, I slow down even more and finally take a breath. Blinding panic gives way to tedium. Bring it, though. I'd rather deal with tedium of going apartment to apartment searching for a pyrotechnic alchemy talisman than the alternative.

I shift down to human form plus wings and land on Tracy's balcony. She's inside at the table, studying. I tap my tail blade on the glass to get her attention, then collapse the extra parts back into my body.

She jumps, startled at the clanking. Once she notices me, she grabs her chest and gives me this accusatory glare... as if I pranked her for no reason. While it is not out of character for me to do so, this isn't a joke. I tug at the door.

Shaking her head, Tracy gets up, walks over, and lets me in. "What are you doing? You know they have stairs, right?"

"Sorry. In a hurry. Where are the girls?"

Tracy looks around, darts back to the table, and checks her phone. "Oh, shit. It's later than I thought. Uhh, they haven't gotten home from school yet. They should have been here like half an hour ago."

We stare at each other in a mutual moment of 'oh fuck'.

The girls don't exactly have a lot of friends, nor do they have a habit of playing outside, especially in this area. Their lateness only means one thing: something happened to them. Tracy's horrified expression begins to crash into guilt. She should have gone to meet them at the bus stop, not rolled the dice and gotten fifteen minutes of study time back.

Part of me wants to tell her not to beat herself up, but I'm kinda pissed... and panicky, so I merely keep my mouth shut.

Eyes closed. Breathe.

"Blood," whispers Tracy. "Use the blood to find them."

I throw mental energy out into the universe harder than I've ever 'psychiced' before. Pandora, where are you?

A sense of 'whoa' comes over me, then a fleeting vision of an alley. I recognize the giant green dumpster behind our building. My panic drops off to bewilderment. "The heck... hang on."

I rush back to the patio and dive off the balcony, stretching my wings after I'm free-falling. They catch the air like a parachute, billowing out to full length. Still dropping fast, I steer around the corner, then the next corner.

Pandora and Ashley are standing in the middle of the alley right behind our building next to a body. Ashley's even poking him with a rusty curtain rod. (Not many random sticks in downtown Philly).

I flare out and land next to them. The greasy, shoulder-length brown hair on the face-down body tells me exactly who he is. Pandora's claws are out. She gives me this casual 'Hi, Mom' look and I just lose it. All the stress from the past five minutes crashes into me and explodes into manic laughter. I'm like freaking out this guy's going to abduct my kid and… big scary arsonist psychopath laid low by a six-year-old. Well, she's hardly a normal child.

Ashley, assuming I'm laughing at what she's doing, prods the guy in the leg again, watching me to see if I laugh more. Wow, this kid's kinda dark.

"Hey," says Pandora, casual as anything. "Did you talk in my head?"

"Yeah. You guys scared the hell out of me." I scoop them both into a hug.

My phone starts ringing.

"We didn't do anything," gurgles Ashley.

Pandora points her tail at the guy. "He tried to give me a pretty necklace, but he really wanted to kill us and everyone who lives here."

I set the girls down on their feet. "Yeah… I just found his hideout. He must have known I was about to catch him. Sec." I pull the phone off its belt clip. Caller ID says Tracy, so I answer. "Hey, the kids are fine. They're right outside the building, in the alley."

"Oh, shit… I'm so sorry!"

"Relax. It's fine. My kid's pretty capable of protecting herself, and Ash."

"Be right there." Tracy hangs up.

"Here." Pandora holds up a gold rabbit pendant. "This is bad. It's gonna set stuff on fire tonight. Can I kill him?"

"You didn't?" I crouch and check the guy's neck. Wow. A pulse.

"No. Just kicked him in the balls and mashed his stupid face into the big trash box 'til he went naptime." She points her tail at a small dent in the side of the dumpster. "You said I'm not allowed to kill anyone 'cept in a 'mergency."

Ashley whistles, saying 'holy crap' with her eyebrows.

"Right. Yeah, good. Don't kill him." I glance at the phone in my hand. Time for the annoying part.

Pandora narrows her eyes. "Are you going soft on me?"

I grin at her, knowing full well she's teasing. "Nah. Too much paperwork on this one. Get ready. We're going to need to talk to the cops."

"Bleh." Pandora sticks out her tongue.

"They're not *always* bad. Just if they come out of nowhere when you're trying to have some innocent fun." I wink.

She holds her arms out to either side. "What are we gonna tell the cops? Why is the bad man sleeping?"

"The easiest lies to sell are the ones closest to being true. You kicked him in the nuts and he fell, hitting his head on the dumpster."

Both girls nod.

"Wings, tail, horns, claws away."

"Eep." Pandora retracts her claws and looks herself over. "Okay."

I dial 911. Game face time.

32

THE CARNIVAL

A small carnival's set up shop in an open lot about two miles away from my place.

It's Sunday, four days after my little 'angel' kicked the snot out of a psychopathic killer. I'm not at all surprised Pandora's run-in with the arsonist had no real effect on her. As far as she's concerned, she punched a bully in the nose. Heck, at age ten, I believed I'd telekinetically killed a guy who tried to lure me into his car so he could molest and kill me. I never once felt regret, guilt, or anything about it. In all honestly, when Dad told me he'd actually killed the dude, it kinda disappointed me.

Anyway... I'm going to need to attend court when the trial happens. Elwood Fletcher—gee, no wonder he turned into a sociopath, right—age forty-one, is being charged with twenty counts of murder by arson, a shitload of property damage charges, and the detectives are trying to connect him via the discovered talismans with something on the order of 150 other deaths spanning the past twenty-two years. The guy got started as a teen.

He didn't wake up before the cops arrived. Yes, they laughed over a six-year-old kicking his ass. It looked way more ridiculous than it was. Pandora's short and noodly. The idea she could kick someone in the balls hard enough to make them trip into a dumpster and knock themselves out is, frankly, ridiculous. A little charm sold it, though. It helps Elwood is pretty small and kinda nerdy.

Anyway, that whole mess is behind us—at least until the trial.

Pandora and Ashley spent Saturday at my mom's place because Jason is home. We tried to cram three weeks' worth of sex into twenty-four hours… and had some cuddle time, went out for food, and basically just drowned in each other's company.

Today, we're kinda pretending to be a family.

Never thought this would be my life.

I'm walking around a street carnival holding Ashley's hand on one side, Jason's on the other. Pandora's riding on his shoulders. It's a nice distraction, something different. They've got a few rides, games of chance, some vendors selling fried treats and such, and even a fortuneteller. Jason did pretty well at the duck shoot. He won a little stuffed rabbit for Pandora. She happily gave it to Ashley and promptly shoplifted another of the same one from the booth via telekinesis. No one noticed the little plushie fall off the shelf and scoot across the ground under the table. Hey, no one caught her, it's fair game. These contests are mostly rigged, anyway. Five bucks for a meager chance to win a plushie that costs less than a dollar? Not gonna yell at her.

"Sorry," whispers Ashley out of the blue.

I glance down at her. "What are you apologizing for?"

She kicks a small pebble aside. "You guys are trying to have a date and you're stuck watching me."

"Nope. It's not *stuck*." I squeeze her hand. "We adore spending time with you."

"They dated yesterday," says Pandora. "Why do you think we stayed at Grandma's?"

Jason coughs, blushing.

I chuckle.

"Besides, this is kind of a date." I gesture around as much as possible while holding her hand. "Carnivals are fun for all of us."

"Okay." She smiles.

A few minutes later, the girls are on a teapot ride. Jason and I lean on the railing watching them go around in circles.

"So, when are you going to transfer to arson?" He pats me on the butt.

I shrug. "No idea. Still don't feel scientifically qualified for it. Probably just gonna help out whenever I can."

"You don't need to be scientifically qualified to investigate magical arsons or use psychic stuff." He kisses me.

"Hah. Maybe. Can we like *not* talk about work today?" I kiss him back. "As long as they don't call us in."

"Shh. Don't dare the gods of burning fate."

I lean against him. "Haven't seen you in three weeks. Glad you had fun over there."

"Yeah. It was fun, but I am *so* glad to be home."

"Is he naked?" asks a shocked woman behind us.

Curious, I glance over my shoulder.

An adolescent centaur boy wanders past carnival booths nibbling on cotton candy. He's maybe eleven or twelve as far as the human parts go, and he's definitely not wearing horse pants. Oh, I think it's the same kid who wandered into traffic the other day. Two nosy women to Jason's right who also have kids on the teacup ride frantically whisper back and forth, unsure how to react to him. All the naughty parts look exactly like an ordinary horse so I don't see the problem. He has kind of a 'farm boy in the city for the first time' wide-eyed expression and may or may not speak English, but he's clearly no threat to anyone.

"So, a centaur in the city?" asks Jason in a low voice. "Wow... no one's losing their mind."

Yeah, the kid—is that even the right word?—is attracting curious stares, but people aren't screaming and running or turning hostile. Just kinda taking it in stride. Another day in Philly. Heh.

"Oh, you didn't hear?" I hug Jason's arm. "The barrier's down. Magical creatures can wander in and out as they please."

"Oof. That's gotta be fun. How many calls? Forty?"

"Yeah, around that. Most are tame. The slugs are the worst. So damn sticky."

He nods toward the centaur. "It's good people are staying calm. Not all magical creatures are dangerous."

I wag my eyebrows. "Some of us are... but only when we have to be."

He kisses me until Pandora and Ashley are done with the ride.

We resume checking out the games and stuff.

Not far from the teacup ride, Pandora points at a man running a ball-toss booth, one of those 'knock down the bottles' things. "He wants to cheat people. I can feel it. I wanna go mess with him. Can we?"

I glance at the dude. Sure enough, his intention is to scam. Probably using weighted bottles and really light balls or some variation, making it really damn difficult to knock down the entire stack.

A roguish grin spreads across my face. "Yeah. Great idea."

---

fin

ACKNOWLEDGMENTS

Thank you for reading *The Burning Alchemist!*

Brooklyn's story will continue... soon.

Also, thanks to Lee Sheridan for editing and Alexandria Thompson for the cover art.

ABOUT THE AUTHOR

Originally from South Amboy NJ, Matthew has been creating science fiction and fantasy worlds for most of his reasoning life. Since 1996, he has developed the "Divergent Fates" world, in which *Division Zero, Virtual Immortality, The Awakened Series, The Harmony Paradox, and the Daughter of Mars series* take place. Along with being an editor at Curiosity Quills press, he has worked in IT and technical support.

Matthew is an avid gamer, a recovered WoW addict, Gamemaster for two custom RPG systems, and a fan of anime, British humour, and intellectual science fiction that questions the nature of reality, life, and what happens after it.

He is also fond of cats.

Visit me online at:

    Facebook: https://www.facebook.com/MatthewSCoxAuthor

    Pinterest: https://www.pinterest.com/matthewcox10420/

    Goodreads: https://www.goodreads.com/author/show/7712730.Matthew_S_Cox

    Email: mcox2112@gmail.com

OTHER BOOKS BY MATTHEW S. COX

- Prophet's Journey

Divergent Fates Anthology

(Fiction Novels - Adult)

The Roadhouse Chronicles Series

- One More Run
- The Redeemed
- Dead Man's Number

Faded Skies series

- Heir Ascendant
- Ascendant Unrest
- Ascendant Revolution

Temporal Armistice Series

- Nascent Shadow
- The Shadow Collector
- The Gate to Oblivion
- The Queen of Discord
- The Burning Alchemist

Vampire Innocent series

- A Nighttime of Forever
- A Beginner's Guide to Fangs
- The Artist of Ruin
- The Last Family Road Trip
- The Phantom Oracle
- How Not to Summon Demons
- Ordinary Problems of a College Vampire

- A Vampire's Guide to Surviving Holidays
- An Introduction to Paranormal Diplomacy
- A Vampire's Guide to Adulting
- How to Stop a Vampire War in Six Easy Steps
- Ancient Vampire Death Cults and Other Annoyances

Standalones

- Wayfarer: AV494
- Axillon99
- Chiaroscuro: The Mouse and the Candle
- The Spirits of Six Minstrel Run
- Sophie's Light
- The Far Side of Promise anthology
- Operation: Chimera (with Tony Healey)
- The Dysfunctional Conspiracy (with Christopher Veltmann)
- Of Myth and Shadow
- The Girl Who Found the Sun

Winter Solstice series (with J.R. Rain)

- Convergence
- Containment
- Catalyst
- Catacombs

Alexis Silver series (with J.R. Rain)

- Silver Light
- Deep Silver
- Silver Quarrel
- Silver Crucible

Samantha Moon Origins series (with J.R. Rain)

- New Moon Rising
- Moon Mourning

- Haunted Moon

Vampire For Hire series (with J.R. Rain)

- Moon Master
- Dead Moon
- Lost Moon
- Vampire Destiny
- Infinite Moon
- Vampire Empress

Maddy Wimsey series (with J.R. Rain)

- The Devil's Eye
- The Drifting Gloom
- Dark Mercy
- Primal Wrath

Samantha Moon Case Files series (with J.R. Rain)

- Blood Moon

Immortal Operative (with J.R. Rain)

- Broken Ice

Four Elements series (with J.R. Rain)

- The Elementalist
- The Black Rose
- The Wakefield Curse

Young Adult Novels

The Eldritch Heart Series

- The Eldritch Heart
- The Cursed Crown
- The Sapphire Soul

Evergreen Series

- Evergreen
- The World That Remains
- The Lucky Ones
- Nuclear Summer
- The Nuclear Frontier

Progenitor Series

- Out of Sight
- Out of Mind

Diary of a Teenage Fey

(Short story series)

- Elder Horror
- The Hag of Barrow Falls
- Babysitter's Nightmare
- Lharakki
- Bauble for a Soul
- Simulacrum
- Amorphous
- Manticore

Standalones

- Caller 107
- The Summer the World Ended
- Nine Candles of Deepest Black
- The Forest Beyond the Earth

Middle Grade Novels

The Adventures of Ubergirl series

- My Dad is a Mad Scientist
- Aliens Ate My Homework
- The End of all Halloweens
- Dr. Infinity and the Soul Smasher

Tales of Widowswood series

- Emma and the Banderwigh
- Emma and the Silk Thieves
- Emma and the Silverbell Faeries
- Emma and the Elixir of Madness
- Emma and the Weeping Spirit

Standalones

- Citadel: The Concordant Sequence
- The Cursed Codex
- The Menagerie of Jenkins Bailey